D0853173

BOUND TO YOU

SWOON READS   •   NEW YORK

BOUND

TO

YOU

ALYSSA BRANDON

A Swoon Reads Book
An imprint of Feiwel and Friends and Macmillan Publishing Group, LLC
175 Fifth Avenue, New York, NY 10010

Our books may be purchased in bulk for promotional, educational, or
business use. Please contact your local bookseller or the Macmillan
Corporate and Premium Sales Department at (800) 221-7945 ext. 5442
or by e-mail at MacmillanSpecialMarkets@macmillan.com.

Library of Congress Control Number: 2017944698

ISBN 978-1-250-10172-3 (hardcover) / ISBN 978-1-250-10171-6 (ebook)

Book design by Liz Dresner

First edition, 2018

10 9 8 7 6 5 4 3 2 1

swoonreads.com

*Thanks to my mom for making me love books,
to all my followers on Wattpad who encouraged me to continue this story,
and to my editor, Holly West, who truly made this book come together.*

CHAPTER 1

"Megan," said Sorelle, my best friend in the world and the pack Beta's daughter. "Stop fantasizing and get your tight ass in a dress. You need to be perfect tonight."

It was my eighteenth birthday and my dad was throwing me a party in the hope I would find my mate. Omega wolves usually found their mate at sixteen, and it happened around that time for most female alpha wolves too. But I'd gone through both sixteen and seventeen without finding him. For a werewolf, even an alpha, I was dangerously close to slipping into old maid territory, which was something no female wolf wanted.

I couldn't *wait* to meet my mate. I so badly wanted someone to love, someone who would love me back. A guy who would hold my hand and tell me I was beautiful. Someone to walk on the beach with. To cuddle with. Someone who was just mine, who'd always care about me and put me first. He'd be strong, an Alpha or Alpha-to-be, and he'd always love and protect me.

"Mmm," I said, turning back to look at Sorelle rather than the ocean just visible from my bedroom window.

Sorelle was very beautiful. She was blond, slim and tall like a model, and had the bluest eyes I'd ever seen on anyone—werewolf or otherwise. Compared with her I sometimes felt average, even if I—with my waist-length black hair, tan skin, and curvy body—was a total knockout. Sorelle was simply radiant. If I didn't know she was a werewolf, I'd suspect she was an angel exiled to earth for the crime of being too beautiful. Or too bossy. Or foulmouthed.

"Wear this one; it's just the right mix of skanky and classy," she said, pulling out a black number that had been one of the top three Mom and I had narrowed my closet down to. "And your hair will be up for once."

"You don't think the blue will go better—"

"No." She held out the dress. "Put it on."

So I dropped my robe, quickly slipping on the black dress. Usually being nearly naked in front of Sorelle wouldn't be a big deal; werewolves learn early to be cool with nakedness since transforming while wearing clothes isn't a good idea. But I had put on a lacy red bra-and-underwear combo, hoping I'd make love to my mate tonight. And I knew Sorelle would quickly pick up on it, since I normally only wore plain black and white undies.

"You gonna do the guy tonight?" she asked, eyebrows raised. Sorelle had found her mate two days before her seventeenth birthday, about fourteen months ago. Despite that, she hadn't slept with him yet, because she was waiting for their "moment."

"No," I lied, and turned so Sorelle would be able to zip me up. "I just read this thing about how what kind of underwear you wear will change how you act. So if I wear sexy underwear, I'll feel sexy."

"Really?" Sorelle sounded like she would sooner believe that little green men might storm into the room yelling, *We come in peace; give us your Mars Bars.*

Eager to change the topic, I asked, "You really think he's here?"

She finished zipping the dress up and I turned to her. She smiled. "You look totally hot!" She paused for a moment, looking toward the door. "And he's totally here. Your dad invited every wolf on the East Coast and then some. He has to be here."

"Yeah. He has to be," I echoed.

Half an hour later, after Sorelle finally got my hair arranged to her liking, we headed downstairs. The party was already in full swing, which made me feel a little bad. This was my party, after all, although I think my dad was also using it to broker some sort of peace treaty between the Boston and New York packs. My dad is this sort of super powerful Alpha—some people even call him the Alpha of Alphas because he is in control of most of the Alphas east of the Mississippi. And since most wolves are omega and follow their Alphas happily, he was pretty much in charge of everyone. I was technically an alpha wolf too, but as an unmated alpha female I was kind of outside the pack hierarchy, so the whole alpha status thing wasn't as important to me.

"Wow," Sorelle said, snagging a bottle of beer from a table. "Your dad really pulled out all the stops for this."

"Yeah," I agreed absently, distracted by my younger sister Rose. She was on a sofa in the corner, reading. Rose was sixteen and had just found her mate a few weeks ago. Said mate, Carter Thorn, was sitting next to her, looking resigned and bored. I reached out and stole the beer Sorelle was sipping and took a swig. Rose had a mate, the thing I wanted most, and she was acting like he didn't even exist! But even though she was acting like an idiot, he was still there and trying to be with her. So unfair. Life sucked.

"Incoming," Sorelle said, taking the beer bottle back and nodding toward a cute blond guy. I'd never seen him before, but then again, that was the point. Most wolves here tonight were strangers, since it was pretty clear my wolf was not interested in picking anyone from my own pack or the other local one.

"Hi," the guy said, stopping in front of me. "I'm Eric."

"Megan," I said, offering him my hand to shake. I didn't quite like the way his eyes immediately dropped to my chest, but I tried to stay positive. Unfortunately, my wolf had no reaction at all to him.

"Nice house," he said, looking around. "Big."

I nodded. It was the pack house and had a lot of large open rooms ideal for gatherings and parties. The great hall, the biggest room in the house, was half the size of a football field and two stories high. I figured it would probably be possible to cram most of our guests into it if we needed to. Possible but not comfortable.

"I like to think it's just the right size," I said, turning away a little, hoping that someone else would come and try a meet and greet. Scanning the room, I spotted Oscar heading my way. He was Sorelle's stepbrother and liked to make crude jokes and ruffle my hair like I was five. "I was actually going—"

"So you're eighteen, huh?" Eric continued, even though I was turning away from him. "You sure you're really the Alpha of Alphas' daughter? It just seems like—"

"Hey, Eric, why don't you take a hint and piss off," Oscar said from behind Eric. Eric tensed—werewolves, especially more dominant ones, don't like anyone sneaking up on them—and turned around, eyes flashing.

"Oscar," Sorelle growled, her voice a low warning. But neither Oscar nor Eric were paying attention to us anymore. Male alpha or beta wolves from different packs tend not to get along. Something about protecting their territory and yada yada. And Oscar was in line to be our pack's Beta, which meant extra tension. He couldn't ever be seen as weak because that would reflect badly on him and his father and our pack.

"Dad," I called, hoping he was somewhere nearby. I also tried to send the message of trouble through the pack bonds. Wolves can't talk to one another through their pack bonds, not with words, but sometimes we can send impressions and images.

"Fucking great," Sorelle swore as Eric launched himself at Oscar. Both of them started throwing punches at each other even as they were transforming into their wolf forms. People drew back to make room for the fight. Clothing tore. Eric got clocked mid-transformation, right in his half nose, half snout. A minute later the guys were both fully changed and circling each other in wolf form. Oscar's coat was reddish and long while Eric's was gray and brown.

"Kyla is going to be pissed he ruined that suit," Sorelle said with a smile that was big enough to rival the Cheshire cat's. "He's like a little kid when it comes to keeping clothes whole."

"At least he's not getting his ass kicked," I noted as Oscar pinned Eric's back leg to the floor. In most werewolves' eyes, getting into a fight was all right as long as you won it.

"There is that," Sorelle said, and linked arms with me. "Let's go."

I let her tug me away, since I wasn't interested in watching whatever this was turning into, and even though Eric's refusal to leave me alone was technically the cause of the fight, I knew they no longer cared if I stayed. It was about the two of them, their need to put the other one in his place and prove who was the better fighter, defending rank and showing that your pack was strong. Mostly, though, it was about kicking the other guy's ass. So really it was pretty much just like when human teenage boys get into fights . . . except with fangs and claws.

I couldn't help but smile along with Sorelle as I glanced over my shoulder. My dad had just shown up and was breaking up the fight, thankfully before either one of them got the chance to do any real damage to each other or to the hardwood floor (although Oscar's suit was no more).

As the Alpha of Alphas, my dad can pretty much just tell other wolves to stop fighting and they do. It's like some weird compulsion forces more submissive wolves to obey, which for my dad was pretty much everyone. Not all alphas have it and most of the ones who do are not as strong as my dad. This was the reason we were able to host more than twelve different packs at our house tonight without World War III happening. There was still a lot of tension.

"Lots of people," I said as we walked through the great hall. I felt like a mix between a juicy steak and a doll being displayed behind a glass window no one could touch. Or talk to. "Why aren't they, like, coming up to talk to me?" I whispered to Sorelle.

"Don't know, but don't worry," she said fondly, squeezing my arm. "There's, like, a couple of dozen hotties around here. One of them is bound to be to your wolf's tastes, right?"

"Right," I agreed.

"I'm going to see if Scott can get us some drinks," she said. Scott, her mate, was six years older than her, always wore suits, and worked at, like, an investment firm, but he could still party and was almost always willing to let us join in.

I wanted to tell Sorelle not to leave me, but I wasn't that kind of girl. The kind who had to have her best friend standing next to her to function. At least I liked to think I wasn't. I'd gotten quite a bit of practice during our senior year because I'd been in lots more AP classes than Sorelle. I was going to get even more practice at college. I'd applied and gotten into my first-choice school: Caltech. I just hoped my mate, when I found him, was open to moving to LA for a few years. Only I had to start talking to some of the wolves and actually find my mate before I could ask him about that.

So I smiled at a guy nearby, which seemed to break the bubble around me, and before long I was in the center of the room, surrounded by lots of guys. Guys who were way too old, way too grabby, way too nerdy, way too smooth. There were even a couple of guys who were way hot, and I tried to convince myself they were yummy, but none of them caused my wolf to sit up and take notice.

"You feel anything yet?" Sorelle asked as she returned a few minutes later. She handed me a red drink with a little umbrella. "When I first felt Scott, it was like a tingling in the air. But some girls claim they smelled their mate before anything else. Others that their voice was like angels singing. Any of that going on?"

"No," I said with a sigh, taking a sip of the red liquid in my glass. It tasted alcoholic and too sweet. "Nothing. What if he isn't here? What if he's—"

"Hello, gorgeous," a deep male voice said from behind me. Both Sorelle and I spun around.

The guy was built, and while his voice was way too deep to belong to an angel, his face sure looked like it could have belonged to some kind of god.

But when the guy reached forward, took my hand, and kissed the back of it, I felt nothing special. There was no tingling or wonderful smell coming from him. I mean, he was possibly the hottest guy I'd ever seen, hot enough I should be totally into him even if he wasn't my mate. But I felt nothing for him.

He was just like all the other wolves I'd greeted tonight.

The guy seemed to realize there was no bond between us, although his eyes said he would be more than happy to take me to bed despite that. But I wasn't interested. Even if he was super hot.

I pulled my hand from his. "Excuse me."

From the corner of my eye, I saw Sorelle give Mr. God Face another look before she followed me. Sighing, I made my way to the back of the room toward the dining room, which held a big buffet. Or it had an hour ago; now most of the food was gone.

"Gaw," I moaned as I leaned against the wall. "Why couldn't my mate just come find me?! My feet are starting to hurt and my cheeks are going to get sore from all this smiling."

"Hey, you are the one who's been dreaming of this since kindergarten," Sorelle said, raising her hands in mock-defense.

Suddenly little voices began to whisper in the back of my mind. *What if I was broken? What if I had some strange defect and I'd never find my mate? What if I was destined to be alone forever? What if destiny wasn't all I'd dreamed it would be? What if, what if . . .*

I knew I was being silly and overreacting, but I'd so hoped to just walk down the stairs and find him. Like a magical path would open up among the guests to guide me to him.

"Sorelle!" Kyla, Sorelle's stepmother, suddenly called from our left. "Your brother just told me you were drinking beer? What's that in your hand?"

Sorelle groaned and quickly put her drink on a side table. "You'll be all right while I deal with the stepmonster?" she asked.

"I'll be fine," I said with a little wave. "I think I'm going to go and get some air."

Sorelle nodded and headed for her stepmother, who was looking disapproving. But then again, disapproving was her standard face when dealing with Sorelle.

I slipped into the kitchen. There was a handful of wolves from my pack there acting as cater waiters (it wasn't like we could have humans do that because of the high risk of them seeing or hearing something they shouldn't). I barely managed not to collide with one of them before I raced through the connecting mudroom to the door leading to the beach.

The night outside was still, only the soothing sound of waves disturbing the quiet. I headed for the water. It would be fairly cold despite the fact that it was summer, but at that moment I wouldn't have cared if it was the arctic sea I was stepping into.

I smiled as I left my shoes behind, glad my dress was short so I could walk knee-deep in the water.

The ocean was like a security blanket to me. Ever since I was just a pup. I'd come out here to watch the ocean and feel it slosh around my feet when I was upset.

It was *my* place.

Then I heard the sound of a lighter being clicked open behind me. I stiffened and tried to catch a scent, but the soft ocean winds weren't favoring me. I turned, slowly, so I wouldn't fall into the ocean.

The man was standing next to my shoes, taking a drag of a cigarette. The smell was horrible, sticking in my nose. I'd never known a wolf who smoked.

But that wasn't something my brain was able to focus on right then. Because looking at him, even across the dozens of feet that separated us, I knew.

The stranger on the beach was my mate.

I moved toward him, my feet nearly slipping as some force seemed to reach out from within me. It was like a rope of air had curled from me to him. The rope was visible, bright white and slightly shimmering for about two seconds, and then it was gone. Only it was still there. I could somehow feel the rope connecting us, binding us together. Forever joining us.

"Oh hell," the stranger—my mate—said. His first words to me . . . not the romantic declaration I'd been hoping for.

I took several more unsteady steps toward him, unable to take my eyes off him. I could only see that he was tall, six feet at least, and broad shouldered. Dark hair. The rest of him was obscured by the moonless night.

When I finally reached the shore I was glad, glad because this close my night vision allowed me to see him. He looked a little older than me. Maybe twenty-two or twenty-three. Not surprising. Most alpha wolves in the house had been older than me as well, since male alpha werewolves often had trouble finding mates. Mostly because an alpha will normally only accept another alpha as its mate and alpha females are rare; only about three in ten of those born with the alpha gene are female.

My mate's skin was pale, his features were appealing, and despite the cigarette, he smelled great. But it was his eyes that captivated me. They were the color of spring leaves, of growing things. Of beauty and new life. I just couldn't look away from them.

"We're . . . ," I started, my throat feeling dry, ". . . we're mated."

"Fantastic," he said flatly.

CHAPTER 2

James

He'd been about to light up his first cigarette in ages when the girl had come running out. It had seemed odd, so he'd gone after her, followed her the few hundred feet to the beach. Not into the water, of course; he didn't like the ocean and was a terrible swimmer.

He supposed he should have known something wasn't quite right when he got the crazy notion to follow her. He was not the type to follow any female, anywhere. In fact, if it was possible, he'd move to an island where there were no females allowed.

He watched her take her shoes off and step into the water. She walked out, and for a moment, he wanted to call to her to be careful. That should have been the second clue. He didn't do concern.

Instead, he lit his cig. The sound made her realize he was there, although he was a bit surprised she hadn't already known. He always knew as soon as anyone was within fifty feet of him. But then again, she wasn't a warrior wolf, as he was, so maybe he shouldn't have been surprised by her failure to detect him.

She turned, and for a moment everything was still. Then it happened. The bond connected. Connected the way only an alpha bond did. The cord, the bond, the light, the magic surged into him. Into her too, he supposed.

They were mated.

He swore.

She walked, no, glided through the water toward him. For a moment he could see her, the beautiful golden skin, the dark mane of hair, and the eyes that reminded him of silver come alive. Then she turned into another woman, a woman he hated. A woman with tanned skin and black hair just like her. He had killed that woman, so the rational part of him knew that this girl wasn't the one he had hated with such passion. Still hated. No. It was just his mind playing tricks.

She stepped close then, looking up at him, young and expectant once more. She was the birthday girl, had to be. The one Robin had been so eager to meet when James's father had ordered them to attend this gathering. Eighteen. God, she was young. He wanted to swear. Then, with the same expectant look still on her face, she'd doomed them both with the true words, "We're mated."

"Fantastic" was all he could manage. *Fucking fantastic.*

CHAPTER 3

There was silence—even the ocean seemed to be still and quiet—as I looked at him and he at me. He seemed detached, unconcerned. Unimpressed. Like finally meeting his mate, the love of his life, was about as interesting as buying socks. I wished there was a mirror so I could make sure a great big zit hadn't shown up on my forehead. Why wasn't he kissing me? Or at least looking somewhat turned on? Holding my hand? Telling me he was glad to meet me? Something?

Abruptly he turned, dropping his cigarette as he walked off. I quickly bent to pick it up. There was no littering on my beach.

"Wait," I called after him as I picked up my shoes in one hand. Putting them on would make following him a lot harder.

I caught him only because he'd stopped outside the door I'd burst through a minute earlier.

"What's your name?" he asked as he turned to me, his hand on the doorknob. There was a faint trace of a British accent when he spoke; at least I think it was British.

"Megan," I said, feeling kind of breathless. And not because of the run from the beach. His eyes were just so green, and the weird bond thing was kind of making me feel dizzy. As if someone had messed with my equilibrium, making my body confuse what was the ground and what was the sky. Making me feel like he was my center of gravity and I was rotating around him rather than being connected to the earth, which rotated around the sun.

"What's your na—" I began, but he'd pushed through the door, leaving me behind. I swallowed, trying to ignore how much his lack of interest hurt, before following him into the house.

It soon became clear to me that he'd been to my house before, because he was walking quickly and without hesitation straight toward my dad's office. Through the kitchen, up the stairs, down the deserted upstairs corridor. Boy, his legs were long. And his butt was cute too.

I hurried to catch up with him and when I did I said, "Hey." Loudly.

He stopped for, like, a microsecond but then just kept on going down the corridor. I wanted to pout and yell at the world, because this was not how this was supposed to go, this was not how my first meeting with my mate was supposed to go, but I managed not to.

Instead I rushed forward and I poked him in the back.

That got his attention; he stopped and spun around. He looked fierce, angry even, and though part of me suddenly felt like a

quivering ball of fear, part of me was pleased he was at least paying attention to me.

"Did you just poke me?" he said, taking a step closer to me. His
voice was a mix of pissed off, annoyed, and a tiny bit amused.

"Maybe," I said, even though I was the only viable suspect.

"It's a yes-or-no question, short stuff," he said, taking another
step toward me, attempting to scare me with his size. Except he
was my mate. He wasn't scary. He was rude and not what I was
expecting, but nothing to fear.

Still, he was more alpha, and that made me automatically give
ground. I stepped back some more until my shoulders were against
the hallway wall. His eyes were glowing slightly, green-green, so
intense. I wondered if he had green eyes in wolf shape.

He put his hands on either side of my shoulders, trapping me,
but not touching me. I wanted him to touch me. Meeting his eyes, I
tried to tell him that without words.

"Yes or no?" he whispered, meeting my eyes and holding them,
rather than forcing them away. He could have done that easily. He
was very alpha, very dominant.

"Huh?" I said, then remembered. I'd poked him and that pissed
him off. I smiled sweetly and lied, "No. It wasn't me." Just to see what
he'd do.

He growled, eyes still unnaturally bright. He leaned a little
closer. I thought it more likely that he'd bite me than kiss me but I
hoped for a hot make-out session. And with him it would be hot.

But before something, anything, could happen, we were rudely
interrupted.

"Well, this looks cozy," a voice said a little way down the corridor. I glanced to the side to see Mr. God Face from earlier.

My mate growled and his eyes kept on glowing but he dropped his hands and backed away from me.

"Hi," Mr. God Face said, walking closer to us and offering me his hand. "I'm Robin. James's Beta." My mate, James, growled as I took Robin's hand.

"Hi," I said, feeling a bit unsteady. "Megan. I'm Megan."

"*Mine*," James said in a low voice, and Robin dropped my hand like it was a hot potato. I glanced to my mate. This was the first matelike thing he'd done or said so far.

"I'll be damned," Robin said, clearly speaking to my mate. "You found your mate."

"So it seems," James said. I looked between the two males. Both seemed way tense for the situation. Then again, my mate had been totally weird since the moment I met him.

"Congratulations," Robin said.

"Thanks," I said when James said nothing. Robin looked at me with an amused expression on his face.

"Let's go," James said, turning to march down the corridor to my dad's study.

My hearing is plenty better than a human's, but it still took me a few more steps to hear that a conversation was taking place in my dad's study.

That there was a meeting going on wasn't really surprising. I knew part of this party was about Dad getting some sort of peace treaty figured out for the New York City and Boston packs. There had been some trouble in both cities: rogues, territorial attacks, a suspicious alpha challenge, and whispers about exposure. My dad was trying to figure out a way to make everyone get along, with as little bloodshed as possible.

I could hear my dad and the Boston pack's Alpha, Jordan, talking. Jordan was a fairly frequent visitor, at least as of late. Something was going on with him and I'd overheard (it's hard to have truly private conversations in a house full of werewolves with supernatural hearing) my parents talking about possible replacements for him. They didn't want Jordan in charge of the biggest US pack besides ours.

The voices quieted as we got closer, probably hearing our footsteps, so all I managed to catch were a few words: *exposure, GPS, missing, government*. Those words didn't sound too good.

Instead of knocking like a normal polite person, my mate simply opened the door to my dad's office and marched us in. Him first, then me, and then Robin.

My dad's study was nice, and pretty cozy for an office. His desk was big and solid, as were the chairs for visitors. Behind the desk, Dad had a big, soft, and worn leather chair. There was a corkboard with pictures of our family, postcards, and some drawings my sisters had made. There was a worn brown leather sofa to the side.

There were two wolves, Alphas, who were vaguely familiar on the sofa. Jordan was standing in the middle of the room, his cheeks flushed with anger. My dad was standing up behind his desk, also looking rather pissed.

"Alpha of Alphas," my mate said to my dad, not bothering to dip his head a little in respect. Which was weird because everyone usually bowed to my dad. He was, as my mate had just said, the Alpha of Alphas. I expected my dad to growl or do something to force James to show respect, even outright challenge him for his disrespect, but he did nothing.

"James," my dad said to my mate, giving him a little bow. That was even more surprising, shocking even, because my father didn't bow to anyone. At least I'd never seen him do it before. Another Alpha of Alphas thing. Normally no alpha would bow down to someone younger and weaker than him unless he'd lost or forfeited a challenge. And my dad was *more* than any other alpha.

That bow made me wonder . . . *Is James more alpha, more dominant than my dad?* That was the only real explanation for James's tone, and the worry and doubt flashing across my dad's face. It felt strange to think my dad wasn't the big bad in this room. My so-far-unfriendly mate was.

"Out," my dad said, clearly speaking to the three other wolves in the room. The two on the sofa looked relieved to be out of there, while Jordan glared at my dad but couldn't hold his eyes for long. That Jordan could even try to challenge the Alpha of Alphas with his eyes like that was proof how alpha Jordan was. After a few seconds, he growled a little but then pushed past us, bumping into Robin, leaving the office.

My dad studied James for a few seconds and then turned to me. "You mated a warrior?" he asked me, looking worried. But there was also that gleam in his eye my dad got when he was plotting something. When he was trying to turn a situation to his advantage.

"No," I said, perplexed. James wasn't a warrior. He couldn't be, could he? The warrior wolves were a fierce class of wolves who once protected our race against wraiths, shadowy creatures that had hunted werewolves. But there were no wraiths anymore, and no one had seen any warrior wolves in ages. "The warrior class doesn't mate with . . . eh . . ." I searched for the right word: normal wolves? Civilian wolves? Regular wolves? In the end I settled for, ". . . us."

"That's actually not true," Robin said helpfully from my right. "We used to take civilian mates into our pack, even though we prefer females with warrior blood. This is quite exciting."

"Why exciting?" I couldn't stop myself from asking as I looked around at the three hard-faced males.

"It's been nearly thirty years since a wolf from the warrior class took a mate," Robin said. "This is a great day. You've just become the new mate to the last warrior alpha."

James glared over my head at Robin. I felt so confused. This wasn't at all going the way I'd imagined it. There were no nice words, no kisses, no nothing. Instead I'd apparently become the mate to a warrior wolf. I knew very little about warrior wolves, but I figured Rose might. She was into magic and books and stuff. I'd have to make sure to have a talk with her.

"Is this a private party or can anyone join in?" my mom's voice said from the doorway.

I smiled and turned, feeling immediately better. Mom and I are very similar; we have the same kind of humor, taste in food, books, music, everything, and we look enough alike to be sisters. She's my favorite person in the family.

"Isabella," my dad said to Mom, nodding to my mate. "This is James, acting Alpha of the Cold Hunt Warriors."

Mom raised an eyebrow as she walked into the room, studying James. "Trist's son?" she half stated, half asked. My dad nodded. I saw surprise in my mate's face. Mom saw it too. "Yes, I've met your father."

James studied Mom for a few moments and then nodded, broke eye contact, and bowed his head to her. I opened my mouth in surprise. James hadn't shown my dad, the Alpha of Alphas, proper respect, but he had to Mom, who most alphas ignored.

Mom smiled at him before heading over to sit on the corner of the big desk. She was fairly short, like me, so her feet were up off the ground. The fact that she stayed on my side of the desk, rather than join Dad behind, it was an important distinction. It meant she thought there were two clear sides here and she wasn't taking either one just yet.

"She's coming with me," my mate declared after a few moments of silence. But it was not *I want her so much I can't stand the thought of being away from her.* No, there was more of an *I'm the boss and this is what's going to happen* vibe to it. Overall it just made me feel weird. Like this was something I had no say in. Which wasn't what I wanted. I wanted . . . I wasn't sure what exactly anymore, but knew this wasn't it.

"Not tonight," my dad said. "Stay a week or two."

"Coming with you where?" I asked, having a feeling it wasn't anywhere near LA.

"Megan," my dad said in a tone that I knew meant *shut up.* Which surprised me. I mean, my dad wasn't always the nicest of guys, but he usually listened to me when it mattered.

"Canada," James said.

"As in maple syrup and hockey?" I asked.

"We got lots of bears and pine trees too," Robin offered helpfully.

"What about LA?" I asked, looking at my dad.

"What about it?" he asked, like he didn't remember at all.

"Caltech," I said. "I got in, remember?"

"Right," he said, and I wondered if he had forgotten. That was a depressing thought, so I did my best to push it away.

"And we're very proud of that," Mom said, then focused on my mate. "How you feel about LA, James?"

"I can't be away from my pack," he said without even pausing for a second to think about possibly moving to LA. Which sucked, but wasn't totally unexpected. I'd always known this might happen, that my mate might be a guy who wouldn't be able to drop everything so I could study at my dream school. Which was why I'd applied to a lot of different schools in different cities. Except no one had told me I needed to look at universities in Canada too.

"Mmm," Mom said, while her eyes narrowed.

"We'll be returning home tomorrow," James continued.

"Tomorrow?" I echoed. "But summer isn't over yet." I turned and focused on my mate, figuring I might try my puppy-dog eyes on him. I do pretty awesome puppy-dog eyes. But before I even could get myself in a position where puppy eyes might work, he side-stepped me, as if getting too close to me might be hazardous to his health.

"This is not a debate," James said, focusing right back on my parents. "My wolf has chosen her and we both know me staying in your territory for much longer would be bad for you." Not a threat but simple fact. I could tell from his tone. "And you know I have business back home that won't keep."

"That business is exactly why we would like to keep our daughter here for a few more days," Mom said. I frowned, wondering just what this *business* was all about.

"It's not ideal," my dad said, and I think it was more to Mom than anyone else. "But I agree that you can't stay and therefore neither can Megan."

"Unless she wants to," Mom said. "Megan, you have a choice—"

There were ways of breaking a mating bond between two omega wolves, but I'd never heard of it for alphas. Mom's words made me think it might be possible, though. Except I wanted a mate more than I wanted Caltech. Which I knew wasn't very modern-woman-hear-me-roar of me, but it was the truth. I'd wanted someone to belong with for as long as I could remember, and now finally I had found him. No way was I giving that up.

"No," James said, not looking at me. "She doesn't. Warrior bonds work differently."

Now I *really* had to talk to Rose. This warrior wolves stuff seemed like something she would have written a paper on, and she might even know something about warrior mate bonds. And if she didn't, I was sure she at least could clue me in on some stuff. Like what was the difference between a warrior wolf and a normal one? There were stories about magic healing, immortality, poisonous fangs, and even a story that some of them had three heads when they changed, like that mythical Greek dog.

"It's fine, Mom," I said, even though I wasn't quite sure what I was saying okay to. Or what was going to happen. I just knew that this was what I'd wanted for so long, waited for. I needed to see it through. Besides, my wolf recognized something in James. I felt something, through the faint link that was our mate bond. Something that was just . . . right. Even if most everything else felt wrong, I was going to hold on to the part that felt right. "I'm sure I'll find a good school in Canada."

Mom turned her sharp eyes on me, probably trying to decide how I felt. I wished her luck with that because I wasn't totally clear on that myself.

My dad nodded and looked pleased. "It's settled, then."

"I'll trust you to keep her safe for one more night," James said gruffly. "But tomorrow, you will make sure she's packed and ready to leave. My wolf wants her safe, in my territory."

"Understood," the Alpha of Alphas said. "But now you must be presented. It's tradition."

MY FATHER GUIDED us to the second floor's balcony, which overlooked the great hall, while Mom and some other members of our pack herded all the wolves in other areas of the house toward the hall. It really was a huge room and it looked like I had been right about all our guests fitting into it.

James was walking stiffly on my father's other side, about as far away from me as he could get. My father had my arm in a tight grip, as if he was worried I'd bolt. But I wanted this—more, it seemed, than both my mate, who hadn't looked directly at me since the whole poking incident, and my father, whose face was in that eerily calm mask he wore when his emotions were churning. He'd worn it that time when I totaled his Mercedes back in seventh grade and when Cordelia, my older sister, had declared she was in love with a human boy and was running away with him (thankfully she hadn't gone through with it).

Once we reached the balcony, my father stopped. I was sort of glad, having had to rush to keep up with them. They both had a lot longer legs than me.

I glanced at my mate. I wanted to see his reaction to all of this, to being presented. Did warriors have a different kind of ceremony for introducing a newly mated couple, or did they have their own rituals? Did this seem strange to him? Was my father embarrassing him? I could read nothing on his face. It was passive, almost bored-looking.

"Silence," my father said, his voice barely above normal speaking level. But the whole room below us went as quiet as the grave and the wolves all turned their attention to us. I forced a smile, feeling strangely cold inside.

Wasting no time, my father held up James's arm, moving him slightly forward, closer to the balcony railing. "I present to you

James, son of Trist the Great, of the Cold Hunt Warriors, and now mate to my daughter."

He kept hold of James's arm as he turned to me. "I present to you Megan Ross, daughter of my beloved mate, Isabella, daughter of my own flesh, and now mate to James, son of Trist the Great," he said as he tugged me forward, raising my arm close to James's.

James and I both kept our arms up as my father let go. The ceremony wasn't complete. James was clearly familiar enough with our customs to know that, which was good. A second later my father pulled a bloodred satin ribbon from his pocket. He looped it once around my wrist, then once around James's, before tying the ribbon, and us, together. James's wrist was, however, covered by the cuff of his black shirt. That wasn't really proper. The ribbon was supposed to be against his skin.

But before I had a chance to point out the mistake, my father pushed us forward and said in a booming voice, "I give you the mated pair James, son of Trist the Great, and Megan Ross."

The crowd erupted in applause, cheers and hollers mixed with a few wolf howls. I could see Sorelle smiling, Scott's arms wrapped around her. I wanted that. I wanted arms wrapped around me.

I turned to smile at James as we lowered our arms. "I guess we're stuck with each other," I said in a tone I hoped was light and teasing, nodding at our still bound wrists. It was tradition to stay tied together for the remainder of the festivities, so I'd hopefully get the chance to get to know him a little.

"You need anything else from me?" my dad asked James, sounding tired and old. I'd never thought of him as old before. "You and yours could stay here—"

"No," James interrupted. "We have a secure location." I felt my eyes get big. No one interrupted my dad when he was talking. My father's eyes only narrowed; he didn't lash out at James. And James . . .

James was untying the ribbon that had tied us together.

"But what about . . . ," I started to argue about the ribbon, but it was already off our wrists and in his pocket. I wanted to argue about everything. Wanted to protest and yell that it was all wrong. But I just couldn't get the words out.

CHAPTER 4

"I've been thinking," said Sorelle, who was helping to fold the last of my clothes and put them in my suitcases. It was about nine forty-five the morning after the party. "This might actually be better."

"What might actually be better?" I said, deciding I didn't want to bring my I BITE T-shirt and putting it in the huge reject pile I had going on, on the bed next to my suitcases. I actually wanted to throw all the neatly packed things on the floor and stomp on them. Real mature, I know. But I didn't. Because I had no reason to be upset, but I kind of was anyway. It was all happening too fast and not the way I'd hoped.

"Canada is a lot closer than California," Sorelle said, pushing some blond hair back from her face. "At least as long as it's, like, the eastern bit of Canada. Is it?"

"I'm not sure. Probably. I mean, if it was Vancouver, we'd be flying, right?"

"So, like, not super far," she said, nodding and licking her lips.

"So we'll still be in the same time zone and it'll be totally easy to drive and see each other."

"Yeah," I agreed, "that's true," before reaching for my extra cell phone bag. It was a specially designed one. You could change the straps so that it either worked like a cell phone shoulder bag or as a mini backpack for when you were in werewolf shape. That way you'd never have to leave your cell phone or cash or stuff behind if you had to change quickly.

"Still fucking sucks that we won't get to go to even one end-of-summer party this year," she said, sitting down on a tiny bit of the bed that didn't have clothes on it.

"Yeah, it's not at all happening the way I was expecting it to," I said, closing one of the suitcases to make room so I could sit next to her. "I mean, I wasn't expecting chocolate and a declaration of undying love the first night."

"Don't lie, you were so expecting that!" she said with a grin.

I giggled. "Okay, maybe a tiny bit, but what I really wasn't expecting was . . ."

"Mr. Asshole?"

"He's not an ass," I said defensively, even though I had no real clue what James was. So far all I knew was that he was distant and bossy. But who knew? Maybe once we spent some time alone, he'd turn into a teddy bear.

"He sounds like one to me," she said, bumping her shoulder against mine. "It's going to be weird. I mean, I'm sort of pre-pared because you were leaving me for movie stars and frost-free winters—"

"Hey, my second-choice school was MIT," I said. Sorelle was going to art school in Boston and so I'd applied to several universities there. Part of it was that Massachusetts had a whole lot of good schools for engineering, but the idea of having my BFF around had been a big bonus. "I can't help that I was awesome enough to get into Caltech."

"I'm pretty sure MIT is more awesome than Calte—"

"Maybe, but LA's got way nicer beaches—"

"Boston's got the Red Sox—"

"Oh, please, you don't even like baseball—"

Our play arguing cut off, both of us glancing toward the door. Someone was coming up the stairs to the second floor; we could hear it and knew what it meant. Time was up.

Sorelle reached forward, wrapping her arms hard around me. I held on to her just as tight. She sniffed some but I knew she wouldn't cry. During all the years I've known her I've never seen her cry, not even as a kid.

"Canada isn't that far away," she whispered close to my ear. "We'll visit all the time."

"Yes," I said, still hugging her, not willing to let go. Sorelle had been my best friend, the one person I talked to and shared more with than anyone in the world, for so long. It was really hard to imagine life without her.

"You ready?" my sister Rose asked from the open doorway. Good. I'd been wanting to talk to her since last night.

"I guess it's time," I said, pulling away from Sorelle's hug. She was so warm and familiar, and letting go of her was a lot harder than it should have been. Letting go of her was like letting go of everything that was familiar and safe.

"Guess so," Sorelle said, brushing some blond hair away from her face. We both stood.

I wiped at a tear that I hadn't been able to stop escaping and forced a smile. "I need a minute with Rose, 'kay?"

"Sure," Sorelle said, smiling tightly. "I'll see you outside."

I waited until Sorelle's footsteps had faded away.

"Spill it."

"Spill what?"

"Everything you got on warrior wolves," I said. "I know you're dying to tell me. This is, like, your field of expertise: magical and weird."

I'd tried to find her last night, but she hadn't been anywhere and there had been so many people wanting to say how pleased they were, lots of people I wanted to say good-bye to, so this was my first chance to talk to her about everything.

"I'm . . . ," Rose started, seeming a bit unsure. "I was never all that interested in them."

"Great," I muttered, but I figured she still had to have more info than me. "What do you know, then?"

"Well," she said. "Warrior wolves all have the alpha gene." Wolves are born either with alpha or omega genes. Alphas are leaders while omegas are happy followers. But the biggest difference is that alpha wolves can change form from birth, while omega wolves don't turn until they are sixteen. Generally alphas have alpha children, but Rose and our youngest sister, Johanna, were omegas, so it wasn't 100 percent certain all of an alpha's children were born alphas. "But they also have another gene that makes them warriors."

"Yeah, but what does that actually mean? Am I mated to Superman or the big bad wolf?" I asked, taking a step back to lean on the bed.

Rose thought hard for a few long seconds. Something seemed to be bothering her. Maybe the fact that she didn't have answers. She liked knowing, being the one who could always hook you up with the boring intel you needed.

"I don't know," she said. "Not really. I don't think they're that different. Other than the fact that they're faster and stronger and live longer than most weres."

"Live longer?" I asked. "Are they, like, immortal? Because I heard a story about that once."

"As long as the pack lives, the one wolf lives," she said, as if that should make everything make perfect sense.

"Wow, that's helpful," I said, standing.

"It means the warrior packs have more magic—from their warrior gene, maybe—and that's what makes them more than most wolves," she said. I thought about that. I guess it made a little sense, even though I still felt kind of confused.

"All right," I said. "What else?"

"That's all," she said, a bit sullenly, like I was being an annoying bitch, not just asking some friendly questions. "Can we go?"

"I guess," I said, and picked up one of the suitcases.

"Good." Rose took the other one. "They're waiting."

AT LEAST JAMES'S car was nice. A black SUV no more than a year old. Not a fast, flashy car, but a good solid one that would get you where you needed to go. Lots of horsepower too. There was a second, almost identical SUV parked on the street. I guessed both cars belonged to James's pack.

"So this is weird," my older sister, Cordelia, said as she hugged me, her hair tickling my nose. "I never figured you'd move out before me."

"Yeah," I agreed, sniffing a little. I'd promised myself I wouldn't cry—suspecting that if I started, I wouldn't be able to stop.

Sorelle slid up to us and gave me a big hug. Cordelia took the hint and headed over to her mate.

"He's hot," Sorelle said, glancing over at James, who was talking to my dad. "In a kind of tough-guy way. And his Beta? Totally yummy! Beyond yummy, even."

"Hey! Aren't you afraid of damaging my fragile male ego?" Sorelle's mate, Scott, said playfully from over by the door. Sorelle rolled her eyes at him, and looked appreciatively over at Robin again.

Sorelle turned her attention back to me. "You'll be all right. You're tough. And you'll be able to practice your insane driving up on those country roads without anyone giving you a ticket," she said, and squeezed my shoulder.

"Yeah, sure." I smiled. "And I'll call you every day."

"You better!" She hugged me again, then went over to Scott. Scott smiled and waved at me before pulling Sorelle closer. She was so lucky to have a mate who lived three blocks away and really, really loved her.

Next were Melody, Johanna, and my dad. Melody was ten and Johanna seven, and both were monsters disguised as cute kids who liked glitter, princess stuff, and squeaky toys way too much for me to ever take them seriously. I mean, I loved them and all, but they were still annoying brats. They both looked bored, which I guess was understandable since this was just a whole bunch of grown-ups standing around.

"Baby—" my dad started, but Johanna tugged at his sleeve, making him turn his attention to her. "What is it, Anna?"

"If Megan is leaving, does that mean I can have her room?" Johanna asked. Johanna and Melody were currently sharing a bedroom (even though there were half a dozen free bedrooms in our house) because they needed to learn to get along better.

"You're so not getting her room," Melody cut in, puffing out her barely there chest. "I'm getting it. Right, Dad? You said that once Megan left home I'd get her room and not have to share with—"

"No, he didn't . . . ," Johanna said.

They began fighting. And let me tell you this: a ten-year-old and a seven-year-old can make a lot of noise and inflict a lot of pain when they are fighting. I rolled my eyes. I was pretty sure neither one of them was getting my room.

"Break it up," my dad said, grabbing hold of Melody's hand just before she scratched Johanna's face. "Hug your sister good-bye and then we'll go inside."

I hugged them quickly, Melody first, then Johanna. Then I hugged my dad, holding on to him hard, even as the girls began arguing again.

"I'm so getting the room."

"No, you're not."

"Am so!"

"Are not."

"Are too. . . ."

"Stop it," my dad said, pulling away from me and turning to them. They both glared at him and then at each other. I half expected Melody to wolf out right then and there or to start yelling and crying. They were good at getting everyone to pay attention to them.

"Bye, Dad," I said, and he gave me a second, much quicker hug before starting to herd the fighting girls back into the house.

I kind of wished he would have stayed to wave me off, but Johanna and Melody were still kids and needed him too. There had always been someone who needed my parents more than I did. That was life in a big family. You learned to adjust your expectations.

Rose had left my bag and then scurried off somewhere, which didn't surprise me. She didn't do emotional. Still, she could have said bye at least.

Mom came over and pulled me close to her. "I love you, sweetheart," she said. "And we're only a phone call away."

"I love you too." We hugged for a minute. I managed not to cry even though when I pulled back I felt a little weepy. Mom's eyes looked suspiciously shiny too. "I'll call once I get there."

Reluctantly I turned and headed over to James, Robin, and another guy who I guessed was part of James's pack too.

The strange wolf put out his hand for me. He was big, about as tall as Robin, who was an inch or so taller than James, but a lot bulkier than both James and Robin. He was like a weight lifter or wrestler or something. His hair was dark and closely shaved and he had a tattoo on his forearm of a big tree. "I don't believe we've had the pleasure. I'm Tobias."

"Megan," I said as we shook hands. I stared at James the whole time, half expecting him to react to this other male, touching me like he'd done with Robin yesterday. But the only thing he did was to cross his arms and yawn.

"Well then," Robin said, clapping his hands together. "How about we get this show on the road!" He smiled broadly. His smile was so breathtaking my mind went blank for several seconds. I'd never seen anyone so beautiful. He was even more gorgeous than Sorelle, which was a little weird since he was a guy. Most guys weren't breathtakingly beautiful—they were handsome or attractive. But Robin was totally beautiful.

"Yeah," I said when I could speak again. "Let's go."

Robin and Tobias headed for the second black SUV at the curb, leaving me alone with James for the first time since the hallway last night. Maybe this car ride was my chance to get him to open up a little. I mean, road trips were made to bring people together, right?

"This is a pretty sweet car," I said. Guys tended to like when you complimented their wheels, and I was hoping that maybe it could be my in. If I could get him talking about cars, that'd be something, and it wasn't like I minded talking about cars. "It's the sports edition, right? With the LED roof lights? Air suspension?"

James only grunted and opened the driver's-side door and got in. Since my bags had already been loaded up, all I had to do was walk around and get in. The seats were a lot higher than what I was used to, leather, and very comfy. The interior was minimal but stylish. There was a high-tech nav system and a digital touch display to replace the analog dials.

I gave a little whistle as I closed the door. "Nice." The car purred to life. "Can I drive?"

"No," he said, and pulled out of our driveway.

The car *had* air suspension. The ride was super smooth. I wondered how it did off-road. I think the car had a compressor assist because it accelerated quickly. I also wondered if he'd hacked the car to remove the speed limiter most new cars had that prevented them from going above 155 mph.

James said nothing. I admired the car for a few moments longer. I was dying to drive it but I was pretty sure it wasn't happening today. But tomorrow was another day.

"So," I said as we hit a bigger street. "This is a little weird, right?"

He said nothing, just focused on driving.

"It's weird for me," I continued when it became clear he was not going to say anything. "I don't know anything about you. Well, other than you're a warrior wolf. And you live in Canada."

James kept on ignoring me.

"And you're rude." That made his lip twitch a little, which could have been a suppressed smile or a suppressed growl. "How about I tell you about me, then? Since you don't seem to want to share."

I took a deep breath. "I'm Megan, which you knew already. I'm really good at mechanical stuff. My gramps loved old cars and he taught me all about fixing them. I love the ocean. I've been best friends with that blond girl back there since I was three years old. I suck at walking in high heels and I have blisters from doing it last night. I have four sisters."

I glanced over to him, hoping he'd say something. But his only response to this was to reach over and turn the radio on. Which really said it all.

"HE TOOK A big bite and it was just gone," Tobias said while Robin shook his head. Right now we were stopped for lunch at a roadside diner, eating cheeseburgers and having a nice chat. Well, me, Robin, and Tobias were. James had eaten, glared at me, and said he'd be outside.

"Your brother ate your finger?" I asked, because the story was just so unbelievable. I mean, I'd heard of werewolf kids chewing up shoes and sofas and stuff, but not fingers.

"Like it was candy," Tobias said, wiggling his little finger with its missing top joint as if to make sure I hadn't forgotten what we were talking about.

"That's not what happened," Robin said.

"It's not?"

Tobias smiled sadly. "No, it was actually an unfortunate accident that occurred when I was helping to build houses for the homeless—"

"That's not what happened either," James said from behind me. I jumped a little in my seat, not prepared for him being there. He was sneaky and quiet. Usually I could always tell when someone was sneaking up on me.

"What, then?" I asked, giving him a little smile.

James ignored the question. "Are you done yet?" he asked, looking at the half-eaten hamburger on Tobias's plate. It was his second double supersized bacon cheeseburger.

"In a minute," Robin said, giving the waitress behind the counter a wink and wave to get her attention. Which had been totally unnecessary because she'd been drooling over him since we all walked in.

"Hurry it up," James said, giving me an extra glare, like it was my fault Tobias wasn't done eating.

I did not understand that man.

At all.

CHAPTER 5

James

Why did he still have the ribbon?

He stared at it, rubbing the red satin between his forefinger and thumb in the hand that wasn't holding the cigarette he wasn't smoking. It was just a red ribbon. It didn't mean anything.

So why did he still have it?

Why hadn't he thrown it away yesterday, or even left it with Megan? He was sure his eager little mate would want it. It would be important to her. Was that why it was important to him? Why he couldn't drop it or let the wind catch the ribbon and take it far away?

"I thought you'd quit?" Robin said, coming around the corner of the roadside diner they'd stopped for lunch at.

"I'm not smoking," James said, quickly hiding the ribbon and his free hand in his pocket. He didn't want Robin to see it, ask about it. He didn't want to give a stupid answer. Or worse, have no answer to why he still had the red ribbon.

"Right," Robin said, coming to stand next to him, watching the smoke rise from the cig. Shrugging, James offered Robin a cigarette from the fresh pack he'd bought at the mini convenience store at the gas station next to the diner. His beta shook his head no.

"She seems cool," Robin offered, clearly speaking of Megan. "A bit gullible, maybe."

"Hadn't noticed," he said, dropping the cigarette on the asphalt. He felt like Robin would be able to see right through him. See everything James was feeling, everything he was trying not to feel, and attempt to "help."

"Attractive too," Robin said, making James fist up his hands. "Can't say you haven't noticed that," his Beta continued with a smile. "But I expect that's part of what's bothering you."

James glared at Robin. "Go see what's taking them so effing long. I'll be by the car."

He stalked off, pulling out the pack of cigarettes again. He knew it wasn't the cancer sticks his body was craving. It was the girl, his mate. Both his wolf and his body were telling him *mine*. Insisting that she was his and that he needed to complete the bond to show her that. Show everyone that. But that wasn't happening.

Robin showed up with Megan a few minutes later. They all looked cheerful. Irritatingly so. This was not a fun day. It was a day of driving for hours upon hours. A day he was being forced to spend essentially imprisoned with his mate.

"Robin," he said, needing a reason not to be alone with Megan. "With me."

Robin stopped for a second, nodded, and then tossed the keys to the second car to Tobias. Megan, who had stopped next to James's car, looked between the two SUVs; then, as Robin turned to walk around to the passenger seat of James's car, she turned toward the second car.

"Where are you going?" James said, taking a step to follow her.

"You smell like cigarettes," she said, turning to face him while wrinkling her nose. "And you don't seem to want to hang with me anyway."

"Hang?" he parroted, not quite familiar with the phrase.

"Yeah, be around me? Listen to me?" She shrugged and bit her bottom lip. He wanted to bite it too. "Share stuff?"

"So?"

"So? I think I'll just go ride with Tobias."

"Fine," he said. He didn't care if she drove with Tobias. He didn't care about her at all. She was just . . . He wasn't sure what she was, but he was glad to be free of her chatter. Of her eyes, which wanted, it seemed, to burrow into him. To figure him out. To fix him. Like that was a possibility.

Tobias was already jumping into his car and looked mighty pleased about his new traveling companion.

James took a step after Megan, suddenly not liking that smug smile on Tobias's face. Not liking how happy Megan seemed to be to have the chance to get away from him. She was *his*. And even though he didn't much like that, he somehow liked the thought of her with Tobias in that car for hours upon hours even less.

Without giving it any more thought, he caught up with Megan and grabbed her arm, turning her around.

"What are you doing?" she asked, struggling a little with his grip. He loosened it some, but didn't let go of her.

"I changed my mind," he said, pulling her with him toward his car. "You're with me."

"I thought you said it was *fine*," she said, but she wasn't struggling with him. "And I can walk on my own."

He resisted the urge to growl at her as he opened the door to the back seat. She scowled at him, as if opening the door for her was the most offensive thing he'd done so far.

CHAPTER 6

was exiled to the back seat.

The back seat.

Like I was a kid.

Humiliating.

I then spent the first hour of our drive glaring at the backs of Robin's and James's heads, while neither one of them paid me much attention. Robin had fallen asleep, his head pressed against the window, the sun glinting off his golden earring every now and again. James had the radio on—some weird station that played rock music—and he hadn't once made eye contact with me in the rear-view mirror.

As we drove on, the quiet and relative sameness and predictability that always comes along with driving on a highway gave me what felt like the first calm moment since last night.

My new life with my mate was so far not going the way I'd expected. Even though I'd known there was a risk that my mate would be an Alpha with his own pack to care about, I'd thought he'd be Alpha-to-be or something. Free to go wherever he wanted— or where I wanted. That I'd get to go to Caltech. But now I wasn't, and that was okay. I was sure there were plenty of good schools in Canada; I'd find one and go to school there. No problem.

What I hadn't planned for, much less worried about, was the possibly that my mate would be so cold and hard. That he would be flat-out mean to me. I was a pretty likable person. I think. I wasn't horrible enough to deserve the way James was treating me. Then again, he seemed to be treating everyone kind of crappy. Something was clearly eating him.

Maybe something to do with being a warrior? I still wasn't sure what that meant, despite my chat with Rose. For a while when I was talking to her, I thought I might be close to understanding, but now I just wasn't sure. In fact I wasn't sure of anything, really. I didn't even know where we were going exactly.

"So . . . ," I said, deciding (after that first silent hour of thinking) that since there were only two front seats and three of us in the car, one of us had had to sit in the back and it wasn't really that rude to put me there. Forcing me to get in the car the way he had, that had been rude, but it also meant he cared. In some weird messed-up way. Maybe I could switch with Robin once we stopped for our next food and bathroom break. Or maybe James would let me drive the SUV. ". . . where exactly are we going?"

James said nothing.

"Look," I said, scooting forward as far as my seat belt would let me. "I get that you're not exactly thrilled about all this, but you will have to talk to me. If you don't, I'll just, like, run away or something."

"You will not," he said, his voice low, but he continued talking anyway. "We're going to the compound, our place outside Tenebri."

"Tenebri?" I said, although what I wanted to ask about was the compound. It sounded like something a crazy militia group might call their headquarters. I really didn't want to have to spend the rest of my days sleeping on a bunk and eating sloppy cafeteria food, so I hoped *compound* was just code for Awesome House Close to Beach. Not likely, but hoping was better than being all negative.

"A city about two hours north of Quebec. You have heard of Quebec, haven't you?" he asked snarkily, looking at me in the rearview mirror for the first time.

"Yeah, I have," I said sullenly. I might not be a brainiac like Rose, but I wasn't totally stupid.

James's eyes in the mirror softened a tiny bit. "Look, short stuff." I bit my lip. Short stuff? He'd called me that last night too. It was a stupid nickname. I was five four, for God's sake; that was average, not short. Well, not super short. "This trip is going to take about eight more hours. And I hate being stuck in a car. Hate it. Makes me twitchy. If on top of that you keep on pestering me—"

"Pestering you?" I said, my voice getting higher. I saw Robin move; our argument was waking him, but I didn't particularly care. "I asked you where the hell you were taking me, not—"

"Whatever you want to call it." His jaw clenched, and his hands gripped the wheel tighter. "Stop the talking."

"Why do you hate me so much?" I blurted out, immediately feeling my cheeks go red. I hadn't meant to ask him that. Part of me was still holding out hope that he *did* like me and was just hiding it. Really well.

"I don't hate you," James said, turning up the radio. "I just don't . . . care."

I wanted to cry and scream at the same time, but instead I stared down at my hands. He just didn't care. . . .

Robin was at this point fully aware of the awkwardness. In an attempt to lighten the mood—at least I think that was what he was doing—he turned in his seat to look at me.

"You speak French, Megan?" he asked, sounding friendly and vaguely hopeful.

"No?" I said. "I took two years of Spanish." And yet somehow I could not speak a word of it, which was kind of depressing, especially since Mom's family—like a bunch of generations ago—was from Puerto Rico.

"Oh."

A few hours later, as we reached the Canadian border, I was getting seriously sick of the tense silence that had enveloped the car. It was like it was sucking all the energy out of me. Thankfully the line of vehicles at the border wasn't that bad, not like when I'd gone with Sorelle's family to Mexico. Once we got to the booth where you were supposed to show your passport, I realized I didn't have mine.

"Here," James said, handing over three passports, one of which had to be mine. I guess my father must have given James my passport, yet knowing that didn't make me feel better. I wanted my own passport, in my own hands. It was *mine*.

"Hey there," said the border agent, a woman with purple hair, as she peered in at me through James's window. "You doing good?" she asked, as if she half expected me to start crying and telling her James and Robin had kidnapped me. For a moment I was tempted to do just that . . . just to see what they would do.

"Yeah." I smiled. "All good here."

Then we were in Canada. It was the same kind of woods, roads, fields, and other stuff outside the car's windows, but somehow it felt different. It felt farther away from everything I knew, everything I loved. Everyone I loved.

I closed my eyes to keep from crying; closed them, and to my surprise—fell into a deep sleep.

Someone shook me awake, and I was glad because I was dreaming of running around in the dark, lost and alone. I glanced outside and noticed it was just as dark as in my dream. I had to have been out a few hours at least for the sun to have set. "We're here," Robin said with a smile.

"Huh?" I managed.

"We're home."

CHAPTER 7

The compound was not what I'd expected. I'd thought there would be some big white concrete building. Actually I'd imagined it looking kind of like my junior high school building—only without the playground.

But what I was looking at was more like a compact castle—taken straight from the set of some Dracula movie. Towers, gargoyles, and hard lines were what the place was all about. Off to the side I could see another smaller building, or the edges of one anyway.

"Not very modern, I know," Robin said as I stared at the mini castle. It had two big scary-looking dragons on each side of its wide entrance, illuminated by a flickering yellow outdoor light. The car Tobias was in drove past us. I wondered where he was going. Was there more around than the castle and the one small house? If this was a "compound," I guessed there had to be more buildings out there in the night, but it was too dark too see much, mostly because the entrance light was ruining my night vision.

"What is this place?" I asked, before jumping a foot up in the air when James slammed the SUV's trunk shut. He held both my suitcases.

"Sandleholm Manor," Robin said, before pushing me forward slightly, indicating that I should follow James, who was heading toward the double doors of the castle with my bags.

"This is the main house," James said roughly as I caught up with him. He pushed open the heavy wooden door and I followed him in. First there was some sort of vestibule with an old bench and a huge oil portrait of a man with a big beard. James went right and then we were in a great big foyer, which opened to the left to a big dining hall and to the right to some sort of living room. Only a fancy one with no TV and art that looked like it should be in a museum.

The living room was full of people. Well, maybe not full. There were only five guys, but they were all so big it seemed like the room was totally full. Two of them were older, one with a lot of white hair that stuck out and another with graying hair and a goatee. The rest looked to be about James and Robin's age, early to midtwenties.

The younger guys and the white-haired man were in the middle of a conversation about beer flavoring while the goateed one was playing chess on his own. But everyone immediately stopped what they were doing to stare at us. Well, me, I assumed, since James and Robin getting home was hardly worthy of such a reaction.

"Hi," I said, and stopped. James stopped too, but didn't look pleased about this impromptu welcome party.

"Wow," said a slightly chubby-faced guy several inches shorter than James. "I thought Robin was messing with us, but you're totally real."

"Yeah, that's me," I said. "Totally real."

"Told you," Robin said from slightly behind me and James. "You not going to introduce your girl, James?"

James glared over at Robin. Robin seemed unnaturally pleased with having pissed James off. I mean, most betas I knew tried their best to make sure their alpha's orders were followed and to keep everyone, especially the alpha, in a good mood. Robin didn't seem very concerned about that.

After a second awkward pause, James put a hand on my shoulder and moved me forward, into the living room.

"Everyone, this is Megan," he said in a stiff voice. He was mostly focusing on the old guy at the chessboard. I guessed that was his dad, Trist. There was something a little similar around their eyes.

The chubby-faced guy who had spoken before headed over to us.

"I'm Tommy," he said, offering me his hand. His face looked young, like a teenager's, but he was big and tall like the others, so I figured he was probably in his early twenties like the rest of the guys.

"Megan." I smiled. "Nice to meet you."

I glanced into the room. Trist was watching.

"Owen," one of the other wolves said. "Nice to meet you!" He held out his hand.

"Hi," I said. Again feeling kind of stupid and weird as I shook his hand. Owen had piercing blue eyes and freckles.

51

"Owen is Tobias's brother," Robin said, taking over the introductions since James wasn't helping. "That's Tio." Robin pointed to a guy who was leaning back on a sofa. He was wide and tall, taller than Robin, even, and as wide as three of me at least. He had half-healed scratches along his scalp, like he'd been in a fight with some big animal, possibly another werewolf. "His favorite hobby is eating."

Tio said nothing, neither confirming nor denying this.

Swallowing nervously, I went over and offered my hand to Tio too. The big guy looked slightly surprised but shook my hand with his giant one after a quick look at James. I glanced back too.

James didn't look pleased but I wasn't sure why. Shouldn't he be happy about me meeting some of the pack? He hadn't seemed to care about Tobias shaking my hand this morning, so it couldn't be all the handshakes.

"James," said the one I was fairly sure was James's dad. It was a command of some sort, because it made James move forward. He put his hand on my back and began shepherding me toward Trist.

We passed the old guy, the one with all the white hair, on the way, and he smiled kindly at me. He looked like Einstein mixed with Santa Claus. James didn't stop by him, and instead moved me toward the goatee guy, who just stared at me intently, looking displeased. Yup. He was totally James's dad.

"Hello! I'm Megan," I said, holding my hand out to him. I had a bizarre urge to curtsy. I mean, I'd never curtsied in my life, and I was wearing jeans and a tank top, which wasn't really the kind of outfit you curtsied in. "It's nice to meet you, Mr. . . ." I realized I'd only heard James's dad addressed by title and first name. I didn't even know my mate's last name.

"Lord Trist Sandleholm," James's dad corrected me. Lord? Was that still a thing? I thought lords and ladies were some sort of medieval thing.

"Right. Wow. Like the house," I said, because it was the only thing that popped into my head. "Cool."

"No, it is, in fact, quite warm," the old guy said before bringing my hand to his lips and kissing the top of it. I wondered if I maybe *should* have curtsied.

"Right," I said, and blushed at the missed cue. I mean, he was technically the one who had misunderstood, yet I somehow felt like the stupid one.

"It's very easy to be dead," he told me seriously, still holding on to my hand. I had no idea what that meant but tried to smile. "Time, time. Time is a lie. Time, time. Do you like time, sister mine?"

I frowned and glanced quickly to James, whose face was impassive. "I guess it's okay. I mean, if there was no time, nothing could change."

"Change," Trist said. "Change is a lie." He shook his head and let go of my hand suddenly, focusing on his chessboard. "It's all a lie. But I'll beat her in the end. I will. I'll stop it." He smiled an odd, savage smile, showing white teeth, then calmly moved a piece on the chessboard.

This was James's dad? He was even weirder than James himself. But at least James only seemed unpleasant. Trist seemed unhinged. Not quite there. Or maybe he was just the kind who waxed poetically about death and time and change. We'd had a kid in my old high school who did that to be dramatic.

Someone came up behind me and I turned, glad to have a reason to not have to talk to or think more about James's dad and his oddness. I smiled a real smile when I saw it was the Santa Claus look-alike.

"This is Dr. Pierre." James nodded to the old guy. "He's our pack medic. He doesn't get out much, but he's a real good fellow."

"All right," I said, offering my hand to him. "Good to meet you. Sorry that you don't get out much, I guess."

"It's quite all right, dear," he said kindly, making me feel marginally better.

I glanced around the room and wondered if I was meant to stay and make small talk. I was so not up for that. I looked over my shoulder to James, hoping he'd see I wanted to be somewhere, anywhere, else. A bit to my surprise, the look seemed to work.

"Megan has had a long day," James said, putting a hand on my lower back. Even through my top I felt the warmth of it. It was also a possessive thing; he was staking a claim in front of his pack. Subtle, sure, but still hard to miss if you were paying attention. "I'm going to take her upstairs."

"Of course," said the doctor. "You must be tired, my dear."

I caught some grins from the younger wolves and I realized they all thought we were heading upstairs to have sex. I mean, that was what newly mated couples did, right? Had lots and lots of sex. Except we weren't going off to do that. At least I didn't think so.

"Was that your whole pack?" I asked in a whisper as we began ascending the stairs, trying to distract myself from thinking about what might come next. "Only seven people?" My pack back home was fifty-plus wolves. This pack was tiny in comparison.

"There is also Markus and Hans, who are out actually doing their jobs," James said as we got to the top.

"So there's nine of you?"

James's only response was a grunt. I guessed that meant yes. This was sure going to be different. Only nine people in the whole pack. That was small. I mean, just my immediate family was seven people. I wondered if they all lived here. It seemed to make sense they would. Most small packs lived together.

I followed James up more stairs and down a bunch of corridors and past lots of rooms. Some were totally empty, while others made me think of museums I'd been forced to visit in school. Huge paintings of people and landscapes. There was even a suit of armor in one corridor. The higher up we got, I saw—mixed in with all the old stuff—more modern paraphernalia, like a cartoon clock, two mannequins, and a swivel chair. I even spotted a beer hat on a shelf next to what I thought might be a stuffed raccoon. The place was huge. I'd no idea how I was supposed to find my way around it.

An empty corridor and a spiral staircase later, we got to what had to be the top floor. I started to wonder if we were going to James's room. I mean, we were mates, and even though he hadn't seemed that interested in me so far . . . that didn't mean he might not want to complete our mate bond. Which was what I'd wanted too. In fact, sex had been one of the things I was really looking forward to trying with my mate. But James had been way too cold and almost mean for me to want that. So I'd have to insist on my own room.

I watched his broad shoulders and strong, muscular body. Part of me wanted him to lead me to his bed and for him to do to me all sorts of things I'd only read and heard whispers about. The rest of me was worried he'd do just that, and because he was so droolworthy I'd let him, despite how cold he had acted toward me. Suddenly I didn't want to get to where we were going; I hoped we'd keep on walking up stairs and down corridors forever. But no such luck.

"Here," he said gruffly, opening a door. He didn't step inside. "This will be yours."

The room inside was twice the size of my room back home, with wood paneling and furniture that belonged in the 1700s. A large painting of a woman in a blue gown hung on the wall. There was only one small window. A thick red carpet was on the floor. It didn't seem to match with the rest of the room, which went in more light tones and blues. In fact, nothing in this whole place seemed to match anything else. James so needed to fire his interior decorator. Not that I really thought he had one.

It was also clear this was not James's room. There was nothing personal and most of the furniture had a decidedly delicate and feminine look. Like if James even thought about sitting in the spindly chair in front of the desk it would collapse.

James put my suitcases down right inside the door. "I'm not . . . ," he began. "I'm not trying to . . ."

I glanced up at him, into his eyes. I swallowed as the silence seemed to thicken. His eyes had little flecks of gold in the green. He was staring at me and his eyes were showing me emotions I think he wasn't even aware of himself. Hunger, anger, confusion, and lust.

"I don't hate you. And I'm not trying to make you unhappy. I just . . ." He pushed his hand through his hair, messing it up. The motion made me want to touch his dark hair, to have his hand touch me. All over. ". . . I'm not good with . . ." He began again. "Just, I don't know, try to be happy here." He looked at the floor, seeming beyond uncomfortable.

Try to be happy? I wasn't sure how that was going to happen. Not with the way he was acting. But at least my new pack seemed friendly enough. A little weird, but all right.

"I will be happy here," I said, despite my thoughts. "My wolf is already glad we're here. I know you . . . your wolf . . ." I tried to smile, but I felt suddenly too weary to even do that. ". . . must be happy too."

James said nothing, and I wondered if I'd screwed up again. Then he smiled, and it transformed him. His green eyes sparkled with it, and the frown I'd seen him sporting during the majority of our time together disappeared.

"I guess so," he said, turning to the door. "And I am not unhappy."

He left before I had a chance to beg him to tell me exactly what he meant by that. In the car and even before he'd seemed so indifferent. Saying he wasn't unhappy gave me a tiny spark of hope, though. James was just a tough nut, but once I cracked him, everything would be fine. And I would crack him.

I reached for the door, hoping I hadn't waited too long and

could still catch him, tell him . . . I wasn't sure what. I'd do whatever I could to make this work—if he gave me, us, the chance? That I wasn't giving up? That I would be happy and he would too? Only once I got outside, he wasn't there.

But I thought I saw a flash of movement at the end of the hall. I hurried toward the bend, my earlier fatigue gone. When I turned the corner I found myself at a dead end, and I realized this wasn't the way we'd come. The stairs were at the other end of the hall.

A slight movement near the floor, behind a solid-looking bureau, caught my attention. I frowned.

There was a girl curled up and half hidden behind the thing. A dirty, badly dressed girl who for some reason made me think of a wild cat. But still, she was only a girl, just a handful of years younger than me.

"Hi," I said, strangely comforted by seeing her. I bent forward slightly to get a better look at her. She was wearing a stained T-shirt and shorts that I thought had once been army green but now were brown. "Who are you?" No response. "What's your name?"

The girl looked at me with dark blue eyes, and her mouth opened for a moment as if she was about to speak. Then she bounced up, pushed past me, and turned the corner. By the time I looked around the bend, she was gone.

CHAPTER 8

James

James's office wasn't the way he'd left it. Which he should have expected since he had given Doc permission to use it. And it wasn't a mess; it was just that things were not quite where he'd left them. The pen he always kept on the right was on the left, the drawer with the paper was slightly open, his map had new pins in it, papers had been stacked on top of the file cabinet, and the drapes were pulled not quite closed.

It was like it was still his office, it had just shifted subtly. Become different while he was away. He had to smile grimly at that. His office wasn't the only thing that had changed. But the change of having a mate, even if he had every intention of leading a separate life from her, was a lot bigger than his pen not being in the right spot. Yet at the same time he felt as if they were part of the same thing: change. And he'd had all the change he was ever going to want when the pack had moved to Canada.

". . . they got rid of it, but it was not a major one," Doc said, and James made himself pay attention to the older wolf.

"You found and destroyed a nest," James said. "That's good work." He would have liked to have been here for it.

Doc nodded but looked tired, and James decided this would be the last time he put Doc in charge while he was gone. Even though the older wolf had been his father's beta for many years and had everyone's respect, it was clear he was getting too old for fieldwork.

"Nothing else?" he asked after half a minute. Doc shook his head. "All right. What about my father?"

"He's doing fine," Doc said. "But he did spend a large part of yesterday searching for your sister. Ended up in the movie room and stayed there until Tommy found him."

"That's strange," James said. Normally Trist didn't go near the home theater room. He hated everything new and modern, and was old enough to think moving pictures were new.

"You joining the boys for patrol?" Doc asked, his eyes tired but a faint smile on his face. "Or are you spending it with your ma—"

"I'm going to see my father," James said. He knew his finding a mate was the most exciting thing that had happened in the pack in years. But he didn't want to talk to Doc about Megan. He wanted to pretend she wasn't even in the building with them. His wolf kept whispering *mine*, kept sending flashes of what he thought James should be doing to Megan, which was making that difficult.

"Right," Doc said, his smile faltering a little. "I guess I'll go down and see what Owen is cooking up for dinner."

James nodded and waited for the older man to leave and his footsteps to disappear before following him out into the corridor. James didn't particularly enjoy visits with his father, which he supposed made him a bad son, but it was the truth. James's father, Trist, had once been a great warrior, good Alpha, and caring father. Now he was unpredictable. Sometimes he was that same man James had loved growing up, and sometimes someone else entirely.

It had all started after James's mother's death. It had taken the madness some time to come creeping in, but in the end it had. That was how it happened most often with alphas of warrior packs. Once their mate died, they began to crack. For some it took days, others decades. But the simple fact was, as soon as a warrior alpha's mate died, the alpha too was doomed. Doomed to start to lose his mind and youth. Another reason not to complete his mate bond with Megan.

Reaching the end of the corridor, James forced himself to knock on the door. There was no answer, but James knew his father was inside. Bracing himself, he opened the door.

His father's room still looked the same as it had while he'd shared it with his mate, James's mother, for so many years. The bed, the bookcases, and the huge wardrobe were all the same. Even the chess set his father was bent over hadn't changed. James remembered helping his father carve the pieces back when he'd been a little runt. How hard it had been to get the grooves and tiny details right, and how patient his father had been as he guided him. But that was before everything changed.

"Father," James said. Trist, completely focused on the chessboard, didn't seem to notice that James was there. "Father," he said again.

Trist looked up. "Give me a minute, boy. I'm thinking."

James scanned the chessboard. "Bishop to—"

"Not about chess," Trist said, waving his hand in the air as if to chase away the notion. "I'm thinking about this mess you've gotten yourself into. A nonwarrior mate who doesn't know about time. What will they all say?"

James wasn't quite sure who these "they" were. Alphas of other warrior packs, maybe? Except there was only one other warrior pack left, in Russia, and the rumor was their Alpha had been killed some time ago.

"So you don't like her, then?" he asked, surprised to discover he wanted his father to approve of Megan.

"Pretty but not too bright," his father said dismissively. "And we can't have her going about dressed like a boy."

"Most women wear pants these days, Father," he offered. "It's not considered odd."

"Well, perhaps the commoners do, but no lady would," Trist said firmly. "She isn't a commoner, is she?"

"No," James said, even though he supposed Megan technically was a commoner. His father narrowed his eyes at him and James got the feeling Trist had no problem seeing through that lie.

"Well, we'll do a proper, traditional induction ceremony," Trist said. "And quick. That way if they question it there'll be little they can do about it. We must do it right. Must do it soon."

"Of course, Father," James said, even though he had planned to induct Megan next month and with as little fuss as possible. But this seemed important to Trist.

"The first night of the full moon is tomorrow," Trist said, moving a pawn on the chessboard. "We'll do it then."

"Tomorrow?" James couldn't help but to ask. Inductions were always done during the full moon, but usually after the new wolf had had some time to familiarize him or herself with the new pack.

"Yes." His father reached out and grabbed James's wrist. There was something feverish and pleading in his father's eyes that made James want to reassure him. "And we do it right, son; no mistakes, no doubt. The Old Ways. Must do it in the Old Ways."

"I will make sure it's all done right," James said, even though he wasn't so sure his new mate would be too pleased with that. But she'd just have to suffer through it, if it would make his father feel better. "I swear it, Father."

"Good," Trist said, and let go of his arm. "She told me . . ."

"She told you what?" James asked, even though he knew it was only ghosts speaking in his father's mind.

"I can't," Trist said, and shook his head, whatever insight he'd been planning on sharing lost. He turned back to the chessboard. His expression became slightly unfocused, the odd intensity in his eyes fading away.

"Father?"

"I've been thinking about something." His voice sounded more calm, more like the voice James remembered from his childhood. Centered, warm, familiar.

"What?" James asked, sitting down in the chair across from Trist.

Trist picked up one of the chess pieces, the black knight, rolling it between his fingers. "Strategy." Trist paused. James waited. "Remember the hunting grids?"

"Of course," he said, wondering where Trist was going with this. If he was having one of his rare truly lucid moments.

"Still working them?"

James nodded. They kept records of where the most wraiths gathered, as it was the best way to discover the nests, where the queens resided. Kill the queen and all the wraiths belonging to that nest died too. They weren't as meticulous as Trist had been back when he was Alpha, though. Trist had been determined to document all attacks, gatherings, and kills. But there were simply too many wraiths out there for the pack to do it.

"They're the key. Must work the grids," Trist said, then unexpectedly changed the subject. "Killed any witches lately?"

"No, Father," James said with a sigh. So much for clarity. "There are no witches around here. We've moved, remember?"

"Of course there are. There are always witches, son. They're everywhere."

"I—"

"Now stop bothering me and go be with your new mate," Trist said with a dismissive wave. "Complete the mating bond." His father stared at the chessboard. "The unity will help you see."

"All right, I will," James lied. He'd already decided he was never going to do that. No matter what his wolf wanted. He would never put himself in a position where he'd risk losing himself to emotions or end up going half mad like his father. Megan would be pack, but their mate bond would stay uncompleted. James would never let anyone control him with emotions again. Never risk losing his mind. Not to love or to madness.

CHAPTER 9

had a serious problem. End-of-the-world serious. Well, okay, maybe not that serious, but still plenty bad: I had no bars.

Not one single tiny bar.

No reception at all.

Zero ability to call or even send a text message.

I'd slept in, as I'd gotten into the habit of sleeping late since it was summer. When I had finally woken up, I'd checked my phone and discovered the unfortunate no-reception situation going on. A situation I was still having some trouble accepting. Also worrying was the fact that my phone couldn't detect a wireless signal. But that had to be a glitch. I mean, how would you live without cell phone reception and/or Wi-Fi? How was I going to be able to message or call Sorelle to tell her I now lived in a castle and my mate was still giving me the cold shoulder? How was I going to get advice on how to deal with the James situation without being able to google stuff? And how would I be able to call my mom and tell her I'd gotten here all right? I'd said I would do that yesterday but I'd been too tired.

After pondering the difficulties of a life without a cell for a while, I decided there was nothing to do but to hope some Canadian carrier got reception out here. I put my phone aside, and I got dressed and decided to unpack. I found a pack of gummy bears in the inside pocket of my bag for breakfast. I really wanted something more substantial, but I reasoned there was no way I'd able to find my way to the kitchen. I'd already gotten lost yesterday chasing the wild-looking mystery girl. One wrong turn and it had taken me at least fifteen minutes to get back to my room.

I wondered who the girl was, why she was in this place, and why she'd run off. Why hadn't she spoken to me? She'd just kind of looked like she was about to and then changed her mind. Like she didn't trust her voice.

A loud knock on my door made me jump and nearly drop the perfume bottle I was holding. Which would have been a shame, as it was a special kind of perfume that smelled good even to a were-wolf's sensitive nose. Although it wasn't so much the knock that scared me, but more the sudden reverberation of my mate bond. It was like for a few seconds it was as solid and new and life-changing as it had been that first night on the beach. It also made me sure it was James who was outside my door.

"Yes, come in," I said, putting the bottle down and taking a deep breath.

James entered. He held something white in one hand, but I wasn't sure what. He was in a long-sleeved dark shirt, the same kind he'd worn every time I'd seen him, and dark jeans. Also the kind he'd worn yesterday. His dark hair, his straight nose, and his green, green eyes were also the same as they'd been before, but he had a little stubble going on today, clearly having skipped shaving. It made him look different. Good different. I wonder what making out with a guy with stubble would be like.

He stopped a little bit inside the door and looked at me. Like he was half-surprised I was actually there. Maybe he'd hoped I was a figment of his imagination. Seeming to realize he was staring, he bit his lower lip and looked away from me. He spent a minute looking at everything in the room but me.

Part of me was impatient about why he was there and part was just pleased. My wolf kept making me think of the bed right behind me and how much fun we could be having instead of just standing around like fools.

"Did you come here to talk?" I asked, stepping a little closer to him, feeling my pulse speed up. He focused his eyes back on me.

"No," he said firmly, his lips pressing together. His green eyes were flecked with gold again. Interesting.

"Oh?" I stepped even closer, not able to look away from him. "So you came here to *not talk*?" I asked, not sure where this suddenly flirty Megan was coming from.

"No," he said, his voice a little lower than I remembered. "I came to tell you . . ."

"Tell me what?" I whispered, leaning closer to him. He drew in a quick breath and then jerked away, his eyes suddenly back to just green. He walked toward the window, a frown on his face.

"We're having your induction into the pack tonight," he said, his voice back to its normal range, placing the piece of white cloth—no, a dress—he'd been holding on a big chair, before turning to head back toward the door.

Induction? Tonight? I swallowed. I wondered if I should have seen that coming. Inductions were always held during the full moon, but usually only after the one joining the pack had time to adapt and learn about the pack he or she was joining. It was a rattling experience to have the pack bonds connect to you—not as intense as a mate bond but intense nonetheless. At least that was what I'd heard; I'd never moved packs and thus had never had to be inducted.

"So soon? Why not next month?" I asked.

He turned back to speak to me. "My father wants it done quickly. Normally there would be attendants, but we haven't had any female pack members. So Robin will fetch you—"

"But there is one other girl here. I saw her," I said.

James looked confused for a moment, and then his expression cleared. "Lucy."

"Huh?"

"That is her name, the wild girl. She's omega and not yet of age, still a child. And she is not pack," James said, seemingly uninterested.

"Doesn't she belong to someone? Where are her parents?" I

asked. I sure as heck wouldn't want to leave my younger sisters with just the company of a bunch of warrior wolves. And Lucy might not be of age, sixteen, but I was fairly certain most people wouldn't quite call her a child. She was probably in her early teens, at least from what I'd seen of her.

"Parents are dead. We brought her here for safekeeping, hoping she'd help us find some extended family, her pack." He smiled grimly. "But she doesn't speak. Tommy feeds and clothes her."

"All right," I said, because I wasn't quite sure that just feeding her and buying her a girl-sized military T-shirt was enough. I decided I definitely need to talk more with Tommy and see if we might be able to come up with a plan to get Lucy to talk and maybe look more like a girl than a wild cat.

Remembering my no-bars problem, I added, "And I was wondering if you, like, had a phone with reception. And maybe what the Wi-Fi password is." Because there had to be Wi-Fi, maybe not in my room, but somewhere in the house.

"The what?" James asked, sounding awkward, almost embarrassed. His expression made his mouth do a pouty thing that made me want to bite his lower lip.

"The Wi-Fi password . . . to get on the internet?" I frowned. Did they call Wi-Fi something else in Canada? I was pretty sure Wi-Fi was universal but what did I know? The only place I'd ever been besides the Hamptons and New York was Mexico. And it had been called Wi-Fi there.

"Right, that," he said, after a few seconds of adorable confusion. "We've been having some technical issues with that."

"I see," I said, worried. "So no Wi-Fi?" I asked, hoping he would say it wasn't so.

"Well, actually it's more the whole internet we're having trouble with," he clarified.

I gasped with horror. No internet. What the heck? How was that even possible? How did you live without the internet? Seriously, I had no clue how I was supposed to live without being able to check my Facebook page, my email, and Instagram. And Pinterest. And Snapchat. And my favorite blogs. And YouTube.

"But there is a phone next to your bed, if you want to make a call," he said helpfully, pointing to a phone. Like one of those with a cord that attached to the wall and then another to the mouthpiece. This specific one was red and looked like it might have been new during the seventies. I reached over to pick it up and found a dial tone.

"It works," I said sarcastically, turning back to him. "Here I was thinking it was an antique and just there to be decorative." Like the rest of the stuff in this house.

He growled, clearly annoyed by my sarcasm. "Use it or not. I don't care." He took a few steps back. He glanced at the white dress—and I use the term *dress* loosely—he'd brought with him. It seemed to remind him of why he was there. "The induction ceremony will be tonight," he repeated. "I brought you the proper attire."

I moved forward and picked up the white, nearly sheer dress he'd dropped on the chair a few minutes earlier. "This thing? What is it?" It looked like one of my beach cover-ups, only most of my cover-ups were in bright, cheerful colors or had prints on them. This one was just boring white.

"It's ceremonial. You wear it and nothing else when you are inducted," he said with a shrug.

"But it's see-through," I said, somewhat dismayed. I'd been comfortable with nudity most of my life, since clothes didn't shift along with you. But I, despite being mated to James, didn't know him or his pack. And if I was being inducted, the whole pack would be present.

"It's ceremonial," he said again. "It's traditional."

"Seriously?" I said. "You really expect me to wear this?"

His face was passive and he pointed to the dress. "This is how it was done in the Old Country. This is how we'll do it."

"I'm not wearing it." I put the dress down. "I'll wear a nice dress, just like I would have back home."

He stepped closer, his eyes darkening. "You will wear it and that is the end of it." It was an order, and if I had not been an Alpha of Alpha's daughter, I'd have bowed my head and done as he asked. But I was an Alpha too, and he couldn't order me around.

"You know, if you wanted to see me naked, you could have just asked," I said sweetly, deciding to try another tactic. "I might even have said yes."

He stiffened and glared at me. "I don't make the bloody rules. I just follow them." He glared down at me, looking between my eyes and my mouth.

"Well, I don't," I said, pissed and angry but also kind of enjoying getting a rise out of him.

"Tonight you do," he snapped.

"Bite me," I snapped right back.

"Don't tempt me." For a moment his eyes held flecks of gold again, and I was sure he was going to grab me and kiss the heck out of me. But he didn't; instead he just gave my lips one last hungry glance, then turned to march out of my bedroom.

CHAPTER 10

James

"What?" James barked as someone knocked hard on the door. He was carving, using the soothing feel of wood and a knife in his hand to try to distract himself from the faces that kept popping into his head.

The first was the woman who had kept him a prisoner with feelings not his own. The woman he had been tricked into loving, the woman he had hated more than life. The woman he had killed.

The second one, his mate, looked so young and lost. So willing to please, so eager yet fierce. Needy and bold at once. Both brought him pain for different reasons. Both were eerily similar in appearance: dark hair, tan skin, and small of stature.

"Relax, man," Robin said as he slid the heavy metal door open. James put his knife and the long-from-finished statue down. "It's just me." He paused. "Tio told me you requested one of the ceremonial dresses be brought out of storage?"

James said nothing, but shrugged. Robin clearly took that as a yes.

"And you expect her to wear it?" Robin continued. "James, you do know we aren't living in the Middle Ages anymore." James rolled his eyes. Neither of them were that old. "And she's your mate. I doubt you'll be happy when we stare at her like a piece—"

"You'll keep your eyes off her or I will—"

"Strangle us very slowly with our own intestines?" Robin offered cheerfully.

James sighed. "My father wants it done as per the Old Ways. Traditions and all that. This is how it is done," he told Robin.

"Yeah, yeah, tradition. Like that would even matter, really. I bet she isn't even a virgin. Pretty girl like that—" James was out of his seat and had Robin pinned against the wall before the other man even had the chance to finish his sentence. James growled; the idea of someone touching what was his, the idea that some schoolboy had touched flesh that should belong only to him, made his wolf want to taste blood.

And it made James the man feel trapped and powerless. He wanted her badly, yet the very idea of letting her—or anyone—have that much power over him made him angry. Angry with her for being so tempting. Angry with himself for not being able to shake his want of her.

"I think you're trying to punish her," Robin said, his face inches from James's. "Punish her for what Marisol did to you all those years ago. You take her from her family, ignore her, and leave her all alone on an empty floor. You might not have tattooed slave bands on her—"

"She is not a prisoner," James said, pulling himself off Robin and hastily covering his wrists and the tattoos there. Tattoos that would forever be reminders of his time spent as something less than he was. Tattoos he did his best to always keep hidden.

"She might as well be. And you are intentionally humiliating her by making her wear that dress. Induction hasn't been done in the Old Ways since we left Europe, and that was half a century ago, James. Think of the girl," Robin said, actually sounding pleading. Which was rare, since Robin always seemed to be more interested in smiling and making jokes than being serious. James wondered if the girl three floors above them had somehow caught Robin's eye and now his best friend was wanting to take his mate away from him. His lips curled back and he showed his teeth.

"It's tradition. Father thinks—"

"We both know the ceremony will be as valid no matter what she wears. At Tommy and Markus's induction, you didn't even bother saying half the words," Robin said, straightening his shirt and touching his one golden earring. "This is just about you exercising control. Not about your father or traditions."

"Robin—"

"No. It's a mistake," Robin spat. "A bloody stupid one if you ask me—"

"But I didn't," James said, voice low and dangerous. "This is my pack, and Megan is *my* mate."

CHAPTER 11

ater in the day, after some tasty food had shown up and I'd
finished my unpacking, I'd called Sorelle on the red phone and
explained I'd been transported back to the nineties. And not
the good parts of the nineties. Sorelle had wondered if any part of
the nineties had actually been good, which had led us to a big dis-
cussion about pop bands, *Xena: Warrior Princess*, and *The X-Files*.
Then Sorelle had had to hang up because she'd promised some
friends she'd go to an end-of-summer party.

The Hamptons had lots of these parties as the townies who
came out for the summer left to go back to New York. Me and Sorelle
usually went to as many as we could, and I felt a wave of longing as
I hung up. I wanted to go to end-of-summer parties too. Instead I
was in the middle of nowhere, about to be inducted to a warrior
pack by my distant mate. I also had no internet.

Thankfully my computer had been Rose's first, and she'd left a whole bunch of documentaries and science movies on it I'd never gotten around to deleting, so I had something to do all afternoon.

After watching aliens blow stuff up and learning all about some weird almost magic fish in, like, an arctic lake somewhere, it was time to get ready for my induction. I found a super sexy, barely there glittery white bikini Sorelle had bought earlier this summer but gifted to me because she was too pale for it. I added the see-through induction dress and checked myself over in the mirror. Sorelle would definitely approve of this outfit. All the white looked totally fab with my tan skin and dark hair. I was pleased with how the bikini made me seem sexy rather than virginal, which was what I figured was the original point of the dress.

It was near midnight when Robin—Mr. God Face himself— came to get me. When he saw my outfit, he grinned and shook his head. I smiled at him.

"You like?" I asked.

"You're going to knock his socks off," Robin said, giving me the thumbs-up. His words warmed both my insides and my cheeks, and I was glad he turned and began walking. I followed.

"Where are we going?" I asked him. We'd walked down, down, down into what had to be the basement, and it felt like we were heading the wrong way. Inductions could be performed anywhere outside where there was dirt, pretty much. But it always had to be outside. It was partly about tying the new member to the people in her new pack and partly about connecting her with the land, her new territory.

"There is a meadow a little bit south of here," he said. He was walking so quickly and I had to half run to keep up. "These tunnels lead all over and will take us close."

Which was good, because I wasn't wearing shoes. Neither was Robin, but he would be changing before the induction, since only the alpha and the inductee were supposed to be in human form during the ritual.

"You find a school yet?" Robin asked conversationally as we walked through a doorway that was about a foot thick. The door was huge and looked to be made of solid wood. I was glad we didn't have to stop to open and close it because it looked super heavy.

"School?" I asked.

Robin looked over his shoulder and grinned at me. "Yeah," he said. "Didn't you say you were going to look into Canadian colleges?"

"I did, yes," I said, surprised he remembered. "But I've only been here a day and that day has been spent without the internet."

"Right," Robin said. "Come find me tomorrow and you can borrow my cell—"

"You have a cell phone that works? That gets the internet?" I asked, grabbing his arm to stop him.

"Sure," he said. "How else would I be able to follow Madonna on Instagram?"

"Madonna?" I asked, and Robin smiled his dazzling smile.

"She's one foxy lady," he said, wiggling his eyebrows up and down.

"You have an Instagram account?" I asked. "Does James have one?" I asked, hopeful. If James had some social media stuff, I could stalk him on there and figure out what he liked. As soon as I got access to a superphone like Robin's, which had just jumped to the top of my to-do list.

"No." Robin shook his head. "James isn't big on embracing modern gadgets. They make his da nervous and freaked out."

"Your Alpha is freaked out by phones?"

Robin shrugged and looked away. "It's complicated." He smiled. "Now we should go or you'll be late to your own induction."

"And that's bad why?"

Robin just shook his head and began heading down the tunnel. After a little while we got to a few steps and a door. Robin stopped and fiddled with the door for a minute; then it opened and we exited into the night.

We didn't talk as he led me down a small path. The sun had set some time ago, but the moon was full and as soon as we got outside she began singing her beautiful song to me. I wanted to howl and shed my human form and run free.

The sky was clear, and thanks to my wolf's enhanced senses, I didn't have any trouble making out our path. Up ahead was the meadow Robin had mentioned. In the middle of the clearing was a stone altar the size and height of a small dining room table. Both Trist and James stood next to it. Robin nodded for me to head toward them, then slipped away into the trees to change into his wolf form. Lucky him. I felt awkward and sad standing in the moonlight in my human form.

Stepping out from the shadows of the trees, I looked straight at James and he at me. I was pleased Robin was right; I could tell the moment James realized I was wearing the sexy bikini and the effect it had on the whole outfit. His expression darkened and his eyes flashed yellow for a few moments. My wolf liked that. A lot. But then his face changed back to his normal passive self. Dang. James was one difficult guy to get a reaction from.

I swallowed and walked toward James and Trist. Trist was looking at something just to the left of me intently enough that I turned to look too. Nothing there. Maybe he was sensing one of the pack? They were here, I knew, even though the only one I could really feel was James.

Once I reached the slab of stone and placed my hand on it, I felt them. There were wolves all around. I'd known they were out there, but as my fingers touched the stone I felt them inside. I pulled my hand back.

"No, keep it there," James's gruff voice said from across the table. I jerked and stared at him. He was in the same dark, long-sleeved shirt and dark pants he'd worn earlier—except he wore no shoes—while his dad wore the more traditional induction outfit, a black wizardlike robe with silver symbols on it. Trist was still looking at something just over my left shoulder, seeming not at all to care about what was going on. I wondered if he was actually going to be able to be part of the ceremony at all.

"Wolves," James called, and the pack, all in their wolf shape, emerged from the forest. They were all big, but I guessed that was part of being a warrior wolf, and most had dark, blackish, or brown coats. The pack formed a circle around us, their eyes glowing in the darkness.

Then, unexpectedly, Trist began to speak, placing both his hands on the altar. Only the words he used were not the words I had heard my father speak when we had our inductions back home. These were in the Old Tongue. Still, I knew what he was asking. Sending a request to the earth to let me become part of this pack, this land.

"Up," James said as Trist's chanting cut off abruptly. At first I didn't realize he was talking to me. "Up," he said again once his eyes had found mine.

I glanced at the stone altar. I had suspected it was for me, only altars were definitely not how this was done back home. But I got up on the stone, James's hand forcing me to lie down on my back. I once more felt the intense connection to the pack, a humming inside me. Everywhere my back touched the stone I felt a faint buzz, like tiny electrical charges. I also felt the moon on my skin, bathing me, calling to me. I wanted to change more than ever before but knew I had to wait. Once this was done, we would all run together, as a pack.

"I will do the rest. In English," he said very softly. The whisper was so close to me it made a shiver of longing run down my spine. I wanted him to whisper more things in my ear, forbidden things, sweet things.

"Great Spirit, we have gathered here to give you a new child of this earth, this place," James began, and I stared up at the stars. In the Hamptons they had never been this bright. "By blood of the earth . . ." I closed my eyes, knowing what was coming. ". . . we ask that she be made ours."

There was a sharp pain on my left wrist and James held my bleeding arm out away from the stone so my blood could drip into the earth. This was part of the normal ritual that I'd seen my father perform.

"By blood of the Alpha . . . ," he said, and turned to his father. Trist in turn cut into his palm too and let his blood drop into the earth. ". . . I ask that she be made mine."

James moved over to coat his left thumb in my blood. Then he put the bloody thumb between my collarbones, at the hollow of my neck. "With blood she is tied to us this night. In the eyes of the Great Spirit and all those gathered, let all know she belongs here."

When his voice stopped, there was wind. Then there was darkness. Like the moon had gone out and the stars too. I knew that hadn't happened, though. The darkness was because of the sensory overload my brain was experiencing. It was too much, blinding me.

I'd been born into my pack; I'd never been inducted. There had been no need. I'd been born Alpha with the links to my pack already there. Only now they were gone, as if someone had cut something that had always been part of me. Cut it to shreds. And the shreds were trying to tie themselves into something else, into a new shape, linked to new people.

A dozen new people, my new pack, became solid and whole in me, yet there was still pain. Unbearable pain, so much I thought the world might have stopped existing. So much that I wondered if Trist wasn't right that death was easy. Right about time being a lie. Because there was no time in the pain. It was endless.

CHAPTER 12

James

She was pale, and he knew that wasn't a good thing. Doc was fairly certain pale meant shock or low blood pressure. Her induction hadn't gone the way he'd expected, but there hadn't been an induction of an alpha's mate since his father took his mother into the pack, so maybe this was normal. Trist, however, had been just as clueless as James about her sudden collapse. Doc had said she'd be fine with rest, though.

He touched her hair and tried to focus on all the ways this girl was different from Marisol. It was only their hair, their skin, and something about their mouths that looked alike. And the fact that they both had trapped him. Marisol with feelings caused by magic. This girl with feelings and desires caused by his wolf.

He did not want to want her. Yet he did. And it made him angry and frightened. Of course he would never share his fears. He was an alpha, and alphas did not show fear. Not to anyone. Yet for the first time in so very long, he was unsettled. Because he was worried about her. Maybe that was what unsettled him so, not the actual worrying but the fact that he was worried at all.

The door to the room opened. Robin and Tommy entered without waiting for James to give permission. They both were dressed in all black. He looked back to his mate, to his Megan. Couldn't make himself care the pack was going hunting.

"Never thought I'd see the day you let a woman sleep in your bed," Robin said, sounding somewhere between astounded and amused.

"What do you want?" James growled, not wanting them to disturb his mate. She'd been unconscious at first, when he carried her back to the house. But now she was in a deep sleep and it would be possible to wake her. But James thought it would perhaps be better if she remained asleep, so her soul, her wolf's soul, could heal.

Because that was what he felt had happened—the pack bonds she had been born with had been torn, a part of her soul destroyed. Then it had been hastily tied back together; attempts to rebuild the destroyed parts had been made. And mostly succeeded. He also suspected the violence of it had been because of the alpha ties that were now embedded in her. She was as much the Alpha as he. His pack would all obey her now.

Only she'd need time to rest while it all settled in her, in the part that wasn't human. The wolf, in this case, was the weak link, not the human part. He smiled at that thought. Usually it was the human part that made trouble, but not with his mate.

"We're going hunting," Robin said, as if it wasn't obvious. "We're leaving Markus since we figured he should rest up a bit, and Tobias—"

"Yes. Go." James waved his hand at them. Unconcerned. They hunted almost every night, attempting to once and for all eliminate the race's enemy. Only the decades they'd spent in cold Canada hadn't made a difference. The monsters were still out there.

"You're not coming?" Tommy asked, his boyish face disbelieving. James supposed the guy had the right to be surprised. Normally James couldn't wait to go hunting for the wraiths. Couldn't wait to kill them, rip into them.

"No," he said gruffly, turning back to stare at the girl in his bed.

"Come on," Robin said to Tommy. Then the pair of them shuffled out of the room. "I didn't think we'd be able to drag him away from her."

The door closed. James felt relieved they were no longer there. They were distractions and he needed to focus on the girl. On counting her breaths, on the beat of her heart he could just about hear if he strained his ears. He needed to protect her, to make sure she'd be all right while she recovered.

The minutes ticked by. James sat in an uncomfortable chair at the foot of the bed, his bed. Only he never slept in it, so he wasn't sure it could be called his. He preferred to curl up on the leather sofa in the corner, in wolf form. Sleeping in human shape was dangerous.

"James?" her sleepy voice said. James jerked, confused as to how and when he'd drifted halfway to sleep.

"Yes?" he said, his voice sounding gruffer than he'd intended.

"James . . . ," she said again, and he couldn't help but like his name on her tongue. It sounded right. ". . . am I in your bed?"

CHAPTER 13

came awake slowly, but as soon as I did wake fully, I somehow knew where I was. Only the location made little sense.

"James?" My voice sounded sleepy.

"Yes?" he said.

"James, am I in your bed?" I asked. Because I knew that I was, on some strange level of my consciousness. Something about the smell of the room, the feel of it. This was my mate's private territory, his inner sanctum. And I was in it. I was sure, yet I did not understand why.

"You are," he said, as if there were no real significance to my current location.

I said nothing, unsure of what to do. James kept watching me, kept those green eyes of his on me, like he half expected me to disappear into thin air.

I wondered if this was the chance I'd been waiting for, the chance to get some time with him, to talk with him. Yet I was a little afraid to do more than sit up slightly. What if he went back to being cold and uncaring when he realized I was no longer in pain? Because I wasn't in pain at all now. I felt newly risen, yet somehow supremely awake.

"Can I ask you a question?" I asked tentatively.

"You can ask," James said, a stronger accent to his words than normal.

I took a deep breath and tried to think up what I wanted to ask, other than the obvious questions about why he was so cold to me, what had happened to him. I figured he wasn't going to answer them. I thought about his accent, about how Trist had used the Old Tongue during my induction.

"When were you born?"

He shrugged. "It's been a while."

"How long is a while?"

He shrugged once more. "My parents were mated at the turn of the century. I was born in 1912. It sounds strange, but a warrior wolf lives as long as the pack is alive. You will live for a long time too." He pushed his hand through his hair. "Perhaps I should have informed you of this before you joined us."

I blinked. Rose had mentioned something about warrior wolves living longer, but 1912? He looked about twenty-two, but he was really over a hundred years old? That was a long time. Like, impossibly long. It was time to meet a lot of women, lots of women more beautiful, more sophisticated, more fitting for him than me. Maybe that was why he was being so cold. He knew I'd never be able to compete, compare, to some other love he'd had.

I nodded. "Okay." I sat up a little farther on the bed. James stayed where he was. "Do you want to ask me something? We could, you know, take turns?" I blushed—like he wanted to play twenty questions with me?

He brushed a hand through his hair, then nodded. Asked, "Do you feel okay?"

Not the most intimate question. Not one about my hopes and dreams. But at least he was taking an interest. "I feel fine."

"That's good," he said, and nodded. Yet he didn't move, just kept on watching me.

"Why did it hurt?" I asked. "It never seemed to hurt when I saw it done in my pack. Was it because you're a warrior?"

"Partly, maybe. It might have been the shock of the alpha power. I don't know. It is possible there was some sort of overload. But you are now much like me in rank. No one can defy your orders; they are second only to mine," he said.

"Really?" I was surprised. Even though it was like that in normal packs, I'd half expected something else for the warriors because everything here seemed kind of backward.

"Yes. You can order them all around." He walked a little closer. "But hopefully you won't do that. That would make them all very resentful."

"I won't," I said, because I had no intention of doing so. I opened my mouth to ask another question but he held up a hand.

"I believe it is my turn to ask something," he said. I nodded. "Why do you want this so much?"

I stared at him for the longest moment. His question was sincere; he really did want to know. Only I had no clear answer to give. Didn't everyone want to be loved? He was my mate; he should understand. Yet he didn't. Which made my skin start to prickle and my breath get fast.

Everything I'd hoped this would be like—the dream of companionship, of love and tender moments—was being taken from me. Had been taken almost as soon as I'd met him. I had tried to be nice even when he was being totally uncool. But now I was angry. He had stolen dreams I'd had since childhood about what meeting my mate would be like. He'd taken my normal life, my parents, and my friends. Moved me across half a continent.

And at that moment I hated him for it. For destroying my dream, for taking my life and for not loving me. For not even understanding why I needed and wanted love.

"Why do you so desperately want to keep me away?" I asked, my voice icy. He looked away from me. I got off the bed.

"Why? Why, James? Why can't you at least try to get to know me? Why be so cold?" I was surprised how steady my voice was. I thought it should be shaking with fear, anger, or rage. "Why? Are you afraid? Afraid your wolf is right and you're going to start to want me? Love me?"

He turned his back on me, his broad shoulders in the black shirt making a wall. Yet it could not stop my words from reaching him.

"I think you are. You're afraid," I taunted.

It happened so fast I had no chance to even form a thought.

One second I was standing with my arms crossed, then I was on the bed, flat on my back, with James just inches away.

His breath was hot on my throat; one of his hands held both my arms, the other pressed me into the bed. His knee was in between my legs, but nothing else of his body touched me.

He growled and the sound was so animalistic, so angry, so final. I shut up. Fast. He was still pinning me down, his much larger hands trapping my wrists. He was so close to me I could feel the heat of his body. If he moved his knee, we'd be pressed together.

"James," I half whispered, half panted. I wanted him closer. I tried to move, tried to free my hands so I could roll over and pull him closer. But his hands held me firm. I'd stopped insulting him, so there was no need for him to keep me trapped. He'd shown me who was the boss. My wolf liked that he'd done that, even though the human part of me still wanted to get to the bottom of the confusion that was James.

"I'm not scared," he said. It sounded almost like he was talking to himself rather than me. "I'm in control here."

There was a slight hitch in his breathing. I realized my earlier words had hurt him. Had upset him. Alphas didn't like to be insulted, to be called weak. Yet this was something more. I couldn't put my finger on it.

Suddenly James moved and I was free to sit up. He was in the shadows, watching me. Watching what I would do next. I felt like I'd just understood something about James, though. So all I was doing was thinking. James had asked why I wanted to be with him, essentially why love and a mate were so important to me. He wanted to know because he knew those things meant giving up control. Which he didn't want to do. Had no intention of doing.

And I knew I couldn't convince him to accept the bond. Not tonight. But I could explain why I wanted it so much, why I wanted to be part of something. Even if it might bring me heartache. Because I somehow knew it would also give me so much more happiness than potential hurt.

"A few years back, me and Sorelle got invited to a party on the beach. There were older boys there, beer, alcohol. We went swimming, drunk and in the dark. The harbor patrol came and broke up the party. Some guy took us home. No one asked where I'd been. Maybe my parents didn't notice I was gone," I said roughly. "There were a lot of times like that. When I felt they didn't quite see me. Sure, that was good sometimes." I smiled. "I could do whatever I wanted. But there were some times they should have paid attention. Like when I was twelve I crashed my father's car. He didn't even notice I'd taken the keys and left the house until the hospital called." It felt odd to speak about my childhood like this, to tell him these things I'd never let myself think, much less speak of, before.

Shrugging, I started for the door. "It's not like I blame them; there were four other girls to look out for and I wasn't really a troublemaker."

I stopped by the door, glanced back at him. He was staring at me, his eyes seeming to glow in the dark.

"That's why I want so desperately to be loved, James." I opened the bedroom's door. "I was never anyone's first priority. Never the one who had someone looking out for me. I was hoping having a mate would get me that. I'm sorry I was under that misconception. I'll do my best to leave you alone from now on."

I left the room, letting the door shut behind me.

CHAPTER 14

While dramatic exits are good and everything, they are less satisfying when the first thing you do afterward is get lost. I'd tried going up, because I was pretty sure my room was higher up than James's room. But after going up two flights of stairs, I ended up in a dark corridor with only one locked door. The door was totally black and something about it gave me the heebie-jeebies, so I headed downstairs again quickly.

Tentatively I tried to sense the pack through my new pack bonds. The bonds felt less solid than those from my old pack and a lot different from my mate bond to James. These pack bonds were more like fluffy drifting clouds in the very back of my mind.

In my old pack, the bonds had felt more solid and focused. I'd been able to sense at least the people I was familiar with, been able to tell them apart, even know them from a mile away. In time I was sure I'd be able to do that with my new pack too. But for now they were more vague, even though I could tell that most of the pack was not close. Maybe not even in the house. Maybe they were out running—it was the full moon. The distance, both physical and emotional, made me feel alone.

I could sense my mate bond to James a lot better than the pack bonds. It was like I had my very own James radar thing. That was how I knew he was leaving the manor. Part of me wanted to try to focus on him, the mate bond, to try to connect, to sense James's emotional state. I knew I should be able to do that. Mate bonds gave you not only a sense of where your mate was located but what he or she was feeling or even thinking.

But I didn't focus on James. Instead I decided a visit to the kitchen was long overdue. My stomach rumbled, agreeing with me. But before I did anything else, I needed a change of clothes. Sure, the pack had all seen me in my revealing outfit during the induction, but I still didn't feel totally comfortable running around in it. As I headed downstairs toward what I thought was the kitchen, I began peeking into the rooms I passed, in hope of a closet or a blanket or something.

I went past a painting I recognized and began to think this might have been the way Robin had taken me on the way to my induction. I opened a door and poked my head into the nearest room. This looked promising. The large room was bit of a mess: stuff everywhere, not even a path so you could get to the rest of the things in the back. No way to get to the window or even see through it because someone had put a Narnia wardrobe look-alike in front of one of the windows, and the other window was just barely visible behind the furniture, boxes of papers, piles of clothes, books, artwork, and just random stuff like a crystal ball and an impressive collection of carved wooden figures.

Leaned against an old bookcase there was a huge—and I mean huge, at least six feet wide and four feet high—framed poster of a gorgeous red Ferrari with a rainy noirish city as a backdrop.

"Oh, you poor baby," I said, headed over to the car poster. "What did you do to get left all alone in here?" I asked while kneeling in front of it, and moving a box to the side so I could sit down in front of it. This was one seriously cool piece of art; why would they stash it in a room that was being used for storage? I mean, seriously, this thing deserved to be seen.

I did some quick calculations on what might be the best way to get this thing up to my new room, where I could admire it every day, but realized it was probably going to be too much trouble and it might not fit through the spiral staircase you had to go up at the end. Maybe I could get someone to help me bring it down to the living room or kitchen. If there was a wall big enough.

"I'll be back for you," I told the poster and stood, checking a nearby chest of drawers. I found a bunch of football jerseys. Holding one up, I decided it would work and slipped it on. It smelled old but I could live with that.

My empty stomach made me resume my quest for the kitchen. But as I followed the scent of what could only be some sort of stew, I made sure to commit each turn to memory so I could find my way back to the car poster room. Once I got down to the foyer, I could sense one of my new pack members was somewhere close, and since there was the scent of food, I realized whoever it was, they were in the kitchen.

The kitchen was big and shiny and the first room I'd seen so far that looked to have gotten a makeover in the last few decades. It was all metal except for a solid wooden bookshelf filled with cookbooks. One of the wolves I'd met yesterday, Owen, Tobias's brother, was checking something in one of the three ovens when I entered.

"Roasted potatoes or french fries?" he asked, his head still half in the oven.

"Fries?" I said hesitantly, not entirely sure he was talking to me.

"Sorry," he said, turning around, a smile on his freckled face. "Only got roasted potatoes."

"Then why did you ask?" I didn't mean to sound so rude, but so far I was having a weird day—or, well, night—and not in the mood.

"Grumpy much?" he said but kept on smiling, apparently not offended. Then he nodded toward the counter space next to where he was working. "Come sit; I'll get you some stew. I do most of the cooking around here."

"Cool," I said, and I headed over and heaved myself up onto the counter. My mom hated when I sat on the kitchen counters at home. "Do you take requests? My favorite foods are pulled pork, spicy chicken . . ." I debated a little with myself. ". . . and sushi. And pizza."

Owen shrugged, then got busy getting a plate done up for me. A huge heap of stew that, now that I was closer to it, I realized smelled a bit cinnamony, and a bunch of tiny roasted potatoes. He only offered me a spoon, but since the meat was so tender it was all but falling apart, that wasn't a problem.

While I ate, Owen seemed pretty content with just making notes in a spotted notebook while checking the oven or some cabinet every now and again. There was something tranquil and at the same time focused about him.

"So you've known James a long time, then? I mean with the whole immortality thing," I asked after I'd wolfed down half the food. I figured this was an excellent time to try to gather some information that would help me make sense of James. Even if I *had* said I was going to leave him alone.

"It's not really immortality. We can die," he said absentmindedly while he took a large roast from the oven and plopped it down on the counter. Like being sort of immortal was no big deal. I was still not sure I actually believed James when he said I'd be like him, like the whole pack. Forever young. Sounded like a song from the eighties. Except James's dad and the other guy I'd met the day before hadn't been young-looking.

"So it's just really slow? Is that why James's dad is old? Is he, like, five hundred years old or something?" I asked before taking another mouthful of stew. It was a phenomenal stew, a little odd since I'd never had cinnamon in a stew (or a whole lot of experience with stew at all), but it was tasty.

"Not quite," he said as he went over and got a big Tupperware container. He took it back over to the stove and poured what was left of the stew into it.

"Then what?" I asked, now genuinely interested in the answer. If aging slowly wasn't the way it worked, then how did it actually work?

"Well, mmm" was his only answer, before he headed over to grab a roll of foil to cover the roast.

I wondered if I could make him answer my question. James had said I was sort of Alpha now too, and that meant I should be able to access that power. Except I had no idea how to issue an alpha command, what it was supposed to feel like or anything. Besides, using my new alpha power to make Owen answer a question he was clearly dodging didn't seem right.

"So," I said after swallowing my last bit of cinnamon stew. "You've known James for, like, a long time, then? Has he always been so . . ." I wasn't quite sure how to put it. *Mean* seemed the wrong word. *Cold*, maybe.

"Not always," Owen said before I got a chance to specify. "Not back before . . ." He trailed off while putting foil over the roast and taking both it and the container with the stew over to the fridge. After putting the food away, he came back over to me. He stared at me with his very blue eyes. "Want to know what my dad always said?"

"Sure," I said, putting my plate down, a little annoyed by the change of topic, but whatever.

"He said: Life is like a stew, and just like some cuts of meat, some people need to simmer for longer before they're done," Owen said.

I blinked. Food metaphors. If I was a better cook that might be more helpful. "So, have patience?"

"Well, kind of," he said. He smiled and shook his head. "It makes more sense in French. Basically the meat still needs to simmer, right? So you can't just leave it in the fridge or whatever."

I thought about what he was saying. I figured he meant James had been in the fridge for a long time and meeting me was like putting the pot on the stove and now I kind of needed to wait. But still make sure the water in the metaphorical pot didn't get cold. Or boil over. The question was, how did I do that?

CHAPTER 15

James

His wolf was becoming more and more demanding about Megan. About being with her. Watching her body, making him crave her. Filling his mind with images he didn't want there. The best way to get his wolf off his back was fighting.

So that was what he was doing.

Tenebri was a hot spot for the wraiths, one of the only breeding grounds left in the world for them and the biggest the pack had found so far. They'd completely obliterated the monstrous race in Europe before learning of this place in Canada a few decades ago. Robin had even convinced James to move Sandleholm Manor, brick by brick, plank by plank. They'd found land as close to the rumored wraith breeding ground as they dared, and yet it was decades later and they'd not been able to find or destroy all the nests, and the wraiths had not moved on. Despite the pack's efforts, the number of wraiths seemed to stay the same.

And so the war kept on while most of the packs in North America were in the dark about the enemy the warriors were hunting. The occasional deaths caused by a wraith having somehow escaped to other parts of the continent was chalked up to accidents or rogue wolves.

It was a good thing too, since it prevented brave young wolves, attempting to prove themselves, from trying to fight. Prevented them from getting hurt or killed. Because no matter how strong of a fighter a normal wolf was, it stood no chance without the venom warrior wolves' fangs held.

On quiet paws James moved easily and quickly, making sure to stay hidden in the darkness. Even though it wasn't strange to see a wolf out in the wilds, in the city you had to be careful. Didn't want to create a wolf panic. But hunting wraiths—or at least killing them—could only be done in wolf form. The special saliva that warrior wolves produced was the only way to kill a wraith.

Wraiths were shadowy figures. They appeared as ghostly apparitions, floating and massless, but in reality they were solid. And strong. Their eyes were narrow slits of yellow, heads flat and compact with grayish thick skin and sinews. Their bodies, despite feeling like nothing so much as skin-covered bone, were durable and strong, and their hands held sharp clawlike nails.

He felt the wraiths as much as he smelled them. They gave off a sort of energy, like an electric field, and one of the requirements for being inducted as a warrior was the ability to sense it.

Fighting was always a mix of aggression and excitement for

James. He suspected some people and even some of his wolves felt fear too, but James didn't. As a pup James had hated to be scared and had just found a way to turn it off.

The wraiths came toward him. To James they seemed like they must be some shadowy creatures from the underworld. Yet they were, he supposed, alive, in their own strange way. Part of this world. They could smell him, hear his blood pumping, his heart beating, sense his energy. That was what they wanted, why they hunted the werewolves. A werewolf's final energy made them powerful; the more they consumed, the stronger they became. Energy, magic, spirit. Whatever you wanted to call it, they wanted it.

The wraiths hovered closer. They knew he was a warrior. They knew to be wary but they also wanted his magic.

A firm believer in preemptive strikes, James gathered himself for a jump and leaped toward the wraith on the left. It reached out for him with its claws, but he'd angled himself just right. He flew past the threat and let his fangs sink into the creature's neck. Resisted the urge to tear or open the wound up more. It was the poison in his fangs that would drain whatever kept the wraiths alive.

The wraiths didn't scream, but there was a sort of hissing from the hurt one. James had barely landed before the second one was reaching for him. Its sharp claws slashed across his hip, but not very deep. He tore into the wraith's arm with his fangs. It felt like fragile bird bones breaking.

He retreated while the first one, the one he'd bitten in the neck, started drifting to the ground, the venom working, killing it. The second one didn't seem as affected.

With a wolfish smile, he gathered himself for another jump. The hit on his hip from before was just a scratch, not enough to slow him down. He exploded up and sank his fangs into the neck of the second wraith. It too hissed. He moved back and watched them die from the entrance of the alley. Watched them fade into the shadows of the night.

CHAPTER 16

A while later I was still hiding in the kitchen, feeling depressed about my disastrous game of twenty questions with James, my big speech about leaving him alone, and Owen's confusing advice. It was pretty clear that I needed some serious BFF time. So I waited until Owen left and then quickly stole some ice cream out of one of the huge freezers, went upstairs, and called Sorelle on my red phone.

"I know you wanted the happily ever after," Sorelle said after I explained the night's events to her. "But I'm not sure there is such a thing."

"There is," I said sullenly. "Everyone but me has one." I shoved a spoonful of chocolate ice cream into my mouth.

Sorelle laughed, which didn't make me feel better. "The happily ever after isn't a destination, you know. Life isn't a fairy tale. You don't go through trials and everything works out perfectly. Life is hard and messy. All the time."

I toyed with the red phone's cord. "I'd take hard and messy," I said. "What I don't want is distant and cold."

"Look, it's clear the guy has baggage," she said. I'd shared my worry about James having possibly dated a lot of women since he'd been around so long. "Just give him some time. Get a hobby. Restore a car or learn to paint with oil. Learn to speak French—which you really should do anyways if you're going to be living in Canada."

"That'll be fun," I said. I'd sucked at Spanish; I didn't have any hopes French would be easier.

"What I'm saying is, just wait him out. You'll grow on him."

"Not if he never talks to me," I said, eating some more ice cream. "He'd probably ignore me forever if he got his way."

"Maybe, maybe not," Sorelle said with a sigh. "The point is: Find something to distract yourself from him for a while. See if you can get into some college classes. Or get a job in town. Learn to knit. Seriously, you can't be obsessing about him all the time."

"I'm not obsessing," I said defensively. Then I thought about it for a moment. "Okay, maybe I'm obsessing a little. But maybe I'll try making friends with the pack and just leave James alone for a bit." I thought of Robin and Tobias. We could be friends. Maybe Tommy too; he'd seemed excited to meet me when I arrived.

"That's good." Someone started playing rock music on Sorelle's end, loud enough that I could hear it through the phone. "Just try to get a life. Try to see James in between if you can, but start small. Then maybe get him to take you to dinner and a movie or something. I mean, you kind of skipped a whole lot of steps because he basically made you move in with him, so you've still got lots of dates to go on."

"You're right," I said, because she was. "I'm going to figure out my life and take this thing with James slow. After all, we apparently have the time."

RATHER THAN SULK the next day away, I decided I was going to be productive. The plan was to A) find Robin and make him give me a working cell phone because the red phone was so not doing it for me, and B) find a computer with an internet connection so I could start figuring out how to get Wi-Fi and research local colleges.

Once those tasks—which were both high priority—were completed, I figured I'd C) track down Tommy. James had said he was the one looking out for Lucy. And while I was sure he'd been doing his best, maybe I could do better. I knew I could at least find her some nicer clothes.

And while doing this, I was NOT going to A) think about James or B) feel sorry for myself. That was the plan.

Okay, who was I kidding, of course I was going to feel sorry for myself. I just wasn't going to let it be the only thing I did. I was probably also going to replay every conversation me and James had had during our short time together. Not that we'd really been together. And by the way James was acting, I doubted we'd ever be. Since the moment we'd met, he'd acted like I was some sort of annoying bug he couldn't wait to squish. Yet at times there was something else, something possessive and hungry in him that he himself didn't even seem to realize was there. He wanted me, I was pretty sure, yet he was acting like he hated me. It was weird.

Beyond weird. I mean, I've heard of girls playing hard to get, but guys were supposed to be all into the chase, weren't they? Was it me being too eager that was making him pull away? Except he'd been as distant since the moment we first saw each other on the beach. It wasn't me, at least not all me. It was something else. The control thing I'd picked up on yesterday? Or more the not wanting to lose it. But that was just an alpha thing, right? Except that didn't explain everything. . . .

But I'd already decided I was NOT going to think about James or *us* today. I was going to meet some of the members of my new pack and maybe be able to check my Facebook. I missed Facebook. And Pinterest. I couldn't believe I hadn't pinned anything in, like, days. And without any Wi-Fi or cell phone reception, I hadn't been able to post any pics on Instagram either, which I was bummed about because of the seriously fabulous food I'd been served and my odd but still kind of cool bedroom.

Using my still-not-fully-developed pack bonds, I went in search of Robin. I was fairly sure it was him I was heading for, at least. Beta wolves have a different feel through the bonds. Unfortunately the place was pretty dead. I sensed a few sleeping people as I passed down various corridors on my way to the second floor. There I found—or more accurately, heard—the first sign of life. Now I was sure it was Robin I was sensing. Low, rhythmic thudding drew me to a door and I knocked. The sound stopped.

"Yeah," a voice I recognized as Robin's said. I opened the door and found myself in a gym of sorts. There were free weights and a punching bag. There was also a section of the room where the floor had lots of claw marks in the concrete. Fighting practice, maybe?

Robin was wearing only low-riding jeans and a fine layer of sweat. He smiled at me, but strangely neither the smile nor his hot bod seemed to do anything to me. Which was both a relief and kind of sucked. A relief because it would have been weird to be lusting after my mate's buddy and second in command, and sucky because Robin was hot and now it seemed I couldn't even get a kick out of admiring male hotness anymore. Instead I started thinking about how hot James might look without his shirt, all sweaty—but maybe not from boxing, from another much more enjoyable activity— which was once again going against my not-thinking-of-James policy.

"Hey," I said.

"You looking for James?" Robin asked before heading over to the side to pick up a white T-shirt.

"No, I, actually . . . I was thinking I'd take you up on the whole phone borrowing you mentioned yesterday," I said hastily as he put the shirt on.

"Well, you can borrow mine," he offered, sliding his hand into his pocket as if to get the phone out. "But just for a while. Madonna's Instagram photos won't look at themselves, you know. Better we get you your own."

"That totally works for me," I said, barely able to contain my giddiness at the thought of having a working cell phone.

"Right," Robin said with one of his dazzling smiles. "Tommy will hook you up. He's our resident tech expert."

"That's perfect." So far my plan was going pretty great. "I wanted to talk to him about Lucy anyways."

"Who?" Robin said, as if he'd never heard of her. Then a few seconds later it clicked for him. "Right, the kid."

"Mmm," I agreed noncommittally. I didn't like how neither James nor Robin seemed to even remember that Lucy was around. I mean, I'd only seen her for a few seconds two days ago, but I couldn't stop thinking about her and how to help her.

"So," I said as we got moving. "Some of these things are totally strange." We'd just passed the suit of armor, which was standing under a huge disco ball. "It's not really . . ."

"We brought a lot of stuff over when we moved. Then added on as we bought new stuff over the years," he said, but he sounded like it didn't much matter to him.

"Right," I said. I was beginning to see a pattern. Everyone here was weird or crazy or totally self-absorbed. James didn't care enough about me to pay me any attention, no one cared about Lucy, and certainly no one cared about making the place look nice. They were just a whole bunch of uncaring idiots. Okay, maybe I was overreacting—after all, Robin was nice enough to help me get a cell phone and Owen did cook for everyone. But still, it wasn't like interior decorating or buying clothes was rocket science.

Robin led me down the stairs to the first floor. I could vaguely sense we were getting close to a few members of the pack, but I wasn't familiar enough with the bonds to tell which ones.

The door swung open, and two of the pack members I'd sensed stepped out. One was Santa Doc. The second one was Tommy, who was naked from the waist up—his chest had a gorgeous tattoo of a wolf and an eagle, and he had a bunch of nasty-looking scratches on his side.

"Hi," I said lamely, wondering who he'd fought to get those wounds. Fights were fairly common in wolf packs, especially among alphas. I remembered Rose had said all warrior wolves had the alpha gene. I guessed that might mean more fights than normal in a warrior pack.

"Hi, Doc," Robin said with a nod to the older wolf, then turned to Tommy. "Megan wants to talk tech with you."

"And about Lucy," I added.

I expected the same blank expression I'd seen on James's and Robin's faces, but Tommy's baby-blue eyes immediately turned concerned, and he looked around as if expecting to see Lucy somewhere. "Is she okay?" he asked. "Where is she?"

"She's fine," I said, wanting to reach out and pat his shoulder. But I didn't know him well enough to do that. And he was still shirtless.

"So what's up?" Tommy didn't seem at all like James and Robin or even Tobias. They seemed almost out of place. Out of time I guessed was more correct. Tommy didn't seem like that. He seemed young. Even though he was probably a few years older than me (or a lot of years with the whole nonaging thing the warriors had going) he seemed so much more relaxed. And happy, or at least carefree.

"Robin said you're the guy to talk to about getting a phone," I started, glancing at Santa Doc, who was peering at us like we were fascinating. "Maybe even an internet connection?"

"Sure," Tommy said. "Come along."

I nodded at Robin and Doc while I followed Tommy. Thankfully where we were going wasn't far and was on the same floor, so I might have a chance at finding my way back.

"Here we are," Tommy said, when we stopped in front of a wide doorway with a dark drapery instead of a door. Inside I could hear a TV playing. "Welcome to the modern world," Tommy said as we walked into the room.

It was a movie theater.

Or at least a home movie theater. There were a dozen plush movie chairs, a huge projector screen, and a popcorn machine and small fridge in a corner. The walls and ceilings were painted black and the floor had a dark gray carpet. It was like a super awesome movie cave.

I was totally relieved to find something in this house that wasn't a hundred years old. Even if the movie that was playing looked really old. It was some sort of Western. I looked over at the screen. It was a pretty sweet setup. But I would not be distracted from my mission by HD video and surround sound.

"Cool," I said, because it was. "But loud." He picked up a remote and clicked it at the projector and the film's sound turned off. "Thanks."

"I'm not surprised your cell isn't working. Most companies have sucky reception everywhere but town," he said before making a little wave to indicate I should follow him.

"Yeah," I said as Tommy took me to a door on the opposite side of the theater to where we'd entered. "I noticed. I don't think I've been offline this long since I was, like, ten. It's weird how you don't know how much you need something until you don't have it."

"True. This is my workshop," he said, holding a thick metal door open. The room beyond looked nothing like the rest of the house. It had bare white walls and some mismatched office furniture. There was a lot of tech stuff. Cords, old hand radios, a few laptops, different-sized screwdrivers, an old TV, a big gray computer that looked to be, like, a hundred, cables, wires, and lots of other techy stuff I couldn't name.

"You have computers," I said, quickly looking back at Tommy, who had picked up a ratty old band T-shirt, covering up his tattoos. "Please tell me you have Wi-Fi."

"Well . . ." Tommy pushed his hand through his hair. "I got the internet." He glanced nervously at the door. "James doesn't *want* to know about it. Or I guess it's his dad. He gets nervous around tech. He's not much for change in general."

I managed not to huff. "I've noticed."

"It's just the way he is. He was real grumpy for a long while after Robin and James decided to induct me and my brother," Tommy offered. "But now he's come around. It'll probably be the same for you."

"Think he'll come around to Wi-Fi this decade?" I asked.

"I decided not to push it," Tommy said, beginning to root around in a cardboard box. "I got a bunch of phones and I'll just need to find you a working SIM card."

"Right," I said, plopping down on a swivel chair to think while Tommy rummaged.

"Why do we need to ask permission?" I asked, looking up. "I mean, it's not like anyone could tell if we did set up Wi-Fi in some areas. And I'm as much the boss as James, aren't I?"

"I guess," Tommy said, banging on the side of a desk before managing to open the drawer in it. "And Wi-Fi is pretty invisible. Except for the box with the blinking light."

"Could you do my room?" I asked, jumping up off the chair in excitement.

"Which one is yours?" Tommy asked, getting an envelope out of the desk drawer. "There is a SIM card; the activation code is in there. The guys are always losing phones so none of these are fancy." He put shoe box full of phones in front of me.

"I think I'll stick with my own," I said, taking the envelope while doing a little silly dance of joy on the inside. "And my room is, well, it's like a blue old-fashioned, very girly room."

"Right, which floor?"

"There's more than one blue girly room?" I asked, and bit my lip.

Tommy smiled. "No, but I have no idea what room you're talking about."

"I guess that makes sense. It's pretty high up and kind of out of the way."

Tommy scratched his cheek. "We'd need a lot of cables to get it up there."

"What about some other room?" I said, suddenly getting an

idea. What if, just like Tommy had created the movie theater room, I could turn one of the many rooms in this house into my own little haven? A nicely decorated one, with the beautiful sports car poster on the wall, and Wi-Fi. A place that could be mine. "On, like, the second floor."

"I could make that work." Tommy nodded.

"Could you help me carry some stuff too? And maybe help me order some furniture from this decade?" I asked, already trying to think up what I might need to buy and what I might be able to DIY into something perfect for a modern but charming hangout space.

"Right now?"

I thought about it. I needed some time to decide what I wanted and maybe find a space to dump all the stuff I ended up not using. "No. But tomorrow?" Remembering the second reason I was here, I said, "I was also wondering about Lucy."

"What you wanna know?"

"I don't know." Something about Tommy made me just like him, so I decided not to be all like, *You shouldn't dress girls in dirty khakis.* I mean, for all I knew, Lucy might like those tomboy clothes. "Like who is she and, well, why is she here? James said her family was killed and that she won't talk, but—"

"You're wondering why we haven't managed to find her pack? Me too," Tommy said, hands on his hips and a half frown on his face. Then he turned and walked over to a big chest and opened it. Inside were files and papers, seemingly thrown in there at random. Tommy rooted around in there for a minute, then came up with a thin file. He tossed it to me.

"Not much in there, but it's all I could find." He shoved his hands in his pockets. "Even had an army buddy look into her. Nothing more. And since she won't talk, there's not much to go on."

"Won't or can't talk?" I asked as I opened the file. There were a few sheets of paper inside, but nothing that looked useful. Most of it looked really confusing. I closed it and put it down on the desk again.

"She sings along sometimes when I play, like, Disney movies for her," he said, pointing out to the movie theater. "So won't."

"All right," I said thoughtfully. "She can speak. She just chooses not to."

CHAPTER 17

Before I left, Tommy asked me to show him to the car poster room. He said he'd totally be able to get me Wi-Fi in there and he'd also see if there was someplace we could move all the stuff in the room so I could start making it my own. It was official. Tommy was my favorite person in this place. He was helpful and nice and actually wanted to talk to me.

I spent the rest of the day exploring, and learning my way around the manor. Around noon, after I'd paused for a lunch break, I developed a shadow—Lucy. She was following me. She was pretty sneaky about it, and once I realized she was there, I tried to get her to talk to me, but that just made her run away. Then, after a little while, I caught her following me again and we repeated the whole me-trying-to-talk-to-her-and-her-running-away thing. In the end, I figured it was okay for her to just follow me around. Hopefully she'd get brave enough to talk to me eventually.

I didn't see James, but that was only because I deliberately chose, twice, to not head toward areas I sensed he was in. I saw no one in the pack either, which I thought was a little odd. But I figured maybe they were off working or whatever. I was curious to meet them all for real but at the same time I was also kind of worried about it. They were immortal warrior wolves. I was just me. I'd never felt like that wasn't enough, except maybe sometimes around my dad, but this was different. I was all alone here. I mean, I was part of something, the pack, but I still was a big-time outsider.

I hoped after spending some time around them I'd feel better. More like part of the pack. Tonight was the second night of the full moon, so I was hoping there would be a hunt—that was the best for bonding within the pack.

"Is there going to be a hunt tonight?" I asked Tommy. We were both in the kitchen, having been drawn by the amazing smell. Dinner was, to my delight, pulled pork. Owen had made one of my favorite foods! "I'm kind of bummed I missed the hunt after my induction yesterday with the whole passing-out thing."

Tommy glanced to the side, then cleared his throat, then took a bite. "No, it's, um . . . Everyone has to get to, eh, work."

"Oh, right, cool. Do you all work nights?" That was kind of weird. Wasn't it?

"Something like that," he said before immediately launching into a story about all the horrible army food he'd eaten back when he'd been a soldier.

It took me a second to realize he was trying to change the topic. Why would he do that? Maybe I was just getting paranoid because of James's distance and reluctance to talk to me about pretty much anything.

"Earth to Megan?" Tommy said, waving a fork to get my attention.

"Yeah, I'm listening," I said, even though I hadn't been. Which wasn't cool. Tommy was totally awesome, and even though we hadn't spent that much time together, I was sure we were going to be friends. So I made an effort to put James and any and all distracting thoughts having to do with him out of my mind.

As we ate and chatted, I learned that Tommy and his brother, Markus, had been normal wolves, part of the other local pack, before James had made them part of the warrior pack a couple of years ago. Also, Tommy was only four years older than me, which, compared with James, made him pretty much "my age" and explained his interest in technology.

No one else joined us for dinner, not even Owen, who had cooked. The other pack members came in and got food and then left again. Maybe they were in a hurry to get ready for work? It still seemed really depressing not to have dinner together. I mean, back home we tried our best to eat as a family most days. And even if everyone couldn't take part, it was still an important ritual for a family and a pack.

I offered to help Owen clean up and he was happy for the help. I wanted to ask him if he was the only one who ever cooked or cleaned up and why. I mean, that seemed totally unfair. There should be a schedule or something, making sure everyone helped out. Then I thought maybe he had volunteered because everyone else just sucked at cooking. I decided not to ask him but to make sure to offer to cook some night in the not too distant future.

"Dinner already over?" James suddenly asked from the doorway, startling me into dropping the plate I'd been transferring from the sink to one of the dishwashers. I'd been so lost in thought I hadn't sensed him coming.

"Oh no," I said as the plate shattered into a hundred tiny shards. I glanced from the plate to Owen and then to James. "I didn't—"

"Don't worry," Owen said. "I'll go get the broom. I drop things all the time."

He hurried over to a door and disappeared.

"We just put everything away," I said to James, squatting down to pick up the bigger shards. "I can get it out again, though, if you're hungry?" Of course he was hungry, or else he wouldn't be here asking about food.

"Don't do that," he said quietly, but his eyes were blazing. "You might cut yourself."

"I'll just get the big pieces," I said, picking the last big shards up and putting them on the closest kitchen counter. "They're not really sharp."

He was still focused on me, seeming to vibrate with some sort of carefully contained emotion. Anger? Irritation? Lust? I wasn't sure. He sure seemed ready to explode into action at any second.

I looked away because the vibes he was sending out felt too overwhelming, and tiptoed around the mess over to the fridge. "Owen made pulled pork and there is some—"

"Forget it," he snapped, and before I could turn to him, he was gone from the doorway.

Last night I'd been the one making a dramatic exit. Tonight it was James. I wondered what had upset him this time.

Right about then, Owen got back with the broom, and he insisted on sweeping up my mess without letting me help at all. Which was totally nice of him and I'm sure had nothing to do with him not trusting me to actually get the floor clean.

Since there was not going to be a pack hunt, I decided I'd change and go running on my own. I might not catch anything, but it'd still be good to let my wolf out and just let all my human worries melt away for a while.

So I hurried all the way back up to my room, where I got a little backpack to put my clothes in once I was outside and ready to change. To my surprise I was able to find my way downstairs after only getting lost once. I was getting the hang of the layout of the manor. Or maybe I'd just learned where a few of the different stairs, corridors, and rooms led, since there was no obvious logic to how the manor had been constructed.

I'd tried to scout out the land around the manor through a few windows, but other than the walk in the dark to my induction, I hadn't gotten a chance to look around all that much. It was all pretty normal. Mostly grass and some shrubs, then lots of trees, all different sorts. It was kind of pretty with the moonlight shining down on it. My wolf was getting seriously excited by the big bright moon just starting to rise.

Was the moon bigger here than home? Was her song louder? I

wasn't sure; all I knew was that I wanted to run as the wolf. Run, run as fast as I could. I stripped out of my clothes and put them in the backpack and then started to change into my wolf shape.

Changing takes a minute—or five—but I wasn't in a rush and that made it easier. Going from human to wolf is faster than the other way around, at least for me, and before long I was standing on four paws, stretching and yawning.

I tried to not to think, to just surrender to the wolf. She didn't care about things I worried about: school, how far away my family was, how unsocial my new pack was, not even all that much about James's behavior. She could always just live in the now, in a way the human me couldn't.

My wolf liked this new place. The smells and the sounds that were so hard to come by in the city were all around us here. I ran for a bit, scared some birds, and even considered making one into a second dinner, but then I heard the sound of running water and turned toward that instead. A few minutes later I found a cute little stream. A stream . . . that might lead to a lake, right? I wasn't sure but decided to follow it for a bit and see.

Ducking under an old fence, I kept running along the river as it bent slightly. I caught a whiff of another animal. The scents translated differently from my wolf's nose and so it took a minute before I could associate it with the sheep I'd seen at a petting zoo once when I was a kid. Part of the scent was irritating, wool and manure, but the rest was making my wolf hungry and eager for a hunt.

No. No hunting livestock. That was one of my father's rules for all werewolves. But my wolf wanted to see. Just see the sheep. Just for fun. Like a game. See how close we could get. Maybe startle them a little.

Since the wind was already favoring me, I figured that was okay. As long as I didn't kill or hurt the sheep, it wasn't really breaking the rules.

With a few quick jumps I hurried up a slight rise and got a view of the flock of sheep clustered together and a farmhouse in the distance. There were some other outbuildings and cars that I doubted had been on the road during my lifetime. There was a faint trace of a human in the air. The sheep's caretaker, a farmer, I presumed.

Now you've seen them, I told my wolf. Told myself. Time to go back. But my wolf wanted to play. These were grazing herd animals, the best kind of prey, and small enough that I could take one down without help if I wanted to.

It'd be fun.

I had to track down closer to the farm to make sure to keep the wind the right way. Didn't want the sheep smelling me before I was ready. So I had to creep close to one of the cars by the farmer's house.

I was halfway across the muddy yard when a chicken I hadn't noticed began to make *caw-caw-crraakw-craw* sounds. Then suddenly a whole bunch of chickens were cawing and a spotlight lit up everything, totally blinding my night-adapted eyes.

I heard the farmhouse's door slam open and the vaguely familiar *crun-crunch* of a shotgun being loaded.

I barely had time to think, *Uh-oh, I'm in trouble* and roll under a nearby car on blocks before a bunch of lead pellets peppered the ground I'd been on a few seconds ago. Close one. But the angry farmer with his gun was still out there and the danger was far from over.

Half crawling under the low car, I listened for footsteps while also trying to figure out a good escape route. There were plenty of buildings, rubber piles, and a tractor off to the side. Any and all of those would make good hiding spots for sneaking away. Except . . . farmer with a shotgun.

I heard the guy fighting with his boots, trying to get them on, and I considered darting over to the tractor. But was the tractor really a better hiding place? It felt safe and snug under the car, even though I knew that was only an illusion. I had to move or else I'd get turned into hamburger meat.

As the farmer's heavy now-booted footsteps made their way down the porch, I considered trying to reach out to James through our mate bond. I should be able to do that, make him sense me and send him my distressed feelings. But what if he didn't hear me? And what could he do? The manor was miles away.

A few miles away . . . but still close enough that James—or someone—should have warned me not to go running in this direction. But no one had. Sure, I hadn't asked, or told anyone what I was up to tonight, so part of it was on me, but the rest was on James. He should have told me not to go running east.

"Where're you, ya bastard?" the farmer yelled, clomping over to the car I was under. I made sure to cram myself close to the only wheel the car still had left, hoping it would hide me. I'd missed my window to escape. "Yar not getting one of 'em."

Apparently other things hunted in this area. Maybe other wolves; more likely mountain lions, lynxes, and maybe foxes. Or some other predator native to here. Maybe bears.

The farmer banged the hood of the car, making my wolf want to bolt. But that was the point. It would be bothersome to get the shot-gun under the car while having to squat down in the mud, and a shot there would most likely ruin the car for good. Not that it looked like it was going anywhere.

Stalemate.

At least for a little bit. I couldn't stay under here forever. Eventually he'd get annoyed and decide to hell with the car. I considered changing back to human, but crawling out in the mud, naked and having to come up with an explanation of how I'd gone from a wolf to a girl, didn't seem very appealing.

The farmer swore some more, complained about someone named Missy being gone, and in general was so busy being mad I'd dared come close to his flock he didn't hear the footsteps. But I heard them. Heavy feet on moist grass and sometimes mud.

"Excuse me, sir?" a familiar voice said, making the farmer turn suddenly. "Yes, hello, have you by happenchance seen my dog? She's fairly big, looks a little like a wolf?"

There was a pause as my savior got closer. I heard the jangling metallic sound of what had to be a chain and collar.

"Well, I, I might," the farmer said.

"She's an expensive one, purebred but with terrible manners,"

Trist said, getting closer. He sounded totally normal, not at all as weird as when I'd met him. "Always slipping off her leash."

"There was a dog, well, I was sure it was a wolf . . ."

I yipped—wolves can't really bark—to get Trist's attention. I wasn't sure if he knew I was there, if he could sense me through the pack bonds. I could only vaguely sense him.

"Oh, you've found her. Thank you, good sir," Trist said, sounding exactly like a relieved dog owner. "Muffin, come out now!"

Muffin?

Now that was just insulting, but whatever. I crawled over to the back of the car, as far from the farmer as I could get and as close to Trist. I peeked out quickly. The farmer had his gun resting in his arms. Kind of like the shotgun was his baby and he was cradling it close to keep it safe from the world.

I darted out and hid behind Trist's dark and slightly dirty pant legs.

"That don't look like na dog I eva seen, mister," the farmer said. "That look like a wolf to me."

"Well, rest assured it's a dog and you've done me a great service today," Trist said, and his hand went into his jacket pocket and came out with a money clip. "For your time." He loosened a number of bills and put them on the car's low roof.

Maybe it was the money, maybe it was Trist's British and very final tone that made the farmer shrug and say, "No problem. I'm glad you found your . . . dog."

Trist nodded and squatted down a little to put the collar around my neck. I forced myself to be still and not growl while he did. Then to follow along like a nice dog, down the driveway until we were out of sight.

Then I pulled free of his loose grip and growled. I understood why the charade had been necessary but I didn't have to like it.

"Not very gracious," he said with a raised eyebrow. He put a backpack down—mine, I realized, the one I'd left my clothes in. "If you let me unfasten the collar, you can go and change."

CHAPTER 18

"Thanks for saving me," I said as I walked out from the trees a few minutes later. And I meant it; I'd been in serious trouble back there. Even if the dog thing hadn't been fun, it had been a smart and necessary move. "How'd you know I was in trouble?"

"I saw you walk off from a window," Trist said briskly. "I figured I'd best follow. Didn't my son tell you not to go running around here?"

"No, he didn't," I said, trying to tame my hair, which always turned into a rat's nest after changing.

"He should have." Trist glanced back toward Mr. Angry Farmer's land. "It's not like him to forget something like that."

"Well, he did," I said defensively. "I'd have remembered."

He stopped and looked at me for half a minute, then said, "I believe you."

"Thanks?" I said, frowning up at him. He reminded me a bit of my own dad. It was probably the I'm-a-big-bad-alpha thing and the graying temples. Or maybe it was some sort of dad vibe all fathers had?

"Do you want to see the stables?" he said, abruptly changing the subject and turning away from me. "We have a beautiful red mare I bought last week who's about to foal. Ever seen a newborn foal?"

I kept on frowning. "I haven't, but—"

"Let's go see what the stable master says; maybe today is the day." Stable master? Trist used the weirdest words for stuff, but since he was seriously old, I guessed that made sense.

"All right," I said after a few seconds. He straightened his suit and then offered me his arm. I took it and we started walking back, first along the road and then across the country for a bit, following the same stream I'd run along but going upstream this time.

As we got closer to the manor, Trist started telling me about how the grounds had looked. About grand gardens, lawns, flower beds, and a pond with water lilies. I doubted, however, those things had ever existed here. Because the pine forest and grassy pasture off to the north surrounding the manor had never been beautiful gardens. This land had never been tamed. Wherever they'd lived before coming here—England, I figured—had had them, and Trist was getting them confused.

Trist took us over to a large timber barnlike building—the stables, I figured. Except I neither smelled nor saw any horses as we got closer. Trist didn't seem to notice, though, and happily walked us over to a door. A solid door with a key code lock on its serious-looking metal handle.

"Well, it's locked," I said after giving the handle a pull.

Trist moved me to the side. "I know the combination." He pressed three fives and a zero, the lock beeped, and he was able to open the door.

He stepped inside and I followed. Even in the dim, pretty much windowless room, I knew where we were. Knew it from the scent of oil and rubber.

"This isn't the stable," Trist said.

"No, it's not," I said. It was something better. It was the garage. A huge garage.

"It's my son. He keeps moving things. The stables must be on the other side," Trist said, then added to himself more than me, "They must. Mustn't they?"

"Maybe? Hey, Trist, would you mind if I looked around here?" I asked, because looking around, I was starting to feel like I'd died and gone to car heaven.

"Of course not, my dear. I'll just wait right outside for you." He smiled but looked uneasily over at the closest car before quickly turning and walking right back out, letting the heavy door close behind him.

"Hello?" I called out. The words echoed back to me. The garage was huge, making me think of a small airplane hangar, and it all looked clean and neat. A bit to my surprise, I found a modern service station with a specialized car computer. I glanced around and came to the conclusion that all the four cars in the garage, except for a beautiful red shiny sports car, were the same make and model. There were five empty garage bays.

I went over and touched the closest SUV's tinted windows. If the pack ever went out together, with each one driving his own SUV, it would look like the secret service, or maybe the mob, showing up. The Werewolf Mafia. That sounded like a rock band. I suppressed a giggle at the thought.

I walked over to a cabinet on the wall that had the shape of a key spray-painted onto it and a keypad next to it and tried the code Trist had used for the door. The cabinet opened. That wasn't very safe. If someone got the door combo they'd have access to the car keys too. The keys were neatly labeled one through nine, with one, four, seven, and eight missing. I closed the cabinet. I wasn't going to be driving anywhere today, even though it felt like ages since I'd been behind the wheel.

A noise from the other side of garage made me freeze. I briefly wondered if it was Lucy, but that didn't seem likely. I hadn't seen her follow us outside, I doubted she had the code, and even if she did, I'd have heard her enter.

"Hello," I called again. Searching the pack bonds, I realized it had to be someone else from the pack. Nothing to be scared of. I was a werewolf, for God's sake. I didn't have to jump at shadows. Still, just to be safe, I grabbed a large wrench from the nearest cart.

I walked until I came to a car with its hood open and a guy in dirty overalls studying the engine. He wasn't anyone I recognized from dinner or around the house or the first night's pack meet and greet, but he still seemed a little familiar.

"Who are you?" I asked, holding on to my wrench. He might be pack but I still didn't know him.

"Markus," the man said, glancing my way for a second, then

back under the hood. "You're Molly, right? Tommy's new pet?" As his eyes came back to mine I realized this had to be Tommy's brother. Their eyes were almost identical. Except Tommy's eyes were nice. They had a warmth to them. Markus's eyes lacked that, and it was kind of weird to see my friend's eyes look so empty, even if it was on another person.

"Megan," I corrected him, not bothering to offer him my hand. "And I'm no one's pet."

"Right," he said, studying me closely before asking, "Did you want something?" in a snarky tone.

"Trist was just showing me around," I said as he went back to work on the car. I wondered if this was his job, fixing the pack's cars? Or was he a mechanic for reals? I'd worked on some cars with my grandfather and knew the basics. Maybe Markus, rude as he seemed, could hook me up with a job? "Are you a mechanic or something?" I asked, looking him over in his greasy overalls. "Like is it your real job?"

"No."

"What is your real job, then?"

"Don't you . . . ," he began but when he focused on me, whatever he saw on my face made him close his mouth and instead say, "Ask James."

"What?" I said

"Ask your mate," Markus said. "He's the one who should talk to you about it."

"About what you do for a living?" I said, and Markus nodded before looking back under the car's hood.

I resisted the urge to bite my lip. Why wouldn't Markus think it was okay to tell me what he did for a living? I was his Alpha too. Sort of. Had James told everyone not to share stuff with me, and if so, why? Whatever the reason, it was clear I needed to have a talk with James about who he was and the fact that whether he liked it or not, I was his mate and Alpha too. He might not want to be with me, but he sure as heck wasn't going to undermine me with the pack.

"Fine," I said to Markus, turning to walk away. "Be that way."

I headed back toward the door to find Trist again. But to my surprise I sensed he was inside the garage. Looking around, I stopped by the last car to the exit, and found him sitting in the back seat.

"Trist?" I asked, and stopped by the car's still open door. "What are you doing? I thought you were going to wait outside."

"This carriage is very comfortable," he said, glancing my way for a second, then back to the still car's front window. "I'm going to get you your gift." His eyes came back to mine, surprise suddenly in them. "Nora? What are you wearing?"

"I'm not Nora," I said. Who was Nora? "I'm Megan, remember?"

"You sure?" he asked, studying me closely.

"Yes," I said. "I'm sure."

"It's good to meet you, Megan," he said, reaching out to shake my hand. Not sure what else to do, I took it. He shook it with a lot of enthusiasm, like meeting me—again—was like meeting someone famous. He smiled widely at me. "Your hair is pretty."

"Thanks," I said, trying to figure out what was going on. This was not the same guy who had come to my rescue earlier. This Trist seemed more like the strange one who I had talked to my first night at the manor. Confused. So confused he had forgotten he'd met me.

"I was going to go down to London," he said as he pulled his hand back. I tried not to look puzzled even though I was. Maybe there was a Canadian London, but the only one I'd ever heard of was in England. "My daughter's naming day is soon," he said. "I'm going to buy her something wondrous. But my coachman seems to have forgotten."

"Oh," I said. Nora must be James's sister. If he really had a sister and this daughter of Trist's wasn't just part of whatever delusion he was wrapped up in. Because I was fairly sure that was what this was: some sort of crazy delusion.

"You want to accompany me?" he asked, looking so hopeful I couldn't say no.

"I'd like that," I said. I wasn't sure if this was what you were supposed to do, indulge crazy behavior. I remembered both Tommy and Robin had said something about Trist being freaked by tech. Maybe the garage and modern cars were causing him to get confused? If so, I probably should find a way to get him somewhere more familiar and comforting. "Let's go back to the house and see if we can find your, your coachman? All right?"

As Trist agreed and got out of the car, I realized how little I knew about James's life. I knew he'd lived a long time, but when I'd heard how old he was, all I'd been able to think about then was all the women a guy like him was sure to have been with over the years. But there was much more to his life than that. A lot I didn't know.

I didn't know anything about his father, or this possible sister. I didn't know about other important people who might have been in his life. Who he might have lost. Maybe he was being cold to me because he didn't want to lose anyone else? It made me sad to think that was the case; no one should give up on finding happiness and love.

As I walked Trist back to the house, I tried to imagine what it was like to be James, but found I had no clue. I couldn't figure him out in the least. Trist, his father, who was both a charismatic and intimidating man and kind of mad, was no help. James didn't want me or understand why I wanted him, yet I was sure he sometimes desired me. But then it seemed he hated me. And he was always so distant, even with his own pack. James was just super confusing. All I wanted was to sit down and have a long talk with him and ask who the hell he was and what was going on inside of his head.

CHAPTER 19

The next afternoon I stood outside James's office. He was alone in there, and the door was already ajar. So it was like he was asking to get surprise visits. I slipped inside. I had this whole thing thought out. I wanted to talk to him, get answers to some of my questions from yesterday. Like what was going on with his dad and why would neither Tommy nor Markus tell me about their jobs?

"Hi," I said. James was standing with his back to the door and me, studying a map with some red, blue, and orange pins in it. "I wanted to talk to you."

"All right," James said, his shoulders tense. I wanted to put my hands on them and see if I could rub some of the tension out. I took a step closer to him. "Talk."

"Wow, you're so charming," I said, walking a little farther into the room. "You should teach classes. How to Be an Ass 101."

"Cut the, crap Megan," he said, rubbing his eyes. "If you want to talk to me, just talk."

"Fine," I said as he turned around. "I decided to go running last night. Since it was a full moon and everything." He tensed. "But that didn't turn out so great because we have a gun-toting farmer for a neighbor. Thanks for mentioning that."

"I did," he said tensely.

I shook my head. "You didn't."

"I did—"

"When?"

"When . . . when you first got here?" It was more of a question than a statement.

"Nope," I said, popping the *P*. "You never told me. But I'm not mad about that." *Anymore*, I added to myself. "Because I realized it's just a symptom of what's wrong with this pack."

"There is nothing wrong with the pack," he said, taking a step forward. I expected my wolf to want to take a step back, give ground to him as the Alpha. But whatever alpha magic I'd gotten from the induction had removed the urge, and I stood my ground.

"Yes, there is." I glared up at him. "No one eats together. Last night was a full moon and there was no hunt. At least I didn't get invited to one." I sucked in a breath and thought about Tommy changing the subject and Markus's weird comment. To talk to James. "And have you been telling people not to share stuff with me? Because that's not cool and totally undermines me, both as your mate and as Alpha."

"I haven't been telling them anything," he said after a moment.

"No? Well, maybe you should tell them something," I said angrily. "Like, anything. Do any of you even talk? Are you even friends? This place sucks."

"Megan, you're—"

"No. I'm not overreacting," I said. "A pack shouldn't be this alone when they're together. So? What're you going to do to fix it?"

"There is nothing that needs fixing," he said, turning back to his board with its pins. I wondered what it was for. It seemed horribly low-tech, but then again, James and especially his dad seemed to like to kick it old-school.

"You have a teenage girl running around this place not going to school, not having friends, not even speaking," I growled. "Your pack barely seems to like one another. Your dad can't be around cars without hallucinating and you, the acting Alpha, won't even spend time with your own mate. Yeah. Your pack is peachy."

"You should learn to mind your own business," he said, turning quickly and stepping so close to me that if I just leaned forward a few inches we'd be able to kiss. His lips looked soft and I wondered what his five o'clock stubble would feel like.

"This is my pack now," I whispered, looking up into his green eyes. "Which makes it my business."

"No, it's . . ." He was looking at my lips and I wished I'd worn lip gloss, but settled for quickly wetting my lips with my tongue. Which was a good move because his pupils dilated. There was a flutter somewhere deep inside where our mate bond connected us. I could see he felt it too; it was in his eyes and in the slight ease of the tension in his shoulders.

We stood that way for what felt like a long, long time. Finally, I moved forward to grab his upper arm and pull him closer, but before my fingers even closed around his arm, he'd jerked away and taken several steps backward.

Disappointment flared in me. I'd been so close. So close to making him forget whatever it was that kept making him pull away, the thing that made him act like he didn't care and didn't want me. But I knew he did; the way he'd looked at me right then proved it.

"James," I said softly. "Why not just give in to this? You want to, I can see it."

"No," he said, jaw tight.

"What's the plan, then? Why bring me here, why induct me if you're just going to keep on resisting what you want?"

"I don't want you," he said, turning away.

"I don't believe you," I said. "You want me."

"No."

"Is that the only word you know? No?" I asked.

"No," he said, his eyes narrowing. "I mean—"

"You are totally impossible," I said, turning toward the door. "And so is your pack!"

CHAPTER 20

James

A *pack shouldn't be this alone when they're together,* she'd said, and he'd had no idea how to respond.

Was it true? He didn't consider himself friends with anyone in the pack but Robin, not really. He was their Alpha, he wasn't supposed to be their friend, and that sometimes made him feel alone. But he'd never thought of the members of his pack as being alone, isolated. Was he wrong?

He tried to remember back to before everything had changed, before the attack, before he'd left, before Marisol, and before he had become Alpha. But it was impossible to compare. Back before, there had been females and children and happiness. Afterward there had only been the mission, the next fight.

But maybe Megan was right. Maybe the pack wasn't as tight of a unit as he liked to think. Maybe something like a hunt would be good. It wouldn't make things go back to how they had been before. Because it could never be like before.

"What's all the sighing about?" Robin asked. They were both busy putting pins into the map in James's office, adding last night's kills and considering locations that might be nests.

"Do you think we should have a pack hunt?" he asked his Beta.

"What?" Robin nearly dropped the pin he was holding.

"A pack hunt," he said, frowning at Robin's surprised expression.

"For . . . for fun?"

James shrugged. "Yeah."

"I think that sounds like a brilliant idea. Megan's, right?"

He nodded. It both annoyed and pleased him that Robin had guessed it wasn't his idea.

"I'll spread the word." Robin grinned, but then it changed into a frown. He asked, "What's with the sour face? You two get into a fight?"

Part of him wanted to tell Robin to mind his own business. And Megan wasn't Robin's business. But another part wanted to talk to Robin. To ask if he agreed with Megan about the pack and maybe just generally get advice on how to handle the whole Megan situation. Ignoring her was making his wolf grumpy, which made him grumpy and unfocused. Besides, she kept showing up everywhere. He couldn't escape her or the feelings she brought out in him.

"How'd you know?"

"Well, it's pretty obvious things aren't exactly hunky-dory." He nodded. Robin was right. This thing with Megan was going to be a lot more complicated than he'd first thought, and right now they weren't exactly best pals. "I get it, man. You're freaked. Marisol—"

"No. It's not about that," he said. And that was mostly true. "Not *just* about that." He thought about it and realized he wanted Robin's help. Even if he was Alpha and hated showing weakness, he needed advice. "I don't know what to do. I thought I could bring her here and just keep her safe. That way my wolf would be happy and I could just go on doing what I've always done."

"But that's not really working out for you, now, is it?" Robin said almost smugly. James narrowed his eyes. Robin had known it wouldn't work. Robin always knew these things. He knew people. Understood them.

"No."

"So maybe talk to her a bit and explain. About your dad and about Ma—" Robin began.

"I'm not sure . . ."

"Look, girls like to understand stuff," he said. "They like when you talk to them and share. It helps them connect, right? I mean, imagine being Megan. She doesn't get why you don't . . . why you aren't as excited as she is."

James knew that. Knew it was an issue. He just hadn't cared much about whether she understood his reluctance or not. But now he did. He felt bad she was hurting, feeling forgotten and like he was undermining her authority. But now he wanted her to understand without having to explain, because he had no idea how to talk to her about it.

"Start small," Robin said, as if he could read James's thoughts. "Just give her a chance to understand."

CHAPTER 21

"It's not my fault," I told Lucy, who was hovering in the doorway to my room. "It's his fault. All his. I tried, like Sorelle said. I tried to have a conversation about some normal things. Sure, pointing out all the trouble around here might not have been the smartest move, but it was about making things better for the pack! What does he say to that? No! Wanting me? No."

I threw the clothes I'd just unpacked a few days ago back into the backpack I'd bought to use for gym stuff, then checked I had everything in my handbag. New phone, old phone, my special phone bag, passport, pepper spray, scarf, peppermint gum, lip gloss. Check, check, check.

"No. No. No. That's the only word the guy knows. No." I glanced over to Lucy. She was looking at me with huge eyes, as if she'd never seen anyone get pissed off before. Maybe she hadn't. Everyone here was probably as emotionally repressed as James.

"You know what's going to make me feel better, though?" I said, snapping the backpack closed. "Getting the heck out of here. Living somewhere with people. And the internet."

Lucy was still staring intently at me. It was kind of creepy.

"Too bad you can't talk. Or won't," I told her. "I could have left a message with you or something."

Except I didn't know what kind of message I would have left with her. I didn't know where I was going or when I'd be back. But I would have to come back soon. This was my pack now. But since James was too chicken to want to be with me, I figured he wouldn't mind me taking off for a while. I mean, he'd be pissed he couldn't be all *I know what's best* and that I'd left, because alphas are possessive, but he wouldn't miss *me*.

I'd miss him, though, which was pathetic since I barely knew him.

"You want to come, kid?" I asked Lucy as I slung the backpack over my shoulder. "I mean, it can't be that much fun being stuck here with all these idiots."

Lucy tilted her head, as if considering, then shook her head no. I blinked, a bit surprised. According to Tommy, she would sometimes indicate movie preferences by bringing him a certain DVD to play, but so far she had mostly run off when I tried to talk to her or communicate.

"Right, then."

I'd been fuming in my room, trying to get through to Sorelle, who wasn't answering, so I figured most of the pack had left by now. They did that almost every night after dinner, got into their dark SUVs and drove off. But they never took all the cars. I guessed because they didn't want to look like the Werewolf Mafia. So I was sure there would be at least one car left.

There were three black SUVs in the garage along with a red Porsche. I smiled. I used the code to get into the box with the keys, picked the small silver one, and pressed the unlock button. The sports car blinked and unlocked. I hesitated for one second, considering taking one of the SUVs instead. But the red sports car was just so amazing. I couldn't resist it.

"Nice," I said as I got in. Someone had been taking real good care of this baby. Leather seats that looked brand-new. No food wrappers or anything yucky. It smelled faintly of lemon cleaning solution.

The engine ran like a dream, and despite everything I grinned. For the first time since my birthday, I was back behind the wheel of a car.

CHAPTER 22
Lucy

Her mother had said not to talk. *It will call them. Be invisible, Lusine,* and wait for your time, she'd said. *Not one word. Not ever.* So she hadn't spoken. Not even to Tommy, who was her friend. But this was different, wasn't it?

Megan was leaving without understanding. Understanding that there was danger. Lots of it. More than even Tommy and James and all the rest of them knew. But Lucy knew, only she couldn't tell them. Could she?

She had to do something, though. But what? She'd watched the car speed away—the car that Megan was in—watched until the lights from it had faded completely while trying to think of something.

It had been several years since she'd gotten here. She'd done her very best to be invisible and it had worked. But if she drew attention back to herself, there could be trouble.

The moon was bright tonight. Lucy wondered if that had

something to do with Megan's rushed decision to leave. In a few years when she turned sixteen she'd know what that was like, to be swayed by the moon. If she lived to be sixteen.

She went down to the big TV room, to the door to Tommy's workshop. Tilting her head, she watched him work. She liked to do that. Liked how his eyebrows drew together when he worked on something difficult. How his big fingers could build tiny things, how he could be so gentle with them even though she knew he was very strong.

Part of her wished to talk to him, and tell him everything. Tell him her past, her secrets, her true name, and trust he would protect her. But telling him all those things would draw attention. She couldn't do that. Not until she turned sixteen. Then she'd tell them her secrets.

Except Megan didn't have that long. Someone in the pack needed to find her before something dark did. Dark and deadly or darkly beautiful, the result would be the same. Megan would die and that would be bad.

She needed to speak. Needed Tommy to realize and help.

"TOMMY," SHE SAID. Her voice sounded strange, different. But it had been three years since she'd last spoken. Her accent wasn't as noticeable either.

"Just a second," he said, focused on his project.

"Tommy!" she said again. Louder. Because she could.

"Lucy?" Tommy jumped off his chair. "You're talking?" He grabbed her shoulders. "OMG, you're talking!"

"Yes, because—" she began but was cut off with a squeak. Tommy had picked her up like she was nothing more than some rag doll and spun her around.

"Say something more," he said, grinning, as he set her down. "Megan left."

That took the smile off his face.

"What?"

"She ang-angry about James and noes and she went and got car," she said, fast, trying to not wince about her accent. "You have to get her before the bad zings do—"

"Wait, slow down," he said, the smile half back on his face. "Megan took one of the cars? How'd she even know the combination?"

Lucy shook her head, because what did it matter? "Make her come back."

"Okay," he said, putting a hand on her shoulder. "We will. We'll find her."

CHAPTER 23

James

His cell vibrated and he considered just leaving it. He wanted to take his wolf shape, run and hunt and forget about the mess of the evening. About his fight with Megan and his talk with Robin. *Just tell her.* That was easy for Robin to say.

But it might be something important. Or maybe Robin had found something that needed checking out. They had been closing in on what they thought might be a nest. He pulled out his phone and frowned. The name on the screen was Tommy, but Tommy wasn't working tonight.

"What?"

"Hey, man," Tommy said. "We have a problem. Megan just took off in Markus's car."

"She did what?" he barked. "Why didn't you stop her?"

"I didn't see," Tommy began, frustrated. "Look, I'm waiting to hear from the GPS tracking service people. They'll find her and—"

"When did she leave?"

"I don't know," Tommy said. "Maybe half an hour ago."

"Then she's already in town, or close to." If she was coming this way. She most likely was; she'd at least have to drive past, since the highway ran just outside of town. Did she intend to drive to Montreal in the middle of the bloody night or would she stop in town? Why was she running off? Their fight? "I'll find her."

"Are you—"

He pressed the end button before Tommy could finish his question. James swore as he slammed the car door shut and began changing into his wolf shape. He knew what he had to do. He had to sense her through the pack bonds, and if that didn't work, through their mate bond.

Being Alpha had its perks, and even though Megan was only a faint wisp of emotion slightly to the west, he could sense her through the pack bonds. He quickly turned and began heading toward her. He sensed she wasn't moving fast, so she probably wasn't in the car anymore. She'd stopped. He wasn't sure if that was good or bad news. Good because she wasn't leaving but bad because in a fast car she was relatively safe. Out in the open she would be an easy target for the wraiths. So mostly bad.

He reached out through the pack bonds to try to get Robin's attention, to call him or at least make him aware he was leaving the area they'd decided to hunt in for the night. But he wasn't sure if the message got through because Robin was some distance off.

Running through the maze of streets and alleys, he couldn't help but to think this was his fault. He hadn't meant to make her angry enough to want to leave. He didn't want her to leave. He wasn't sure what he wanted—to be friends? To be mated for real? Maybe if he could keep her safe, be sure he could never become like his father, it might be worth the risk.

Through the pack bonds he could feel himself closing in on her. As he cut through an alley that would take him close to where he wanted to go, he sensed the wraiths. He had no way of knowing if it was a coincidence or if they'd somehow picked up on Megan being nearby. But it would be best to take care of them before they got anywhere close to her.

So he changed his trajectory, turning left instead of continuing on toward Megan. A minute later, down a small garbage-littered street, he found the wraiths.

Two of them. As ghostly as always, maybe more than usual because of the bright full moon.

He snarled at the wraiths as they floated toward him. The area was empty of people, which was good. Humans couldn't see wraiths—their minds simply couldn't process them—but a witness might call the police to report a wild wolf fighting air.

The wraiths both came at him at once, but weren't coordinated enough to be a problem. He took the first one out with a running jump, scoring it with both his teeth and claws. It hissed as it died and that, along with his worry, was enough of a distraction for the second wraith to come at him from the side, its long claws slicing into him.

The wraith hissed in satisfaction as James felt the claw leave his liver, bringing fresh waves of pain. His head spun as he tried to focus. If he didn't act fast, he was going to die. Even if he did act, it wasn't very likely he'd ever see the sun rise again. Liver wounds were bad. It had taken him a week to recover when Marisol had stabbed him, and all he had to do then was lie on the cold floor, not fight.

He sank down, attempting to mimic falling unconscious. He wanted the wraith to think he was down for the count while he gathered his strength for one last attack. There was just one. One little wraith. He could kill one. One more.

Focusing on it, drawing on strength he didn't know he had, he launched himself at the wraith and bit deep into its neck. It made a strangled sound. James had never seen them talk but wondered if they maybe communicated through the odd sounds they made. There was clearly something intelligent about them; they had patterns. Hunted in specific ways, kept close to town and people. Returned to their nests and their queens during the day. Still, James doubted the noise this wraith had made was anything more than a dying sigh.

The fight finished, James slumped back on the ground. His body was shaking with the adrenaline still pumping through his system. He couldn't shift, couldn't crawl somewhere a human might find him and take pity on him. He couldn't even find Robin with the pack bonds.

He couldn't reach out to him because the mate bond was dulling those connections. His bond with Megan was new, hadn't settled yet, making it the one his wolf had easiest access to. He hadn't realized that was happening until now. Not until he needed his pack and all that he had was his mate bond.

He was bleeding too much; he could feel the sticky liquid soaking his fur. The blood and adrenaline were turning his body into the enemy. An enemy his mind had to defeat or die.

As the world began to fade away, he latched on to the bond that tied him to the girl he'd tried to drive away, the girl he'd done his best to separate himself from, hoping she'd sense his pain and come to him.

CHAPTER 24

The barista tapped my order into the machine. She had absurdly long nails that were painted like candy canes—I was amazed she could tap on the keys with them, they were so long—and contact lenses that made her irises look bright purple.

After I'd paid for my double hazelnut and caramel wonder latte, I went to sit by the window, even though there wasn't much of a view. Just a street, and a little ways off, the parking lot where the beautiful Porsche I'd "borrowed" was parked.

I wasn't sure what the plan was, but driving for hours and hours by myself in the middle of the night—that was how long it would take to get to Quebec, according to the car's GPS—didn't seem like a super smart idea. But I really didn't want to head back to the manor either.

"Thanks," I said as the waitress with the candy-cane nails and freaky eyes put my drink down in front of me a minute later.

She nodded and spoke to me in French. *"Profiter de votre café, rougarou."*

I had no clue what that meant but gave her a little smile. The double hazelnut and caramel wonder latte was one of those over-the-top coffee-ish drinks with syrups, whipped cream, and a cherry on top, and it tasted fantastic. This wasn't a chain or anything, but clearly they knew how to make coffee. It was pretty damned near magical, and for a few minutes it seemed to make all my troubles float away.

Tommy had called two times, probably to tell me to come back. I didn't pick up because I didn't feel like explaining why I'd taken off or what my plan was. Mostly because I didn't have one. And if I talked to him, he'd convince me to go back to the manor.

Once I'd finished my coffee, I thanked the purple-eyed woman in French as I went over to throw my cup away. I knew, like, three French words, but *merci* was one of them, and she nodded. She really had made me feel better with that coffee. I wished I could have left a tip, but the only cash I had was an American fifty-dollar bill.

Just as I was opening the coffee shop's door, the pain hit me. It was like the time Terrance Long had accidentally pushed me off the bleachers and just for a moment after I'd hit the ground I hadn't been able to even breathe because of all the pain.

Gasping, I slumped against the door, helpless. The pain ebbed and was replaced with a need to go . . . somewhere. I just wasn't sure where. There was just the need to get there. My head started to pound; my chest felt tight. I needed to go *somewhere*.

I pushed off the door, nearly falling over because everything was spinning. But then after a second the world righted itself and I knew what was going on. My wolf knew too.

Our mate was calling. I froze. My wolf wanted to run to him. But that wasn't what I wanted to do. I was taking a break from him and his "no" way of life. Was James using the pain to make me come back to him? Was that possible? If so, he was even more of a jerk than I'd first thought.

But a voice inside of me insisted James was in trouble. Real trouble. *What do warriors do?* They fight. They fight and they get hurt.

Yet if I went to James, I'd be stuck. I was sure he would be pissed and be all like you-shouldn't-be-out-alone and then he'd probably change the combination for the garage and keys to keep me "safe" or something jackass-y like that.

Except there was the pain. I didn't think James would send pain to me to stop me from leaving. I wasn't even sure it was possible to send pain through a mate bond without a reason. So he had to be hurt, and judging from the level of pain, I guessed pretty badly. I swallowed. If we'd been together longer I might have been able to feel him clearly—feel what he felt, sense what he sensed—but I just couldn't. And now he might die. At least it felt like he might. Just the thought of James dying—of him being dead—made my mind up.

I needed to go to him.

I rushed outside to the car, suddenly not able to waste a single second. I let my wolf lead, because her reactions were faster. She got things done when they needed doing. And now was the time for actions.

"Where to? Where to?" I muttered as I used the remote to unlock the car. Trying to focus on where James was, I found myself suddenly dizzy and out of breath. I felt him then, abruptly but clearly.

He was close. Close enough that I didn't need the car. So close I could find him easily on foot. I turned toward the edge of the parking lot.

It was like there was a weird compass thing inside of me, where James was north and I was simply following the little arrow. Freaky.

The night was still fairly warm, but it could have been scorching summer afternoon or a chilly winter's night outside and I doubt I would have noticed.

I reached a dark, smelly alley but I kept going, fishing out my pepper spray from my bag. I was close.

Finally reaching the end of the alley, I stopped. There was a furry heap on the ground.

CHAPTER 25

moved like I was in a trance until I was standing close to the body. No. He was breathing. So not body. Not just yet.

"Oh God," I whispered as I sank to my knees next to him.

James's head lolled to the side when I touched his scruffy neck. I could see that his fur was coated in something blackish red and I could smell the metallic tang of blood in the air. His whole side was covered in it. I wanted to reach over to find the wound and attempt to press it closed, but instead I pulled out my cell phone. I had ten missed calls from Tommy. Yikes, I should probably have answered.

I pressed the call-back icon and it rang for what felt like forever but was probably just a few seconds.

"Megan?" said Tommy's familiar voice.

"Oh God, Tommy," I said by way of greeting. "You have to come. He's all bloody and bleeding and—"

"Megan, are you okay?" Tommy said through the phone, sounding shocked. "What's going on?"

"I'm fine," I sobbed. It was so good to hear a friendly voice, someone I figured could help me. "But James is, oh God, James is—"

"Where are you?" he asked, clearly recovering his cool.

"I'm not sure," I said, looking around, but that wasn't much help. "I parked a few blocks off the highway by a coffee shop and then I don't know—"

"Robin should be close. Try to call him," Tommy said.

"I don't have his number," I said in a panic. Why hadn't I gotten Robin's number when I had the chance? I was so stupid.

"No, I mean with the pack bonds. You're Alpha. He will have already sensed something is wrong, but use your—"

I took a quick breath, dropping the phone, as James moved, his ears flicking. I'd thought he was too unconscious or too almost-dead to do anything more than lie there.

"James? James? Can you hear me?" I wasn't sure if him waking up was bad or good. On TV being awake usually meant good, but I thought that might be wrong since being conscious also meant some of his energy was being used for, well, staying conscious.

Then I realized he wasn't waking up, he was transforming back into his human shape. Not good. You weren't supposed to shift when you'd been hurt; it made it harder for the body to heal.

"No, James," I said, reaching over to touch his neck. "Stay wolf. Stay like this."

But it was no use. He was already changing, and I leaned away from him as he changed. When he was no longer covered in fur, I could see the wound much better. I could also see everything else.

Unfortunately, I couldn't appreciate all that naked hotness and the really cool but scary tattoos he had, because he was half dead.

"Right," I said, tugging my jacket off and draping it over his hips. Then I pulled a scarf from my purse and pressed it against the still bleeding wound. He groaned and tried to move away from my hand. "Shhh," I said, "I need to stop the bleeding."

"Marisol?" James suddenly moaned, his green eyes opening wide.

"No, I'm Megan," I said. Who in the world was Marisol? "Just lie still and it'll be all right."

I winced because I knew enough to realize that losing this much blood was bad. Really bad. But I still said it was going to be okay. I pressed the scarf harder against the bloody wound, hoping—praying—Tommy or Robin would get there soon. That they'd come and help me, because there was no way I could get James back to the car without some assistance. I might be a werewolf, but James was probably twice my weight or even more since he was solid muscle.

It seemed like I sat there, pressing my hand against James's bleeding wound, for a very long time. But at the same time there was no time. I was thinking about who Marisol could be, trying to not think about what it would feel like if the mate bond with James shut down. If he died.

Then there was a noise.

Keeping my hand against James's lower chest, I turned. There were two . . . things in the alley's opening. Shadowy and floating with yellow eyes. Like they were there, but not. I stared and tried to figure them out. They made me think of nothing so much as Dementors but with claws and glowing eyes instead of hoods.

When they moved they looked like shadows, drifting in the wind, but they weren't drifting. Their yellow eyes were focused. They were coming for me and for James.

Danger. Kill. Danger. My wolf was going crazy. I needed to change or there was no way I'd be able to fight these things. But changing would mean having to let go of James's wound, which might cause him to bleed out and die. Besides, they'd be on us before I could complete my change.

I reached for the pepper spray I'd dropped in my rush to get to James. James growled, reacting to the creatures even though he was unconscious. Swallowing, I tried to remember the range of the pepper spray. The monsters were still a few dozen feet away.

Not that I really believed my pepper spray would actually be able to defeat them. But a girl had to hope, right? Pepper spray is pretty damned nasty. I knew because I'd gotten some on me when Sorelle and I tried it out. So maybe it would drive them off at least?

It could happen.

I mean, humans were good at making powerful weapons. They had invented the atom bomb, tear gas, and lip gloss with cherry flavor. So it wasn't out of the realm of possibility that pepper spray might repel these awful floating magic demons. *Right?*

The creatures floated closer, eyes glowing. Man, I was going to have nightmares about tonight for the rest of my life. These creatures just gave me the willies: their eyes, the way they moved, the aura of something *other* around them.

I remembered the pepper spray was supposed to have an extra-long range and gave the button a squeeze while I turned my head away. I heard a stream of the pepper spray leave the bottle. I gave it a second, then turned back to see.

The creatures were still coming, but a bit slower, maybe? Their eyes didn't seem affected, but maybe something about the stuff still repelled them a little?

Closing my eyes and turning away, I held the bottle up high and in the general direction of the wraiths and just sprayed, moving my arm slightly. Like I was using air freshener.

Then the *spppiii* sound of pepper spray leaving the bottle stopped. I was out. I turned and stared dumbly at the bottle for a second. The wraiths were really close. I wanted to close my eyes but somehow that seemed more terrifying.

This is it. I'm going to die.

"Hey, motherfucker," someone called from the mouth of the alley. The shadow monsters turned. A shot rang out, startling and loud in the night. Then one of the monster's heads exploded. Except the thing's body stayed floating, like a headless chicken. A huge wolf came flying through the air, its jaws clamping around the monster that still had a head. Then a second wolf went for the headless one.

The cavalry had arrived.

Since A) the creatures were busy and no longer focused on me or James and B) it hadn't been very useful, I threw the pepper spray aside and put that hand on James's chest too, both to comfort him and to convince myself he was really alive. He moved a little and I pulled back to look at him.

James opened his eyes. Their greenness was almost unnatural. He looked straight at me, seeming confused. "Megan," he whispered.

I felt some strange, absurd weight lift off my chest. He'd called my name, not whoever this Marisol person was. He knew I was there. That I was the one who had saved him.

CHAPTER 26

"Megan," Robin said, gently squatting down on the other side of James. "Megan, you can move now. Let Markus take a look, okay?"

I glanced up and saw Markus standing behind me. How had he gotten there? His dark eyes stared down at me. He was holding something. A red bag with a cross on it. Medical stuff. Tommy and Markus had been in the army. Markus would know how to fix James. Save him.

Robin helped me when I wobbled as I stood. I wasn't hurt but I felt very unsteady. My hands—my bloody hands—were shaking. I let Robin lead me a few feet away but looked back to James when Robin tried to get me to focus on him. I needed to keep watching over James. Needed to see he was alive, that they were taking care of him.

"Megan," Robin said, taking hold of both of my shoulders. "Take a breath."

I swallowed and breathed in. The stink of the alley and James's blood filled my nose. Not comforting scents.

"It's going to be okay," Robin said, hands still on me to keep me focused on him. "They're working on him. Tio is coming around with a car."

"Those were wraiths," I said, glancing over to where the two monsters had been. There was no sign of them now. No bodies.

Markus working on James's bleeding body was the only proof of what had occurred here. James. I wanted to go back to him, make Markus let me help, but I knew that I'd just be in the way.

"Yes," Robin said. I turned my gaze back to him.

James was hurt and it was because of me. I'd left and he'd come here to look for me. That was the best explanation for why he'd been so close. But it was also James's, Robin's, Tommy's, and even Markus's fault. Because they hadn't told me about this. About the wraiths. If I'd known, I wouldn't have left in the middle of the night. None of this would be happening. James would be fine. If he'd told me, we wouldn't be in this mess. If anyone had. If Robin had.

"Yes? That's all you have to say?" I cried, taking a stumbling step back from Robin. "They're supposed to be gone. Extinct. No need to fear. Just a fairy tale to tell misbehaving pups."

"James would have—"

"James would have what? Told me?" I said mockingly. "Because he's such a big sharer. No. You should have told me!" I pointed at Robin. "Once you realized he wasn't going to, you should have told me. This was something I deserved to know—"

"Really? You think so? You were running away," Robin said before nodding toward James. "This is your fault—"

"No. It's yours. All of yours," I yelled, directing it toward Markus and the two wolves in the alley. I knew it wasn't true. Part of it, maybe. But the fault was mostly mine. I was the one who had left without talking to one of them. I'd betrayed them. I'd caused this whole situation.

If James died it would be my fault.

"He's not going to die," Robin said, almost as if he'd read my mind. Maybe he'd sensed my feelings through the pack bond.

Just then a car screeched to a stop right at the mouth of the alley. The huge Tio stepped out and came over to us, moving with surprising grace for someone so big.

I attempted to move forward as Tio and Markus lifted James up and got him over to the car, but Robin's hand on my arm stopped me.

"Let me go." I tried to pull free. "I need to go—I need to go with him—"

"Calm down," Robin said, holding on tighter. "We'll be right behind them; my car is just a block away."

"No," I cried, flinging a fist out toward Robin's face. The blow hurt my hand more than I think it hurt his nose. And he didn't let go. "Nooo." Tio slammed the door to the back seat and got in the driver's seat. He glanced my way for a second before taking off.

Robin let go of me.

I ran down the alley. The car's taillights were already too far away. James was gone. Too far away. I stopped, shaking and angry.

He needed me. I needed him. I needed to make sure he was still breathing. Being taken care of.

"Come along, then." Robin, with a small trickle of blood coming out of his nose, waved for me to walk with him the other way. "I'll take you back. Okay?"

Glaring at his back, I followed him. I was glad I'd made his nose bleed. But only for a minute. Then I started to feel horrible about it. I wanted to cry, about James, about learning about wraiths, about the whole situation.

Robin's car was parked down a narrow alley, too small to drive through, which I guessed was why we'd had to wait for Tio. To go around. In the car, Robin put the heat on high, and only then did I realize I was shivering.

"He's lived this long," Robin said as he started the car. "He'll live. Okay? We're tough. If it doesn't kill us instantly, most likely we'll live."

"There was so much blood," I said, staring at my hands. "And the, the wraiths. They were horrible."

"I know," Robin said as we pulled out onto the highway. "I'm sorry I didn't tell you. Maybe I should have. Maybe I didn't think about it too much. I should have. We should have made you feel more like part of the pack," he said quietly as the car picked up speed.

"I wasn't really leaving, not forever," I confided. "I just feel so . . . like, what's the point? Why am I here? James should have just left me back home."

"You know what James asked me about earlier?" Robin asked,

turning to me. "Having a pack hunt. We haven't had one of those in ages. So you are making a difference."

I managed a smile even though I was still super worried about James. "Really?"

"Really."

"I'm sorry I hit you," I said. "I didn't mean to."

"I was keeping you from your mate. Your hurt mate," Robin said, wiping at his nose. It had stopped bleeding and he was still as handsome as ever, so I guessed I hadn't broken it or whatever. "I kind of deserved it. But I couldn't let you go with them. You'd have been a distraction."

"I know," I said, because I'd realized that too. Unfortunately the knowledge didn't make me feel any better.

WHILE ROBIN DROVE, I looked back on the time I'd spent around James to see if the knowledge that wraiths existed somehow made sense of his behavior. Had he kept me at arm's length to somehow protect me? Was that what it had all been about? I wasn't sure if I wanted this secret to be the reason he'd treated me the way he had, or not.

As I rubbed my hands against my jeans, trying to get the blood off, I decided it didn't make sense. James had been cold to me since before we even got here. Even if he was worried about me being shocked or unable to handle the wraiths, he could still have been nice to me. Wraiths existing didn't make his detachment toward me make any more sense.

I glanced at Robin, who was focused on the road. He went out and fought the wraiths every day—or, well, night—and so did the rest of the pack. They all went out to fight monsters the rest of the wolves thought were extinct. James had been hurt, almost killed tonight, by one of them. Yet no one knew. No one but the warriors knew this battle was still going on.

"That's one big secret to keep from all the wolves. Isn't it?" I said thoughtfully. I needed something to distract me. Asking questions seemed as good a way as any to do that.

Robin glanced my way. Hesitated. "Your father knows; several of the more powerful Alphas around do too."

I nodded. That made sense. My dad knew everything.

"One of the reasons so many packs have moved south and west is because we want them farther away from the wraith breeding ground here in Tenebri. It's worked pretty well so far," he continued.

"Why wouldn't the wraiths just move too?" I frowned. "I mean, they kill wolves; that's like their mission in life. Why stay here and get killed and not go somewhere else where there are no warrior wolves?"

Robin paused and looked my way. I thought I saw a bit of surprise in his eyes.

"We think certain areas have special things they need to nest. This place must have those," he offered with a shrug. "Or maybe they don't understand there are other places they could go."

"It's still strange, isn't it? For them to stay?"

Robin seemed as if he had never thought much about it, but agreed. "Perhaps it's a little strange."

Maybe wraiths weren't all that smart. That was kind of comforting. Made them less scary in my mind. Except when I closed my eyes and saw the whole horrible scene with James bleeding and the wraiths coming my way, their eyes hadn't seemed devoid of intelligence. No. There had been something in them. Something calculating and cold.

"And your mission is, like, to kill them?"

He shrugged. "We hunt the wraiths, and once we find them in bigger concentrations in certain areas, we go in and destroy their nests and their queens," he said. "Once you destroy a nest and its queen, that takes out all the wraiths connected to her."

Biting my lip, I thought about that, and the map with the pins in James's office. That must be what it was for, right? Tracking the wraiths and finding their nests? Surely there had to be a more efficient way to do it. Like some computer program that let you flag locations.

"So if you destroy all the nests . . . ," I said, leaning back, "they'd all be gone? No more wraiths, no more hunting them, no more danger?"

That sounded good. Except since I knew they'd been living at the manor for several decades, it clearly wasn't that easy.

"Yes, that was what warrior packs usually did: come to an infested area, kill all the wraiths and destroy any nests, and then move on. But we've been hunting here forever and—"

"There are still wraiths," I finished for him. A never-ending battle. "Why not get help? My dad has a lot of wolves that are good fighters."

Robin shook his head. "Only the venom on a warrior wolf's teeth can kill them."

Interesting. I wanted to ask more about that, but my mate bond told me we were getting closer to James. We were almost at the mansion. Just a few more minutes, then I could see James.

As if Robin could sense my eagerness, or maybe because he wanted to see that James was okay almost as badly as I did, he stepped on the gas. We were on the private road that led toward the manor, so there wasn't any chance of getting stopped for speeding. I remembered how free and happy I'd felt just a few hours ago when I'd sped out of here in the red sports car down this road.

How quickly the world could change and become a much darker and scarier place. A world of monsters. That was kind of funny. As a werewolf, most humans would probably classify me as a monster. But tonight I'd seen something that had scared every part of me. When I thought about the wraiths and their glowing eyes, it made the fear I'd felt in that alley come back almost as strong.

THE LIGHT OF the manor showed up in the distance. Finally. James was in there. I needed to be with him. Close to my mate. He needed me. I needed him, needed to see that he was okay. I jumped out of the car before Robin had fully stopped in front of the manor's doors. He swore as he hit the brakes, but I was already halfway to the door.

CHAPTER 27

When I'd come rushing into the house, Tommy had just barely stopped me from bursting into the surgery room. At first, I was angry. Just like when Robin had prevented me from going with James back in the alley. But Tommy's way of restraining me had been much better than Robin's.

Tommy had hugged me and said, "I'm totally glad you didn't die. But next time you ignore my phone calls I'll strangle you myself." That had made me feel better, and calm enough to wait until Doc said I could go in to see James.

But now that I was in the room, I was scared to look at James. Instead I studied the room's door. It was white. The handle was silver. It had a dent about knee high, like someone had kicked it real hard. I stared at it for the longest time before turning around slowly. The room looked like a hospital room, without windows. A red plastic medical-waste trash thing in the corner. A white counter with a sink. Stainless steel.

Soap in a pump. Plastic glove box.

And on the other side of the room, a bed. A medical one, with bars on the side and wheels. This place was much better equipped than the medical room at my old pack house.

I finally dared to look at James. He looked a little paler than usual. A little less tense. Almost peaceful, which was a little scary as well as nice. There was an IV in his arm and a bandage on his side.

But I barely noticed the bandage, I was so distracted by the tattoos on his chest, arms, and wrists. I'd noticed them earlier in the alley but I had been too busy with trying to stop his bleeding to examine them. They were done in red ink and were nothing like other tattoos I'd seen. For some reason, the more I looked at them the more they scared me.

I picked up a metal chair that stood just inside the door and sat it by the bed.

"Hey," I said to him even though he was unconscious. "Quite a mess I've made of things." I took his hand. "You know I'm kind of annoyed with you," I continued. "Not for not telling me about the wraiths. That's so you. I can't be mad at you for being you, right? I can be mad at Robin and Tommy and all the rest of them for *that*. You want to know why I'm mad at *you*?"

There was no response. If this had been a sappy movie, he'd have woken up and looked tenderly into my eyes and realized he loved me. But alas, it was not, and he just kept on being unconscious.

"I'm mad because you almost got yourself killed. That's not cool."

I wanted to touch more of him; I wanted to know what his skin felt like. How his hard muscles would move under my touch, catalog his response, but for some reason I also really wanted to touch the tattoos. Needed to. There seemed to be several different ones, all intricate in their designs. Some were embellished words of the Old Tongue. Others were symbols I recognized—like a Celtic knot—and others I did not—like a snake curled around a five-pointed star on his chest. They were red and scary, like dried coppery blood etched on his skin.

I slid my hand up his arm. His skin was warm, and I wanted to stop and enjoy it, but I found my fingers moving up and touching the nearest tattoo. It was more than just an ink marking. These tattoos meant something. I didn't know what, but something about them was special.

Then his hand did move a little, as if trying to escape my touch. His face became even paler and the muscles in his neck strained. His fingers curled, gripping the blanket. He said one word, one name: "Marisol."

That was the second time I'd heard him say that. In the alley it had depressed me, but now I wasn't quite sure what to make of it. The way he said it . . . there was no reverence or warmth. Not the way a lost lover's name might roll off one's tongue. And if Marisol was not a love, she must be someone else. Something else to him. I was determined to find out what.

After a few hours of waiting for him to wake up, I fell asleep in the chair, leaning on the side of the bed. When he was still out in the morning, I let Tommy convince me to come upstairs for some breakfast.

Robin and Owen and Tio were all in the kitchen. It seemed that for once, part of the pack had gathered to eat together. All it took was their Alpha almost dying.

"You don't think he's, like, in a coma or something?" I asked nobody and everybody. I'd never heard of a wolf in a coma.

"Naw," Robin said while loading his plate with roast beef and scrambled egg.

"Yeah. Don't worry, he'll wake up soon, he just . . ." Tommy chimed in, but then trailed off because a furious-looking Markus had just entered the kitchen.

Markus hadn't exactly been the friendliest wolf in the world to me—or anyone—but right then he looked downright scary. Like he could stare down a wraith and it would run off with its tail between its legs. Not that wraiths had tails. Or legs.

"What did you do with it?" he asked tightly while stalking toward the table, stopping right in front of me.

"Do with what?" I asked as his dark eyes burrowed into me. "I didn't do—"

"The Porsche," Markus growled.

"Oh," I said, suddenly remembering. My hand flew to my mouth in horror as I realized that I'd left the Porsche in that abandoned dark parking lot. Worse, I'd unlocked it in my hurry to get to James. I clearly remembered unlocking it but never relocking it. "Oh crap."

Markus looked like he wanted to strangle me.

"Bro, it's just a car," Tommy said beside me. Except the way Markus turned his glare to Tommy made me think it wasn't just a car. But I was glad his eyes were on Tommy rather than me. They were so angry and dark.

I couldn't believe I'd stolen Markus's car and then left it unlocked in a deserted parking lot. That poor beautiful car.

"It's not there," Markus was saying. While I was despairing over the car, Tommy had told his brother something about the GPS tracking service. Markus focused back on me. "Where did you leave it?"

"There was a parking lot. By a coffeehouse." I debated about whether to tell him I'd left it unlocked. I decided honesty was probably the best policy. Better than him finding out later. From how pissed he seemed now, he might murder me in my sleep if I hid something from him. "I may have . . . Imayhavelefittunlocked."

Markus gave me such a look then. It wasn't anger or hate. Well, it was both of those things, but it was something else too. Something desperate and oblique. Like a child whose favorite toy has been forever lost.

"I'm really sorry," I said, meaning it.

Markus didn't acknowledge that, just turned and left.

The others started up a quiet conversation while I stared after him. After a minute I turned to Tommy to maybe say sorry to him too. Or to ask why the car was so important. But just then I suddenly felt a confused roar coming from my mate bond—one that somehow blocked out all other sound in the room, all other feeling.

"Something is wrong," I said, almost stumbling and having to grab hold of the kitchen counter.

CHAPTER 28

James

She wasn't there. She had been but she was gone now. Gone. Alone. Had to find her. Had to protect.

"Be calm, please."

There had been wraiths. Last night. He needed to find her. To make sure she was safe.

His.

"James."

They were trying to stop him from getting to her. He needed to get to her. He needed her.

The wolf. If he was the wolf, they couldn't stop him. Even when he was hurt the wolf still had teeth and claws. That was what he needed.

He began to change.

CHAPTER 29

There was a howl and then a crashing sound, one that we heard even from the kitchen. James had changed into his wolf shape and he was coming this way. Coming to find . . . me. Coming to save me. Except I was already safe.

All eyes turned toward the door that led to the corridor where the medical rooms were. We all knew what was coming. It was like hearing a train approaching and knowing that there was no time to get out of the way. No way to stop it. The train was going to come roaring past, and if anything got in its way, that thing would get shredded.

The door was thrown open, partly splintering around the lock. James in his wolf shape skidded on the tiled kitchen floor.

I took a step back, because James's wolf was big. His head was almost as tall as the counter, with wide shoulders and heavy paws. A normal wolf would have looked like a small dog next to him.

James also had a mouth full of fangs, which he was displaying to everyone but me.

Sidestepping, I moved away from Tommy. I was very glad I hadn't changed clothes into the scrubs Doc had offered last night. James's wolf was clearly in control, and smelling plastic or someone else's scent on me might have triggered an attack.

"Megan," Tommy said, but I kept moving away from them. Not quite toward the out-of-control werewolf, but not away either.

James took his attention off the rest of the pack and turned to me. His eyes were wolf gold. I wasn't sure how clearly he was thinking, how much was the wolf and how much was James. Normally a wolf would never hurt its mate, but our mate bond wasn't complete.

Suddenly he moved. For a second I thought he was going to go for my throat, kill me right then and there. But instead he got up on his back paws and placed his two front ones on my shoulders. He was big enough that he could do it comfortably. It wasn't as comfortable for me, though. His paws were heavy. He nuzzled me with his big wet nose, rubbing against my neck, almost as if checking for a pulse.

"James," Robin said softly. "You're scaring her. You don't want Megan to be scared, do you?"

I wanted to protest. I wasn't exactly scared. Startled was more like it. Even though I'd grown up in the pack house, having a huge wolf walk up and pin me to the wall was a first.

But before I could say anything, the wolf stepped back, sinking onto all fours, and shook himself. Then James began the change back to human and I glanced to Doc, who had just shown up in the doorway. Changing when you were hurt wasn't a good idea. It slowed the healing. James had already gone from wolf to human once. Now he'd gone from human to wolf and was attempting to change back again. That wasn't smart.

The change took a long time. Changing back to human usually did take longer, but this dragged on and on. For a minute he seemed to be trapped between human and wolf, not quite either, looking like a werewolf from a horror movie. Then finally he lay on the floor fully human, his face pressed against the cold kitchen tile.

I thought he was unconscious, but after a few seconds he turned to look up at me. His eyes were the wolf's eyes, making sure I was all right. That was why he'd come. I hadn't been there when he woke up so he'd come to find me. To make sure I was safe.

I didn't say anything, but I held his eyes. There were a lot of different things in them, more emotions than a wolf could feel. Slowly the gold faded to James's normal spring-green ones, but a glimmer of those feelings was still there.

James was half-conscious, and after a quick look at his wound, Doc declared he'd need to be stitched back up again. With Robin and Tommy as crutches, he hobbled back down the destroyed hall. I walked behind them, admiring the view.

We passed the room James had been in. The door, which had only had one dent when I'd been there earlier, now had several and hung sideways on only one hinge.

I stopped to look while the guys continued on, taking James into the next room. I'd been in this room a little under an hour ago. But it looked completely different. It was like a tornado had gone through the room. The medical waste container had been turned over, trash was scattered all over the floor, the bed torn up and on its side. The wallpaper had chunks missing. The chair I'd been on had a bent leg.

"I guess he really wanted to see you," Tommy said from the doorway with a grin. I glanced back at him, then at the room again. James had done this to get to me, to make sure I was okay. I felt a smile spread across my face too.

CHAPTER 30

As I'd predicted, that night I had nightmares about the wraiths. About being back in the alley with James bleeding out and them coming for us. Then it changed and I was no longer being attacked by a wraith; I was a wraith, swooping down to kill an unsuspecting werewolf.

Once I finally managed to wake myself up, there was no way I was going back to sleep. But even awake, I kept replaying what had happened in my head. I'd never felt that helpless. Never thought I might actually die. Even living in a large pack where fights happened frequently, this was the first one I'd seen where the stakes were truly life and death. And I'd been totally useless.

I needed to change that. I had no desire to ever see a wraith again, but if this city, which Robin claimed was totally wraith infested, was going to be my home, I needed some way of being safe. I needed to learn how to defend myself from the things that lived and thrived in the dark.

A shiver ran down my spine and I got out of bed and turned my lights on, wanting to chase all the shadows away. The lady in the portrait looked down at me. I wondered who she was. She was young, maybe my age, blond and petite. James's sister maybe. Or mother. Or just some lady with no connection to anyone. Just some painting that had ended up in the pack's care. Like the car poster.

For a minute I wondered if this woman might be Marisol. James had said that name twice when he was unconscious, but his voice had been so odd when he spoke it. I wasn't sure what their relationship was. Would he keep a portrait of her? I didn't think so, but the idea bothered me.

I wondered if Marisol was the reason he didn't want to be my mate. I imagined it had to have been a pretty bad breakup for him to end up being so closed off emotionally. For maybe a long time, since it seemed everyone was pretty used to the way he acted. But maybe things were changing; the fact that he'd come looking for me when he'd woken up after being hurt had to mean something. The broken hospital room had to mean something.

Still, knowing there was some woman—maybe the one whose portrait was on my wall—who had hurt him in his past made me growl. Whoever she was, I hated her. Even though she was clearly not part of his life anymore, maybe even dead, I hated her for what she'd done to James . . . and to me.

A little shuffling sound from outside my door diverted my attention from the portrait and Marisol. Even though the rational part of my mind told me it was highly unlikely that a wraith or burglar was creeping around outside, I quickly unplugged a nearby lamp and turned it upside down. It was made from heavy ceramic and I figured I could use it as a club of sorts if I needed to.

But when I opened the door I thought at first it had been my tired and maybe slightly paranoid brain playing tricks on me. Then I saw Lucy, blinking up at me from the floor. There was a fancy-looking red velvet pillow with gold tassels next to her.

"Lucy?" I said, not quite sure why she would be there. "Are you sleeping out here?"

I didn't expect an answer, she normally took off when I tried to talk to her. But she nodded, sitting up.

"Don't you have a bed somewhere?"

She rubbed her eyes and shrugged. It was a slightly annoyed gesture. As if she was confused as to why I was disturbing her sleep. I decided she must have a bed somewhere but she'd probably wanted to be close to someone after the craziness that had been the past day.

"Well, you shouldn't be sleeping on the floor," I said, taking a step back from the door. "Come in and sit with me?"

I expected this to make her run off. But instead she came into my room. She didn't sit down on any of the delicate furniture but instead looked around, her attention first focused intently on the portrait lady, then the curtains and an antique clock that had stopped.

"It was you," I said, realizing it and immediately feeling stupid for not having done so sooner. In my defense, I'd had other things on my mind. "You told Tommy I'd left. Or wrote him a note or something."

I sat down on the bed, watching her. "You knew . . . you know about the wraiths, right?"

Then something that I wasn't at all prepared for happened.

Lucy spoke.

"Yes," she said, sitting down on the bed next to me.

I blinked at her.

"What? Wait!" I swallowed. "You talk?"

Lucy shrugged and stared at me with her big blue eyes, then she nodded. "Yes."

"But you haven't—I mean, Tommy said . . . ," I began, not sure how to deal with this sudden change.

"I do not talk to others. I talked to Tommy. I talk with you. Now." She spoke oddly, but I guessed she was a bit out of practice. Or maybe used to speaking some other language? My first thought was French—we were in Canada, after all—but her accent was too harsh. Russian, maybe? I wasn't good with accents.

I frowned. "Okay. But why? Why haven't you talked to them, told them where you are from, about your pack, about—"

"No." Lucy jumped up and shook her head and took several steps away from the bed, suddenly looking more wild than she ever had. I could see the whites of her eye around her pupils and her voice was shrill when she spoke again. "I promised I'd not. I'm *hewdevi* or they come. Mother said I—"

"Relax, Luce," I said, standing and reaching out to her, wanting to calm her. She slipped away and I didn't try again, not wanting to cause her to run off. "No one is going to come here or do anything to you, okay?"

Lucy looked doubtful, but after a few moments nodded, the matter apparently settled.

"Do you want to stay with me tonight?" I said, walking over to the bed and getting in. "The bed is surprisingly comfy."

I hoped she'd say yes. Both because it would make me feel less scared about going back to sleep and because it would mean she trusted me. She thought about it for a minute, tilted her head, then came over and crawled into the bed.

I turned the bedside lamp off and snuggled into the covers next to her. Lucy's small, cold hand found mine. There was something very desperate about how she held on to me. She was afraid. I closed my eyes and thought of the nightmarish wraiths. I felt like I understood fear in a way I never had before. But I didn't want Lucy to feel scared. I wanted her to know I would protect her, that the pack would.

"You're safe," I told her as I squeezed her hand. "I will keep you safe, okay? I swear it."

I wondered if that was a smart thing to promise. My world had gotten a lot scarier, literally overnight. I already knew neither I nor Lucy stood a chance against a wraith. Maybe Lucy was right to be frightened. Maybe I was a fool for thinking she, we, were safe.

Her fear and worry made me more determined, though. I was going to learn to protect myself—and, if there ever was a need, Lucy too.

CHAPTER 31

The next morning when I went looking for James, it was a little harder than I'd thought it would be to find him. He'd reached out and let me in when calling for help the other night, and our mate bond had been more open while he was unconscious and when he was wolf. But now it seemed closed off again. I figured that was because James was hurt. That made everyone more defensive. Or maybe because he was pissed he'd been told to stay in human shape for at least two weeks by Doc yesterday. He hadn't liked that one bit.

I wished there was some kind of guidebook on how mate bonds worked. But they were all unique. I did know trust was an important part of it. And consent. You had to want a mate, consent to forever be part of each other, for it to work. For a short while, James had wanted me close, but it seemed like it was only out of necessity, to save his life. Now we were back at square one.

When I finally did find him, he was in the otherwise empty

kitchen fiddling with something. I wasn't sure what it was at first, then I realized he was carving something out of wood. Something small and delicate-looking, at least in his hands. The way he used such small, controlled movements to whittle away at whatever he was making was fascinating. I just watched him from the doorway for a bit.

"I heard you lost Markus's car," he said, not looking up from his work. I felt a little flutter of surprise. James had never initiated a conversation with me before.

"It was an accident," I said, walking into the room and around to the table so I was facing him. "And mostly your fault."

Surprisingly enough, that made his lip twitch, as if he wanted to smile. James smiling, or at least almost smiling, made me feel warm and happy inside. I liked this new James who was talking to me and almost smiling at me.

But thinking of having lost Markus's car made me feel crappy . . . I was going to need to do something about that. Maybe I could find him a new one? "I'm sorry about it. I'll be a lot more careful next time."

"Next time?" He looked up. "The next time you run away?"

"The next time I need to drive somewhere," I corrected him. "You're not going to change the code to the garage, right? I'd never forgotten to lock a car before, I swear."

"I'm not worried about losing another car," James said seriously after a few moments. He gave me a look that was almost . . . tender.

I felt happy tingles all over, because James had just admitted he cared about me. That I was important to him. Not James's wolf,

James the man. And his eyes, they were saying just as much. I'd never seen him look at anyone or anything like that. It made me feel truly hopeful for us for the first time.

"I think that's the nicest thing you've said to me," I said, pulling a chair out and sitting down across from him. I tried to figure out what he was carving but couldn't. He held the carving knife and the wood expertly, though, despite them being small and his hands large.

Thinking of James being good with his hands was seriously distracting, but I wasn't here to dwell on his kind words, the look, or his hands. I had sought him out for a reason: to convince him to teach me to fight. That was my goal. "Is there some weapon that works on the wraiths?"

"Robin said he explained it all to you," he said, a little wrinkle appearing between his eyes.

"He did. He said only a warrior wolf's bite can kill one. But he shot it and that slowed it down. Is there some magic bullet or something?" I hoped there was. If I could get myself a gun with bullets that hurt wraiths I'd feel a whole lot safer.

"No magic. But most things tend to get distracted when you put a few lead projectiles in them." He frowned, studying my expression, which I was keeping carefully neutral. "Why?" he asked, suspicion suddenly radiating off him.

"I just wanted to know. If they had, like, some other weakness. Something to make them less scary," I said carefully.

"You don't have to worry about the wraiths. As long as you're not in town at night, you're safe." He sounded like he was totally sure about that, which was comforting. Not that I had been worried wraiths would descend on Sandleholm Manor—well, maybe a little.

"That's not what it feels like," I said quietly. "Ever since I saw them I can't . . . I feel helpless."

"You don't—"

"And because that's a really sucky way to feel, I came up with a plan," I said in a rush. "I need you to teach me to fight."

"Megan—"

"Come on!" I said, trying to stop him from rejecting the idea.

"I wasn't saying no," he said, but he was still frowning.

"You didn't sound like you were saying yes either," I said, and crossed my arms.

"I wasn't."

"Look, I don't want to become a warrior and go out kicking ass or anything," I said, hoping that would wipe the frown off his face. "That's not why I'm asking. I just don't—The other night really scared me. So teach me to defend myself so I won't have to be scared."

"All right."

"It's not right—wait, what—okay?"

"Yes," he said.

I grinned and just barely kept myself from jumping up, rounding the table, and giving him a hug. I wondered what he'd have done if I had. Would he have hugged me back? Run his hands over me? Kissed me? Pushed me away? I decided it didn't matter. James had agreed to teach me to fight, to be safe.

CHAPTER 32

James

He had been surprised at her request to learn to fight. Surprised but not opposed to it. Not really. Ever since waking up after the attack, he felt a gnawing worry whenever she wasn't close. If he knew she could at least take care of herself a little, if he could teach her just the very basics, he'd feel calmer.

Or maybe he'd agreed for the selfish reason that he wanted to spend time with her. Before, he'd been so desperate to get away from her, overly concerned with the mate bond. Afraid the smallest act of kindness or lust toward her would call the magic. But it hadn't.

Perhaps that was because both of them were holding back.

Megan probably wouldn't admit it, but her mate bond wasn't totally open, ready to embrace him. Maybe because of the way he'd acted when they first met. Maybe because she was an Alpha too and alphas protected—both others and themselves. They had to be strong. Letting him in would be harder than she realized.

Whatever the reason, it meant he could spend time with her, maybe even give in to the lust he felt for her, as long as he kept his guard up.

"I understand wanting to be able to protect yourself, your pack, your territory," he said. "You're Alpha. It's part of who you are."

That made her smile widen. "Who *we* are."

"Yes," he agreed.

Who we are.

Him and Megan as a *we*. He wasn't quite sure what to think about that. His wolf liked it. Maybe he did too.

He watched her eyes. There was something in those gray eyes, a light. It, he realized, was what made her so captivating. The rest of her was beautiful, but her eyes. The light burning in them, her spirit, almost made it hard for him to breathe. He wondered how he could have missed it before. Maybe he hadn't dared to look close enough.

"James, who is Marisol?" she asked quietly. But the words felt huge. Like they were booming inside his head.

Robin had said to talk to her. Share. Explain. Suddenly he was desperate to do that. He wanted her to understand him. The problem was, he wasn't sure he understood himself. He desired Megan for sure; just having her be in the same room, her scent, the soft-looking bare skin of her arms, made his body respond. But even though he knew Megan, even from the little time he had spent around her, wasn't like Marisol, he didn't want to ever be bound to anyone again. Especially not when the bond breaking would send him down the same path as his father.

What he did feel he owed her was an explanation. Even if he wasn't sure about what he wanted for the future, he needed her to understand his actions toward her.

"You caught me by surprise," he started, which immediately made Megan frown. He decided to try again. "I never wanted . . . You were never part of my plan."

She tried to avert her eyes, but he saw the hurt flash in them. This wasn't going the way he'd hoped. He wanted to make her understand, not feel worse. Robin had said to give her something small, to trust her just a little. James wasn't sure how to do that. His story was all wrapped in a series of events that didn't make sense without being told in order.

"My mother was killed in an attack when I was about your age. Most of the pack was killed," he told her. He didn't tell her about the horror of waking up the morning after the raid, finding his mother's body. Searching for his sister but not finding her. He didn't want to put those images in her head. They haunted him enough.

"I'm sorry," she said softly.

He nodded.

"We couldn't find my sister, so I went in search of her." He went back to working on the carving, not sure he could get the words out while looking at her. But he couldn't carve because his hands were shaking. He had to put the knife down.

"Nora."

"Yes," he said, a little surprised she knew his sister's name. She must have heard it from his father. He was the only one who spoke of Nora. "There was someone I heard rumors of. Someone I thought could help. Marisol." He paused. Wasn't sure how to go on. How to explain. "She was witch born. She had magic."

"But she didn't help you, did she?" Megan said. He felt the dryness in his mouth, thinking back. No. She hadn't helped him. She'd trapped him, taken his will. For too long he had been too weak to get out. He couldn't tell Megan about that. He couldn't talk about it at all or the feeling of being forced to feel and do things he hadn't wanted to would suffocate him. But for her to understand, he had to.

"No," he said, putting his carving to the side and sliding up his sleeve to show her one of the tattoos. "She bespelled me, and when I tried to break free she used these to bind me to her tighter."

"I'm sorry," she whispered. He kept staring at the tattoo. How he hated it. "I—"

He looked up at her. "She made me love her when I hated her. And I couldn't stop it." Megan's eyes were full of emotion he couldn't quite identify. Was it pity? Horror? Revulsion at his weakness? Sympathy? Fear? Love?

She reached out, as if to take his hand, but he ignored it. He grabbed the little statue instead, looking away from those eyes. The emotions he couldn't understand.

"I killed her." He squeezed the wood, feeling the statue tremble under the pressure. "In the end I killed her."

She surprised him then, by saying, "Good."

He marveled at that response for a while. He was right before. She was an Alpha too. Maybe she did understand. Not the helplessness he'd felt. Not that. But the need for violence, the need to stop one's enemies . . . maybe she was stronger than he had first believed.

"By that time Nora was long dead," he said, needing to continue because he wasn't sure he'd ever be able to restart telling this story and he wanted it all out, wanted her to understand. "My father was already spiraling into madness."

"Because of everyone who died?"

"Because of my mother," he said. He hated having to explain this to her. In the beginning he'd hoped she knew, about the madness that came with an alpha warrior losing his mate. But of course she hadn't. It wasn't the same for normal werewolves. "When she died, the mate bond broke, unraveled, and with it his mind. The same happened to my grandfather before him . . ."

"James," she said softly while biting her lip. "None of that was your fault. Not your mother, not your sister, not your father. Especially not Marisol."

He wished that was true but it simply wasn't. Yet he was thankful that she said it, and her words were so heartfelt that he, without thinking, reached for her outstretched hand.

CHAPTER 33

Twenty-four hours later, my head was still spinning from everything I'd learned. There were still many questions, yet everything about James suddenly made so much more sense. His distance toward me wasn't because of actual malice or dislike of *me*. It was his own fear and guilt.

He'd been bespelled by a witch, forced to love her because of magic. While the mate bond wasn't able to force anyone to do anything, I could still see why he would fear it. Why he might feel I was attempting to do the same. To bind him with magic—wolf magic, but magic all the same.

There were also layers of guilt. Guilt for surviving when most of the pack had died in the attack that killed his mother, guilt over not having been able to resist Marisol, and, I thought, guilt over his father's condition.

But him telling me, trusting me, had to mean something. He was letting me in, moving past the fear and guilt and all that baggage.

Sure, there was the bit about the alpha beginning to lose his sanity when his mate died. I understood his fear; he'd seen it happen to his father. But it wasn't like I had plans to die any time soon. Loving someone always came with the risk of losing them, didn't it?

Besides, now he was going to teach me how to fight and I'd be able to keep myself safe. I might not be able to guarantee I wasn't going to die before him, but in all fairness, he was the one out there hunting wraiths every night, not me.

Speaking of fighting, it was time for my first training session with James, which we were doing in human shape since he couldn't shift yet because of his wound. I kind of remembered the way to the gym and used the vague sensation of the mate bond to help guide me.

Once I got there, the door was open. It looked like I remembered. Mats, boxing gear, and other workout equipment. It was big and bright, both from the sunlight coming through the two windows and the fluorescent lights.

James was standing in the middle of the mats, stretching. His dark jeans and dark T-shirt looked out of place in the gym, as did his handsome and fierce face. Instead I imagined him in a forest long ago, a warrior who didn't live by any rules I had ever known, and found it was easy. He belonged there. In this gym . . . not so much.

I'd never seen his bare arms before (except when he'd been hurt, but I'd been too distracted then) and took the chance to study the tattoos on his wrists and arms as he moved. I'd thought there was something odd about them but I hadn't understood until yesterday that what I'd been sensing had been traces of magic. Even though they'd been put on his skin with evil intent, there was a certain beauty to them.

"Are you going to stand there all day?" he asked suddenly. I startled and felt myself blush a little. I'd just stood there ogling him for two minutes.

"No," I said, hurrying inside and over to him. "Hi— Good morning—I mean . . ." It was after lunch.

"Let's get to it, then," he said, all business. But it bothered me less than it would have before, because I knew the reason for his brusque manner. "You can't kill a wraith in human shape," he said.

I tried to focus and get into serious study mode, but James in a tight T-shirt was surprisingly distracting. And his mouth was too. I loved how his lips moved, how his faint accent made everything sound smarter and more interesting somehow.

"And killing one shouldn't be your objective anyway; running should. Best thing would be for you to try to never meet one again."

I agreed with that sentiment, but at the same time I wanted to be prepared if I did end up face-to-face with one of them again. "Right."

"But it's useful to learn to fight as a human too." He walked over to the punching bag. "You might not have time to change." Like the other night. I nodded. "It will also be easier for me to instruct you, at least until I can change or we have someone else assisting."

He walked back over to the mats and motioned me over. There was a slight stiffness in how he held himself, but other than that he seemed totally recovered from his injury. That was amazing. Even my dad, who was Alpha of Alphas, didn't heal as fast.

"So first rule of self-defense?"

"Don't die?" I guessed with a smile. He didn't look amused.

"Be smart," he said, his eyes narrowing. "Don't go into town at night because that's where the wraiths are. Before you do, think. Think about where you might be in danger and avoid those places." I walked onto the blue mats as he talked. "Easiest fight is the one you never have to get into. Second. Your most important weapons are your legs." He patted his thighs. He had nice legs; even with the jeans he always wore I could tell. Why hadn't I noticed them before? Maybe because there were so many parts of him that were totally droolworthy.

"Both in the sense that they'll let you run away and because trying to use your fist to knock someone out is more likely to break your hand than their face." He held up his closed fist. "Lots of little bones in your hand. Hurts like hell to break them."

I flexed my own hands and brought them up. Thought of all the joints and how small my hands were, especially compared with James's. I remembered punching Robin and could see why it might not be a good idea. He stepped a little closer. He smelled wonderful, and the competent way he was instructing me made me feel safe.

He took one of my closed fists. Little tingles radiated from his touch as he looked straight at me with his intense eyes. "If you are going to throw a punch," he said, so close I could feel the faint tickle of his breath, "thumb goes outside the fist."

"Okay," I said softly. He abruptly stepped back, my voice breaking the spell. The warm and bubbly feeling from being close to him faded.

"So, step one; run. If you can't do that, the second is, kick. Aim high, for the center mass on a wraith. On something more human you go for their knee joints. With us warriors the wraiths tend to go for fast kills, but with someone . . ." I think he was going to say *defenseless*, but he changed it. ". . . less skilled they like to kill by choking, drawing out the death."

That sent shivers all over me. "That's horrible."

"But good for you," he said, moving a little closer again. "It might save your life. With them close like that, you can try to break their fingers and poke out their eyes." He put both his hands loosely around my neck, wrapping them around, putting a little bit of pressure on my windpipe. "Fingers are pretty easy to break. As long as you get a good grip and twist or pull hard."

I looked into his eyes; the fingers around my neck were making my wolf worried. The wolf didn't like to be dominated, threatened, not even by our mate, and she wanted to get away, but the human part of me understood it was just an exercise and actually couldn't help but enjoy the fact that James was touching me.

"Try."

Tentatively I reached up, trying to get one of the fingers wrapped around my neck off. I didn't pull hard—I didn't want to accidentally snap his fingers—but I found that it wouldn't have been hard to yank with a lot of force.

"Yeah, like that," he said, leaning a little closer. God, he was close, and he smelled so good. And his eyes were so green. "And if your attacker is this close, you can try using your head. The head is like a big bowling ball; knocking it into someone's face can really mess them up . . ."

James seemed to realize then that he was once again mere inches from me. I could feel his warm breath caressing my face. His hands slid around my neck and I was sure he was going to step away, pull away from me like he had every other time I'd been close to him.

Instead he moved one hand to my shoulder and the other one up, to cup my cheek.

I wanted to yell at him to kiss me already, wanted so badly to just lay one on him. Instead I moved just half an inch closer to him, wishing he would come to me, longing for him to kiss me.

And then he did.

James's mouth was on mine, soft and careful. I froze. I had wanted him to kiss me for so long, and now that it was happening I wasn't sure what to do. Then I felt James begin to pull away— probably because I wasn't kissing him back. I quickly grabbed his arm and began returning the kiss.

I felt dizzy as I kissed him; my wolf was ecstatic. *I* was ecstatic. My senses were alive, his hand on my neck tingling almost as much as my lips. Part of me couldn't help but wonder if this was all a wonderful, vivid dream. But James's mouth was so hot on mine, going from questioning to demanding, it couldn't be a dream, it just couldn't—

James's hand on my shoulder moved the straps of my tank top and bra to the side, baring my shoulder, stroking with his slightly rough hand. I leaned into the touch. My wolf was in high heaven, wanted to be with him, right there in the gym. Wanted to open up and embrace all of him and be bound for good.

James growled. "You want me." His voice was low. One hand in my hair and the other curling around my waist, he moved me so my back was against the wall.

"Yes," I murmured, looking up into his eyes. He knew I did. Just as I, at that moment, was very sure he wanted me too. As much as I did him. There was no past, no future, only the now.

He growled again, leaned in, and nuzzled my neck, then went on to kiss my shoulder. Slowly, I moved my hands up to his shoulders. The muscles under my fingers tensed but he didn't move back. Instead he moved his hands to my hips and, as if I weighed nothing at all, picked me up and pushed me against the wall, his big body seeming to cover me, pressing into me. I grabbed on to him harder.

"Mine," he whispered. "Mine." He kissed down my exposed neck and shoulder, his teeth scraping against me. The feel of his mouth and skin against me made me feel dizzy. But in a good way.

I reached for the hem of his shirt with one hand. I wanted to be closer, closer. James's hands weren't pausing either; they were moving all over me while his hips ground into me.

But when my hand brushed at the skin of his lower back, he stopped, and before I had a chance to even think, he'd grabbed both my wrists and pinned them over my head.

He stared at me for a few seconds, golden flecks in his eyes dancing. I tried to get my hands free for a second, but when he wouldn't budge I figured it didn't matter. And he wasn't hurting me, just holding my hands. *Control*, some part of me whispered.

I didn't mind, though. I moved forward, putting my mouth on his earlobe, then down to his neck. Nipped him playfully, pulled back slightly. Looked deep into his eyes.

"Mine," I said, letting him see the wolf in my eyes. "All mine."

James smiled a slow, lazy smile. "Got it all figured out, do you?" His hands dropped away from my wrists and pulled back slightly, enough so that I had to let go of his waist and stand on my own. I managed, even though I felt like spaghetti and my body was screaming *NOOO*.

"What's wrong?" I asked, but he put a finger over my lips.

"Someone's coming," he said, taking a few steps back from me just as the door to the training room was suddenly flung open.

"Megan!" Tommy cried, clearly not realizing he was interrupting a moment.

The moment, actually.

"I got your Wi-Fi working!"

CHAPTER 34

While I wanted to be totally furious with Tommy, I couldn't be. Because he'd fixed the Wi-Fi for me. But his timing sucked.

"Really?" I took a few steps toward him on my still slightly unsteady legs.

"Yes, I . . . ," Tommy said. At that moment, he seemed to understand, probably from my disheveled appearance and puffy lips, that he'd interrupted something. Tommy glanced to James, who was looking a bit rumpled too. "Is this a bad time? I didn't mean to interrupt."

"Yes," James said, much to my surprise. I think Tommy's too, because he looked unsure of how to proceed. I looked to James, and was pleased see he was still looking at me with the same heated look as during our make-out session.

I felt torn. I was beyond thrilled to finally be able to go online. I wanted to rush up to my room and get my cell and laptop and just log on to Facebook and check my favorite blogs. But I also wanted Tommy to leave. Because if he did, maybe James and I could go back to what we'd been doing—which had been a lot better than anything online could ever be. I mean, I'd made out with James. That was amazing. Crazy amazing.

James gave a sigh but asked, "What's the problem?"

"No problem," Tommy said, seeming a bit tenser than normal. "I just . . . I got the Wi-Fi working."

"I told him to do that," I said quickly, because I wasn't sure if James was okay with that and I didn't want Tommy to get in trouble. It had been my idea. "And just in my room—well, not my room-room, and it's not like it's something your dad can see or anything so it won't bother him."

"What is this other room of yours?" James said, sounding a little gruff. I wasn't sure if that was from our make-out session or annoyance at something.

"I'm . . . ," I said, moving a bit closer to him. "I'm kind of fixing one of the big rooms up a little."

"Why?" He seemed genuinely confused.

"Well, James," I said carefully. "This place isn't exactly . . . Let's just say I think we need a new nice cozy hangout place. A place the whole pack can spend time, that looks nice and isn't so . . . ."

"Messy? Old?" Tommy offered from the door. "Ugly? Museum-esque?"

James seemed to think this over for a few seconds, then he said, "Okay." He put his hand on my lower back and moved me toward Tommy. "Show me."

His touch made me flash back to our kiss. I still couldn't quite believe I'd kissed him. Not just kissed, but made out against a wall. And now he wanted to see the Wi-Fi room! Things were truly getting better: he'd shared about his past, we'd made out, he'd touched my back and been interested in my project.

To top it off, Tommy had gotten the Wi-Fi to work. It was crazy how much I missed it. Sure, I'd been able to use the internet down in Tommy's "lair," but it was so weird to be on a stationary computer and it was impossible to relax sitting on his uncomfortable chairs. But now there was actual Wi-Fi.

Even James's hand dropping away from my back couldn't dampen my excitement. This was a new chapter for the whole pack. There was going to be a room with Wi-Fi. But not just that; it was going to be a nice and cozy room for everyone to socialize and relax in. It would bring them all together.

"The range is good, but not great," Tommy said as we got closer to "my" room. Maybe it should be called the Wi-Fi room instead? "Once you leave it gets blocked pretty easy. Because of how thick the walls are. But inside the room, signal strength is great."

We entered the room. It was still kind of messy, although both Tommy and I had done our fair share of moving and packing stuff down. But at least now you could see the second window and I'd found a dumbwaiter—like an old mini elevator thing—that went to a corridor right outside the kitchen.

James walked in and then around (as much as he could with all the stuff), stopping to glance at a few things. I watched him nervously out of the corner of my eye while Tommy showed me the shelf with the router and things. I didn't really care how he'd made it work—all I cared about was the fact that I'd have the internet! I'd be able to chat with Sorelle, check for schools, and just generally rejoin the twenty-first century.

"I think this used to be a ballroom," James said after a minute of looking around.

"Really?" I asked him, moving over to him while Tommy stayed back with the tech. "That's cool. And it does have a pretty floor. But Tommy said he'd help me fix a new wallpaper because this one is all worn and cracked in places, if that's okay? I figured I'd make it kind of modern. Not super modern or anything. I want everyone to feel like they can hang out here."

I'd already sketched out where I was going to put the furniture I'd ordered: a big U-shaped sofa that everyone would be able to fit into, a TV cabinet that could be closed if Trist was present, a few cozy chairs next to the fireplace (next to some bookcases that were already in the room and too heavy to move). I'd also ordered a nice big table where we'd all be able to eat fancy meals for Thanksgiving and Christmas and birthdays.

I began telling him about it all, showing him where I imagined things being placed. He watched me intently, as if my description and plans for this room, the pack, and a special TV cabinet for his dad was the most interesting thing ever. Which was really nice and made me feel all tingly. Almost as good as kissing him had been. I still couldn't quite believe that had happened. Could almost not believe that this new version of James was real. But he was.

"I'm not sure when the stuff gets delivered. Did I tell you about the dining table? It's going to be so nice. Maybe we could have dinner together. On it. I mean to try out the table. Once it arrives, I mean," I finished.

Oh, wow, Megan, smooth. Way to go. Like he wasn't going to see through that lame excuse to get him to spend time with you. Or maybe he wouldn't. He could be clueless sometimes.

He looked at me with a raised eyebrow. "To try the table?" For some reason when he said that it made me think of him and me on the table having an even hotter make-out session than the one in the training room.

"Yeah," I said, glancing away. "If you want?"

"Sure," he said, smiling some more. I loved that I was making him smile. "We could do that."

CHAPTER 35

"See," Sorelle told me. "All you had to do was have a little patience."

And nearly die, and find out wraiths are real and that my mate was bespelled by a witch. Except I couldn't tell Sorelle that. It felt strange to be talking to her and not sharing everything I'd learned over the past few days. I'd always told Sorelle everything. But these were different secrets, not mine to tell.

"It's pretty great," I said, thinking back to earlier. Making out with James. James being interested in the Wi-Fi room. James smiling. Our plan for a sort of, kind of date once the dining room table arrived. "It's just . . ." I wasn't sure how much to share with her. ". . . James . . . it's not about him not liking me. It's the whole mate bond thing. Not having a choice."

Sorelle made a *hum* sound, then said, "Sounds like he kind of maybe . . ."

"What?" I asked, eagerly wanting to know what she was thinking.

"It's a bit stupid. But it sounds like maybe he just wants to fall in love normally. As a guy, not because of the magic of the wolf," she said. "Which is really sweet, right?"

I thought about that as I leaned back on the beanbag—I'd found it stuffed in a closet when I got lost earlier—which, except for the few bookcases I was keeping, was the only thing in the Wi-Fi room at the moment. Me and Tommy had been busy getting it cleared out this afternoon and it was actually a bit echoey because it was so empty. But hopefully soon stuff would start being delivered. I hoped they'd hurry up with the table. James and I could have our date and maybe even have a sexy make-out session on top of it.

"Maybe," I said finally. But I wasn't so sure James wanted to fall in love. He wanted me, I was sure about that. I wanted him too. But love, just like the mate bond, would require him to open up. Besides, if we made love, I thought that would complete the mate bond. Which he didn't want. And I had no idea on how I could change his mind about it.

"Sounds like Mr. Asshole is getting over himself, though," she said. "With agreeing to train you and the whole make-out in the gym. Maybe you're wrong about him being scared? Maybe he just needed to warm up to you a bit?"

"I don't—"

"Maybe you should just jump his bones and get it over with."

Sorelle grinned. "Once the bond is complete, it's complete, right? No take-backs. So just seduce the heck out of him."

"That's your advice?" I said, amused. Then I thought about it. About mate bonds and her and Scott. More specifically about her not having sex with Scott. It seemed odd—I mean, I couldn't keep my hands or thoughts off James and we'd only known each other a few weeks. Sorelle and Scott had been mated a year. "Hey, Sorelle, you and Scott . . . why haven't you? You know? Seduced the heck out of him?"

"It's not the same," she said, but she didn't say anything else. Didn't elaborate or explain.

"How is it not the same?"

"I don't know," she said after a bit of a pause. She was fiddling with something on the desk, offscreen so I couldn't see, and not meeting my eyes. "Scott and I are just . . . it's not like with you and James."

I frowned, not understanding. I also wanted to push her, to make her tell me more. About why and how it was different. How and why she thought me seducing James was a good plan. Yet I didn't, because she clearly wasn't comfortable talking about it. Next time I saw her in person I would ask her more about it, though. This felt like an IRL conversation. Instead I said, "How is Scott, anyway?"

"Weird about Boston." She rolled her eyes. "I think he's trying to get a job there or something. Which is sweet but unnecessary."

"When are you leaving again?" I asked, since I was kind of planning to live vicariously through her until I could find a college somewhere around here. And I was probably never going to get the fun dorm-room experience since my closest city was totally wraith infested.

We talked for a while about her preparing to move, the Boston pack she was "transferring" to, and generally how everything was back home. Hearing about how ordinary everything was made me feel odd. Like how could everything be just the same back home when the world I lived in had changed so much?

Afterward I checked my emails. I'd gotten a reply from Caltech. Before calling Sorelle I'd written to the admissions department and the woman I'd been in contact with in the mechanical engineering department, Karen, to say I wasn't coming to California. Karen had written me asking if I was all right and if I wanted to defer admission a semester or year and that the department had been looking forward to having me. She was so nice I wrote back that I was fine and would consider it. Who knew, maybe all the wraiths would be defeated and next fall the pack could relocate to California. Okay, that didn't seem likely, but a girl could hope.

Then I googled "how to play chess." If I could learn, then maybe Trist and I could play and become friends. Or something. I'd seen him play it a couple of times during the evenings since I'd arrived, always alone. That couldn't be all that much fun. Playing against someone was probably better.

Unfortunately chess was rather complicated. And it also wasn't helping that as excited as I was to rejoin the modern era, part of me, a big part, couldn't stop thinking about what happened in the training room this morning.

I had made out with James! And he had hung out with me afterward of his own free will. Even almost twelve hours later it was hard to really believe it. If only Tommy hadn't shown up . . .

But before I started down the slippery slope of imagining what could have happened if Tommy hadn't interrupted us, I closed the computer lid and rather ungracefully got off the beanbag chair and headed for my bedroom.

Sitting around and fantasizing wasn't going to make me feel any better. In fact, there were probably only two options: a cold shower or two, or following Sorelle's advice. Go and find James and see if he was up for continuing the make-out session from earlier in the day . . . and this time without any chances of interruptions.

Except I wasn't sure if I was brave enough to seduce James. Today in the gym had been a kind of spontaneous thing. Actually seeking him out, that would be something different. Maybe he would try to be all cool and distant.

But he hadn't acted like that. Not after nearly dying. As I walked up the spiral stairs toward my bedroom, I thought about how things were finally starting to turn around. James was realizing that having a mate was a good thing.

Maybe I could initiate something. If the make-out session today had been any indication, he wouldn't turn me down. He was letting me in, letting me know about his deep, dark secrets and training me to be safe.

I should do it. I wanted him and he wanted me.

Okay, maybe that was my wolf and the sexy red lacy bra I'd found in a drawer this morning—the very same one I'd worn on my eighteenth birthday—speaking. But from the way James had looked at me earlier, with such heat and hunger, and with him opening up, it didn't seem like such a stretch to think we were ready to complete the bond.

Once I got to my room, I threw my computer on the bed and got the sexy red underwear combo out of the drawer.

I imagined James seeing me in the lingerie. I knew the red lace looked good against my tan skin. I imagined him taking the little bits of lace off me.

I had a red silky robe that would complete the outfit. I changed into the underwear set and went over to the mirror.

My hair looked good, my skin too. My reflection looked—or I hoped looked—ready for what I was about to do, for what I wanted. James wanted it too. I knew he did.

Reaching for the robe, I looked around for shoes, but in the end decided I didn't need them. I tied the red silk cord of the robe closed and smiled at my pink cheeks and dilated pupils. My body and my wolf knew what was going to happen.

All of me was ready. I just prayed James was too.

I stepped out into the hall.

I knew the general direction James was in, due to our mate bond, and I had been to his room after the induction. Yet getting there again proved harder than I thought it rightly should be.

Through the pack bond I suddenly felt someone coming my way. Oh crap. I *so* didn't want someone seeing me all dressed up (or was it dressed down . . .) and ready for seduction.

I ducked into the closest room, gently closing the door and

hoping whoever it was wouldn't come right past here and wonder what I was doing in this room. Which seemed to be an overfull library.

Brushing away invisible wrinkles from the robe, I wondered if I should just turn back. I mean, what was I doing? Was I really going to seduce James? Maybe I should just go back to my room and pretend I never even started in on this plan. I should just wait. Not push James so much. Let him take the lead.

My wolf thought that was a stupid idea. I did too when I thought about it some more. I wasn't a coward. I was a wolf and I wanted this.

Once I was sure there wasn't any risk of running into anyone from the pack—most of them were probably out hunting because I could only sense a few of them in the house—I left the library. I was determined to find my way. It couldn't be that impossible.

I walked for few minutes more—getting even more lost, it seemed—before Lucy suddenly stepped out from a doorway. Her blond hair was somewhat tousled and I saw a leaf and two twigs in it even from twenty feet away.

"Hi." I smiled, trying not to feel weird about wearing just a silky robe. It was just Lucy and the robe was modest enough—it went to my knees—and was closed. Maybe she just thought I had been on my way to take a shower. Only I had a full en suite bathroom. Maybe she didn't know that. Maybe she didn't even care. Whatever. It didn't matter. I needed help finding my way . . . even if that meant Lucy might realize I was planning on seducing James.

"Will you help me find James's room?"

Lucy tilted her head, bit her lip. Paused in that intense way that meant she was thinking. It was like I could see the cogs, gears, and wheels turning behind her forehead. She looked me up and down, seeming to be evaluating me.

"Okay."

"Thanks," I said. I got the feeling she definitely understood what I was about to do. I blushed but she just turned and took off down the corridor. I followed.

I kept my focus on the pack bonds, figuring if I sensed someone else I'd hide again. I really didn't want one of James's wolves finding me running around in just a robe. I mean, Lucy was one thing, but it would be so awkward if I ran into Doc or Trist.

After a bit I could feel by the mate bond that we were getting close to James, and I even recognized a painting of a fox hunt I'd seen when leaving here after my induction. This was the hallway where James had his room. Lucy stopped, pointed, and nodded, then bounded off down the stairs, more doe than wolf at that moment.

James would know, would feel that I was coming to him. I ran a hand through my hair as my pulse picked up speed.

I was outside his door very quickly. Almost too quickly.

I stood for a moment, then knocked. Heard James's muffled "Come in." And opened the door.

It was dark, only a faint glow from the half-closed bathroom door illuminated the room. James was standing in that light, jeans hung low on his hips, his face shadowed while his hair was illuminated. He moved a step closer to me, and I couldn't help but to study the wonderful display of muscles that was James's chest and abs. How did a body like that even exist? The tattoos, even knowing their real evil purpose, were somehow beautiful because they were part of him. I licked my lips. James should totally go shirtless more. Like All the Time.

"James," I said by way of greeting as I closed the door behind me.

He stared at me, his eyes glowing. His eyes went from my face to my robe and then my bare legs. He growled. I suppressed a smile. He wanted me. I had known it, yet seeing it, feeling his eyes on me, was different.

James stalked toward me, making parts of me want to run. Making me feel like a little scared bunny he was about to gobble up.

He stopped inches from me, his eyes back on my face.

He reached out and touched my hair, brushing it back. "I like your hair." His touch was gentle, yet I could see the hunger and ferocity in him, waiting to be let loose. "I've liked it since the beginning."

I wasn't sure what to say, so instead reached forward, wanting to touch him too. His hand caught my wrist before I'd even moved a few inches.

He took a deep breath. "Megan—"

"Shhh," I said, and used my free hand to loosen the robe's tie. I felt nervous, yes, but this was right. "Don't think. Do."

I tugged at the knot and it fell away, letting the robe open. There was a spark of shyness and nervousness but mostly I just felt good. Powerful. I wanted this, I knew he did too.

James took in my body, his green eyes turning gold and hungry, turning me on and scaring me a bit at the same time. He put his hands on my shoulders and backed me over to the bed, where he sat me down.

He knelt in front of me, sliding the robe off, letting it pool behind me on the bed. His touch was as light as a whisper. His fingers trailed up my arms, over my collarbones. Lingered at the pulse in my neck. It was beating fast, both from what my body wanted and because of the small part of me that was utterly terrified. Desire was so confusing: wanting something so badly yet being somehow scared of it.

I reached forward, wanting to touch him too.

"Don't," he said, tensing and pulling back from my hand. I stopped. Something about the edge of his voice. I remembered him grabbing my hands, stopping me from touching him in the gym.

"Okay." I let my hand drop. "I won't."

He paused, then resumed his soft exploration of my body. Neck, shoulder . . . who knew someone touching your shoulder could feel so erotic? He let his fingers drift lower and touched the tops of my breasts. He moved his hand over my bra, under my breasts, stroked my ribs. I was thankful I wasn't ticklish because the sensations were plenty enough on their own, making all of me tingle, burn, and shiver.

James leaned forward, kissing the inside of my knee, his hands on my hips. His breath was coming in short puffs, his hot breath caressing my leg, the pulsing place between my legs, my stomach. Yet he was holding back. Like he was *always* holding back.

I could sense the overwhelming want coming from him through our mate bond. Just as before, when he'd been hurt, I could truly feel what he was feeling. But this time, instead of pain, there was want and fear. He wanted me, but he didn't want to lose control. The two were warring within him.

Desire and control. There had to be a way to give him both . . .

"I have an idea," I whispered. I tugged the silky cord out from the robe, looping the cord first around my left wrist, tying a knot, then around the bed's metal frame.

"Megan," he said as he watched me, eyes still hungry. But he managed to make his voice calm and steady. "This isn't what you want. You want the fairy-tale shit."

"I want you," I said. I wasn't 100 percent sure about this, but it wasn't like I was going to cuff myself to the bed. Heck, I could probably just pull really hard and tear the silk. The point was, he needed to feel like he was in control. This would help with that. Besides, it was kind of hot, the idea of being completely at my mate's mercy.

Decision made, I tied the red silk around my other wrist and used my teeth to secure it. Then I looked up at him and smiled slightly at the look on his face as he stared at my bound arms.

His eyes came to mine and we looked at each other for a long moment. He seemed to relax and tense at the same time. As if something had changed in him. Like he'd just decided he wanted me and nothing in the world was going to stop him.

I let out a groan as he covered my body with his, burying his face in my neck and pressing his lower body between my legs. I so wished he wasn't wearing jeans; I wanted him to be inside me, to complete the mate bond so we'd be bound together for good. But at the same time . . . James was all muscles and power. Compared with me he was very big, and I was beginning to worry just what that would mean in terms of certain body parts.

He nipped at my neck, teasing, surely leaving little marks. I arched and twisted under him, not to get away, but to get closer. Nothing I'd ever done to myself had felt anywhere near this good and it just kept getting better. He teased my breast through the lace, and I felt my nipples harden as he sucked on them through the material. He looked into my eyes—his eyes weren't gold, yet there was something wolfish in them, and I could see desire burning in them. I wanted him too, so badly, and I hoped he could see it.

He moved down my torso, his hands squeezing my hips, pulling me closer to his lower body, positioning me just right. I wanted to be rid of my little bits of lace, to be naked. Wanted to be lost in him. He kissed his way around my belly button, licking, tasting my skin. He trailed his mouth lower, lower.

I moaned as he toyed with me, the tiny bit of fabric giving me no protection from his mouth. Then even that was gone and I was bare to him. I felt so good. But it was more than just my body's pleasure, it was the mate bond wrapping around us. Like a wonderful warm cocoon being built around just the two of us with tiny but still-strong strands.

My left wrist got free of the knot and grabbed for James's hair. He looked up at me, grabbing the hand that I'd touched him with. It wasn't a hard grip, but it was firm. I worried for a second that my touch had made him wary and he was going to pull back. I couldn't stand the thought of that. But he didn't.

"You're not very good at keeping your hands to yourself," he said.

"No," I whispered. He kept a gentle hold of my wrist and began kissing and biting his way up to my elbow, my shoulder, neck.

My body was humming and only James's touch was important. The vibrations, the humming of our mixing emotions, were getting stronger. The mating bond was finally connecting, or getting close to it. He pulled back for a second and I felt a shot of fear. But then he came back to me, jeans gone.

I felt a little drunk. Like the world wasn't quite real, like only this room, like only he and I existed. I wondered if he felt the same or if he was holding back too much to be able to feel all that I did. I hoped he wasn't. I wanted it to be amazing for us both. But he had to be feeling it. There was no way he wasn't. Then I wondered if all mated pairs were like this when they were together. If so, I wondered how any of them ever managed to leave their bedrooms.

But around that time my brain stopped functioning properly and the wolf took over. Suddenly there was nothing but the pressing need to mate, to bond, and all I could see was his face.

I just wanted. Wanted James.

He kissed my mouth gently, too gently for the hungry look in his eyes, before putting both hands on my hips. When he entered me for the first time there was pain, there was fullness, and there was the mate bond connecting us, reaching out. All the while I just kept looking into his eyes and he into mine. It was the strangest sensation, like both my body and mind were just flowing out and away. I felt the bond wrapping me and him together, binding us with warm golden light. It was safety and desire. And love. It was wonderful.

Except as I reached for him with everything that I was, it changed. He looked away from my eyes, and as I lost that contact, it felt like the mate bond closed. The warmth turned cool and I felt like I was falling—that horrible pinch in your stomach before hitting the ground replacing the wonderful feelings of the mate bond.

James was still inside me but the mate bond was shut down. Totally closed off. Rejected. Less accessible than even that first night we'd met. I found I didn't even want to try to reach for it for fear of experiencing the empty, desolated feelings from a second ago.

"James?" I whispered, my voice thick. I realized I had tears on my cheeks. When had I started crying? I reached for him, wanting him to look at me, but before my hand was halfway to his face, his weight was gone from me.

Cold to the bone, I reached for the covers as the door to his bathroom slammed. I wiped at my tears. What had gone wrong? It had been so great. Now I felt cold and alone and *sore*. And all I wanted was to run and hide and never see James again.

CHAPTER 36

James

James splashed his face with cold water, trying to get his pounding heart to slow down and the buzzing in his ears to go away. He wasn't sure how he'd done it, but he'd managed to be with Megan without the mate bond connecting, defeated the magic when it tried to claim him. He'd done it!

Too bad that once he knew he could control the magic, he'd become shaky with it. Realizing he could have her without the bond had threatened to consume him, had made him feel wild. But she had been a virgin, and he imagined the hunger for her he had felt at that moment would have scared her if he'd acted on it. So he'd had to stop, leave, and calm himself.

In the mirror his eyes shimmered with gold. His wolf thought he was a fool for leaving her like he had. That Megan had come to him, wanting this. She wasn't scared. He was the one who was. Scared that if he lost himself in the passion, in her, he wouldn't be able to stop the magic. But James knew he could. He'd left her because he didn't want to upset her by wanting her too much. Being too rough. Not because he wasn't in control.

Realizing this and drawing a few more breaths made him feel calm. Soon his eyes were back to their normal green. He had bested the magic and his wolf's desire too.

As he headed back for the bedroom he thought this was probably not how Megan had imagined her, their, first time. It wasn't how he had seen it either. Interrupted without either one of them getting any real pleasure out of it. But he knew he could control the magic now. He could be with her.

Next time it would be better. Much better.

"Megan?" He frowned because she was reaching for her discarded little robe. The expression on her face wasn't one he could read, and while she glanced his way when he said her name, she wasn't meeting his eyes.

Something was wrong. There was pain in her eyes.

Surprising himself, his first instinct was to reopen the mate bond, to try to get a feel for her emotions. But instead of the emotions and warmth he was used to feeling, he got . . . nothing. She was still there, connected to him, but now she was as closed off as he had been.

And she was getting dressed. Her body angled away from him, saying *don't come near me* even more effectively than words. She wasn't going to let him make it better. Explain. He needed to stop her, yet he understood her desire to escape. The passion in the room had gone, making it feeling huge and empty while at the same time claustrophobic.

"You're leaving?" It wasn't really a question. Still he walked toward the bed, wanting to reach out to her. He may not be able to reach her through the mate bond, but maybe a physical touch, a comforting one, would make her stay. And he wanted her to stay. He hadn't realized how much until this moment. The moment she was leaving.

"I, just." She swallowed loudly as she wrapped the robe around herself and looked away. "I need to . . . I can't—I have to go."

"Megan—" He reached for her but she jumped off the bed before he could touch her.

"I'm fine," she said, and smiled a stiff smile. "I just need—I just have to leave."

She bolted for the door. He wanted to follow, grab her, hold her close and somehow say the right things to make it better. Take the hurt away from her eyes. But when he'd tried the mate bond it had felt closed off. Not because of him, but because of her. When he'd tried to reach out to her physically, she'd run.

That made him think that he couldn't fix how wrong the night had gone just then. He just wasn't good enough with words for that, and even if he was, he doubted she would be willing to listen.

So he let her go.

was crying because I was angry. Really. These were angry tears and sobs. Not heartbroken ones. Because I'd read it all wrong. James *wanted* me, sure, but he didn't care about me. Wasn't starting to *love* me. That had just been all in my head. He didn't want to be mated, didn't want to let me or anyone in.

I was angry at myself for being stupid enough to think him spending a little time around me meant so much. That because he'd shown interest in the Wi-Fi room, smiled at me, he was opening up. He'd told me from day one, both with his actions and words, that he didn't want a mate. So I was angry with myself for not listening. For thinking I was special enough to change him. I clearly wasn't.

And I was angry at James for not making it clearer. For not telling me, I might desire you but I don't want you. Don't love you. Because he must have known that was what I wanted, what I thought tonight was about. Love and the mate bond.

I leaned back in the tub, submerging my neck, my chin, my whole head into the warm water. Enjoyed the odd, muffled way the world sounded for a few seconds before emerging and taking a deep breath.

What was I supposed to do now?

I couldn't stay in my huge bathtub for the rest of my life. Not even the rest of the night. No matter how tempting the huge tub with its warm water was. Despite the comfort it offered for my body and spirit, the warmth and the escape. The way my tears just disappeared when they hit the water. My fingers had already turned into raisins.

Could I leave? I'd come to Canada to be with James. Given up on school and everything familiar back home. For what? To live in an ugly castle where no one cared about anything? I didn't want that. Maybe I should go. Not in some foolish attempt at running away that ended in disaster but actually properly leave to go home. Or to go to Caltech. I could start over in LA.

Except James was still my mate. Even if the mate bond was closed off and he couldn't ever love me, we were bound together by the magic. He'd mentioned that warrior mate bonds worked differently back in my father's office. That I had no choice but to go with him. There had never been an explanation of what that meant exactly. And I needed to know.

I didn't want to be half bound to someone who couldn't love me. Who did his best to reject me the very moment we were supposed to be the closest. He had told me he had a past and I'd just realized that past made it impossible for him to let me in. But that didn't lessen the hurt I felt. I knew it wasn't truly his fault, but right then there was no one else to blame.

I stepped out of the bath, expecting to feel cold again. But I didn't. I just felt numb. My head hurt from the crying, but at least the tears had finally stopped and I didn't even care enough to be horrified by how puffy my eyes looked in the mirror.

James had rejected me, shut down the mate bond. Even pulled back from me physically . . . which didn't really make sense; I'd seen his hunger, his lust for me. And then he'd just let me go afterward. Hadn't even tried to explain what it was that had messed it all up. If he'd at least done that . . . but it was clear he didn't care. And I didn't want to keep on trying. I'd tried so hard. Tonight was supposed to be a dream. Not a nightmare.

Putting on my most comfortable pajamas, I crawled into my bed. I was exhausted, not just from tonight but from the past few weeks. Tired from trying so hard to make this thing with James work. And now I was done. I wasn't sure what came next, but I did know I didn't want to keep trying.

CHAPTER 38

James

When he couldn't find Megan through the mate bond—she was still keeping it closed off—he checked the pack bonds and noted something interesting. Most of his pack seemed to be gathered together on the second floor. Megan wasn't with them, but instead up in her room.

He figured since she was still blocking their mate bond she was still upset about the other night. Which he understood. He pulled back too when things got intense or something out of his control happened, and that night had clearly upset her. Still, he had hoped to talk to her about the pack hunt. He thought she might want to have a say in which location. There were lots of places to hunt deer, but maybe she'd want to try for elk or bison. They didn't have lots of those down in New York.

He'd have to talk to her about it later. For now he decided to investigate what the whole pack was doing gathered together. It was rare, most of them being rather solitary, or preferring to socialize in smaller groups.

The smell of the paint hit him first, cluing him in to what the pack was doing. They were painting the room Megan had shown him the other day, the small ballroom she was converting into a "hangout" space for the pack. He remembered her excited eyes as she'd told him all about it. How alive and vibrant she'd looked; just being around her had made him feel more alive than he could ever remember feeling before. But she wasn't in the room with the rest of the pack. Which seemed odd.

He was right. Once he got there, he found almost the whole pack was painting or working to prepare a section of the room to be painted.

"What's all this?" he asked Tommy, stopping next to him and Robin.

"Painting," Tommy said, not quite looking at him.

"I can see that," he said. "But this room is Megan's project, isn't it? Where is she?" James couldn't help but ask, glancing around even though he knew she wasn't in the room.

"It's a surprise for her," Tommy said, with a shrug. "She seemed kind of upset yesterday. Sad. And when the paint arrived this morning, I thought that helping to fix this for her would make her happy."

James nodded. Because it was a nice thing to do. It probably would make Megan happier, knowing someone else in the pack had cared enough to fix her room. But it should have been him, not Tommy, who came up with it and executed the plan.

"And the rest of them? How'd you get them all to help?" James looked around at the pack all working together.

"I asked," Tommy said. "They all volunteered."

That surprised him. His warriors didn't normally volunteer for anything. Then again, what he normally asked them was to go out into the night to kill wraiths. Perhaps painting a room to make a young woman, their Alpha female, happy, held more appeal.

As he looked around, he found he was pleased to see them all together. Robin and Doc fixing something by one of the doors, his father and Tobias joking about something. Hans on a ladder, painting. Owen and Tio over by the dumbwaiter. Even though they were all working, they were also having fun. Together. This was a pack at its best. This was the way it was supposed to be. The pack joined together by a common purpose.

"Where are the paintbrushes?" he asked, turning back to Tommy. This might not have been his idea, but he was going to help. Maybe that would count for something.

Tommy grinned. "I'll show you."

A FEW DAYS later he once more tried checking on Megan and found the bond still closed. He frowned at himself. She was still shutting him out. And it bothered him.

It bothered his wolf too, making him feel restless and tense.

While he understood why she might have shut it down after he'd pulled back from her that night, understood that she'd been upset, he just didn't see why she was *keeping* it closed off. It had been days.

She'd been the one who had come to him. She must have known—he had told her quite clearly about his past—that he wouldn't let the magic of the mate bond consume him. She'd seemed to understand he needed the control.

Perhaps Megan had changed her mind about it all. Maybe he was finally getting his wish of being left alone. It certainly seemed so. The irony of it was . . . he no longer wanted her to leave him alone.

She'd always been the one who sought him out and he had been sure this would be no different. Once she felt less upset, after seeing her freshly painted room maybe, he'd figured they'd probably talk about it—she liked talking—and she'd understand that he hadn't meant to hurt her—not mentally, physically, or with the bond. He'd never meant to hurt her at all, in any way. And he would fix it somehow.

Except she didn't seem to want to fix it. She just wanted to ignore him. She left the room when he entered, turned away when he tried to catch her eye. She was acting just like he'd wished she would when he first brought her home.

And he hated it.

He kept thinking of things he might tell her, of little things he'd never thought about before. The pack hunt, a thought about the wraiths, even a stupid memory he'd had of his sister. He also couldn't keep from thinking about touching Megan, holding her and being with her again. Of ways to let her know that if she ever needed him, he'd be there for her. Except she was avoiding him, taking great pains to not even be in the same room as him.

He missed her.

It was a fairly startling realization, but nonetheless true. He missed her: her smile, her scent, and the way she cared. Even though he hadn't asked it of her, nor even deserved it, she cared about him.

Or she had.

Now? He didn't know. What he did know was that he was going to use the one real excuse he had to see and talk to her. Training. It was something she'd asked him to do for her. Their one lesson hadn't exactly gone as he'd planned, but he'd had no complaints. He wouldn't mind their next lesson ending with her against the wall, legs wrapped around him. In fact, he'd welcome it. He wanted to be close to her again.

He knew she was in Tommy's home theater room, and even with their mate bond shut down, he could find her with the pack bonds. Robin was with her and so was Tommy. As he got closer he could hear them talking.

"Hey, give me! Owen made the cookies for me," Megan said as he looked inside the room. "You have to at least save me *one*."

"I don't know. We agreed to watch a movie about robots falling in love. I think you owe us the cookies," Robin replied.

Suddenly Megan looked up and saw him. An emotion he couldn't name flashed across her face and then . . . then she turned away. It hit him almost like a physical blow.

What made it worse was knowing she was only acting the way *he* had acted toward her in the beginning. And the message she was sending was so very clear. As clear as it had been that night when he returned to bed and she'd pulled away before he could even touch her. But he didn't want to turn away and leave. He wanted the connection; he wanted her to be okay. For them to be okay.

James entered the room. Megan was in the front row of movie chairs with Robin and Tommy sitting on the floor, leaning back against the seats next to her. James had to fight down a growl at that. He didn't like how close and yet casual they looked. The simple connection of just sitting together, shared between them and his mate.

"He's right, we need cookies for this—" Tommy stopped talking when he noticed James.

"Need something, boss?" Robin asked. His eyes were focused on the movie screen, trying to seem relaxed, but he was tense. So were Tommy and Megan. He was too, for that matter.

"I came to get Megan for a training session." He answered Robin's question but was paying close attention to Megan.

She seemed startled at his words, as if that was the last thing she expected him to say. Then she pressed her lips hard together and said, "I'm busy." Her eyes quickly moved from him to the two men sitting next to her. "Besides, I'm going to be training with Robin and Tommy from now on."

"I don't think so," he said, anger, worry, fear, and jealousy flaring up in him. She didn't want to spend time with him. She had changed her mind. She preferred Robin and Tommy's company to his. That wasn't right. She was supposed to be *his*.

"You don't get a say," she said, eyes flashing. "Besides, I figured you'd be happier without me bothering you."

James swallowed. He wanted to explain that wasn't the case.

That she'd gotten it wrong. That he wanted to spend time with her more than he'd ever wanted to spend it with anyone. But how the bloody hell could he do that without sounding weak and emotional, especially in front of his Beta and Tommy?

"Go," he said, glancing at the two other males in the room. It was an order, and both Tommy and Robin started to get up.

But Megan reached out and put a hand on each of their shoulders. "No. I want them to stay." She glared at him. "And I want you to leave. Now."

He wasn't sure if it was her tone or her eyes, but the rejection was clear.

Fine.

Lifting his chin, he backed out of the room. If that was how she wanted it, so be it. He'd been fine without her. He'd learn to be fine without her again. If she didn't want him around, he had no idea how to fix this. No idea. She made everything so confusing. She'd seemed to want him so much, just days ago. Now she couldn't wait to get away from him. How was he supposed to handle that?

Halfway down the corridor, he heard footsteps. For a second he hoped it was Megan, but the steps were too heavy. It was Robin. He didn't need to look behind him to know that.

"That's it, huh?" Robin said in a rather mocking tone. "Giving up without a fight? That's not like you."

"Back off," James growled as he kept moving away.

"I don't know what the fuck you did, but—"

"What I did?" James stopped and spun to face his Beta. "I'm not the one shutting her out. She's the one doing it to me."

"I'm betting she has a pretty damned good reason for it," Robin said angrily, fist clenching. For the first time ever, James thought Robin might actually slug him. "She's acting all down. Like someone kicked her puppy or something, and she skips out of a room as soon as she senses you coming. You must have noticed. And now she doesn't want you to train her. You did something—"

"She was the one who . . . ," he tried, but he wasn't sure if what was going on was his or Megan's fault. She'd come to seduce him. When it hadn't gone the way she wanted, she'd just pulled back completely. That hadn't been what he thought would happen.

What exactly did you think would happen? a little voice inside his head asked. *You take a girl's virginity, shut the mate bond down, leave her without even showing her there are good parts to being bedded, and then don't explain. No wonder she isn't talking to you. Isn't willing to open herself up to you again.*

"I don't care what you did or she did. Things were starting to get better, I sensed it in the pack bonds," Robin said, eyebrows knitting together. "Then something fucked it all up. And I don't think it was Megan."

"It wasn't. It was . . ." He wasn't sure how to explain it. But he was beginning to realize he'd made a bigger mess of things than he'd thought. He'd been so pleased for staying in control. But that control had been the opposite of what Megan had wanted.

"Well, find a way to fix it." Robin's jaw clenched. "And do it soon."

"You don't tell me what to do," he said with a growl. But there was no heat behind his words. Robin was right. James knew all too well that time didn't fix things, it just made wounds fester.

"I'm not trying to tell you what to do. Or, well, I guess I kind of am. I want to help, James," his Beta said. "That's all. Will you let me?"

"Help," he said after a few seconds. "How? How do I *fix* it?"

"I'm guessing whatever is going on is beyond giving her a little bauble and saying you're sorry?" Robin said.

He nodded. "You saw. She doesn't seem interested in spending any time around me," James said. "Hard to say you're sorry to a girl when she'll barely talk to you."

"I don't know," Robin said. "But I think the most important thing is to actually let her in."

James frowned. "I have. I did what you said. I talked to her."

"But you didn't complete the mate bond," Robin said.

James said nothing, but he knew Robin was right.

"So to fix it, I guess you have to let her in. Truly let her in," Robin offered. "Question is, do you want her enough to do that?"

James thought long and hard about that. Being with Megan and keeping the mate bond locked down had made him realize he was in control. It made the idea of the bond, the magic, less like what Marisol had done to him and into something he could choose.

But did he want to?

CHAPTER 39

Telling James that Robin and Tommy were going to be my new sparring teachers had been a spur-of-the-moment thing, but as soon as I said it I realized it was a smart plan. I *did* still want to learn to protect myself but I *didn't* want to be around James. It would be too painful. Even though the fact he had come to ask, well, *tell*, me we were going to have fight training was interesting. I wasn't sure what it meant . . . maybe . . . NO! I wasn't supposed to be thinking about James today. I wasn't doing it. No more. He was banished from my thoughts. Totally not thinking about him . . . Wait. Was thinking about not thinking about him thinking about him? Ugh.

Robin had gone to follow James, and I waited until their footsteps were gone; then I asked Tommy, "Is that okay? Would you train me to fight?"

"Sure," Tommy said, but frowned. "What's going on with you and James, anyway?"

"Nothing," I said tensely. "Absolutely nothing."

Tommy gave me a look that said *I don't believe you for a second*. But it was the truth. Really. I wasn't interested in being around James without it meaning something. He didn't want that. I wasn't going to be able to give up what I wanted and neither was he. That left us with an unresolvable problem.

That left us with *nothing*.

CHAPTER 40
James

" I had another delivery this morning," Markus said. "And not the half-cow Owen keeps asking about either. No. A sofa. A big one. They loaded off and it's taking up the half the garage. I don't mean to complain, Alpha, but what am I supposed to do with all of it?"

"Did you tell Megan?" James asked, more focused on the carving in his hand than on Markus.

"I haven't," he said with a scowl. "She hasn't been around much anyway."

"Well, I guess the stuff is for her, so I don't know. Park a few of the cars outside or find somewhere in the house to store it until she wants it," James said.

Hopefully he'd find some way to get through to Megan, show her . . . well, he wasn't exactly sure, but something that would make things go back to how they were. Megan would be happy and she could do whatever she had planned to do with all the furniture and crates and boxes that Markus had complained to him about over the past week.

"Fine," Markus said, but didn't sound overly pleased by the advice James had offered.

He left, and James went back to his carving. He wanted to get the wolf done. It was his first real attempt at anything other than leaving Megan alone, which had been what he'd been doing—without result—for days now as he tried to figure out his next step. He'd decided giving her a gift would be a start, hoped that would make her want to at least talk to him.

At first Robin had tried to get him into *online* shopping, since James was less than excited by the idea of a visit the local strip mall. James had agreed to try it, even though he hadn't spent much time on the internet, figuring it was kind of like ordering things from a catalog.

Except once he'd attempted it, he'd realized there was a lot more *stuff*. Too much. How were you supposed to pick? In the end he'd given up and decided he'd make her something. This was, in fact, something he had learned from the internet too. That gifts you made yourself were apparently better, more treasured, so he was carving a small wolf statue for Megan.

It was practically done; all that was left was a careful sanding and oiling. He'd have to leave it to dry for twenty-four hours, then he'd give it to Megan. He was oddly worried about how she would receive it. It wasn't a useful gift, but Robin claimed buying Megan a winter jacket (which James had thought made sense, as it was both practical and would show her he was thinking of her well-being) or a gift card for the jewelry store (so she could pick what she wanted for herself since he was unsure of what she liked) wasn't a good idea. Women, according to Robin, didn't want useful or practical gifts.

James just hoped she'd appreciate the wolf, and when she saw he was trying, maybe let him back in.

CHAPTER 41

"You did really well with the running jump the other day," Tommy said. "But you kind of have a tendency to over-balance your landing. So first we're going to focus on that and just getting that all to work as one smooth move, cool?"

I gave him a nod and we got started. We were having a training session and I was in wolf shape. Tommy was a good instructor, not distracting (like James was), encouraging and clear with instructions, and mixing things up enough so it didn't get boring. He still worked me pretty hard, though, maybe a little bit of leftover drill sergeant from his army days or something.

But by the end of our session I was starting to actually manage to get all the bits kind of right and together. Running jump, bite, land, and quick dart away. Hopefully I was never going to have to use these moves, but knowing at least something that could help me defend myself against a wraith made me feel a lot better.

"Hey, Megan," Tommy said as I was heading for the door. "Some more stuff arrived for your room . . ."

Tommy had shown me the Wi-Fi room all freshly painted and mentioned furniture being delivered, and I'd tried to make myself care.

But what was the point? I wasn't even sure I wanted to stay. I mean, it was nice of the guys to paint the room for me. It showed they kind of wanted me around even if James didn't. That should have been enough to cheer me up. But holding the mate bond closed and trying to deal with the fact that things with me and James were never going to be the way I wanted—and had hoped for pretty much my whole life—was exhausting. It was like I had lost something, like a part of me had just . . . died.

"I just thought you should know, you know?" Tommy said, sounding a little bit uncertain. I wanted to reassure him that it was all fine, but I wasn't sure it was or even if it ever would be. I turned away from him and headed out the door.

I didn't want to disappoint Tommy, but I knew I had. He was trying to get me to feel better, wanting to get me excited about the Wi-Fi room . . . and all I could do was run away.

In my room I changed back to human and took a shower. As soon as I got the hot water going I began to cry. I'd been doing that a lot, crying, but only in the bath or shower. If I started to let myself cry at any other time or place I wasn't sure I'd be able to ever stop.

It had been more than a week, I tried to tell myself. I needed to get a grip. I knew about being second and even fifth best. I had never been anyone's number one. I had been foolish to think I'd ever be James's. But the longer I stayed around here the worse I seemed to feel. Maybe it was keeping the mate bond shut or the fact that I had no future at all. Coming here had stolen both my school and future professional dreams as well as the ones of having a mate who loved me and a family of my own some day. It all seemed so very bleak, and there was no escape. I was stuck here, with nothing to look forward to.

I was almost done in the shower when I heard a knock on my door. I knew what it was. Breakfast. Owen had started sending food up for me because I rarely went down for meals. Just like Tommy, he was being nice, trying to make me feel better.

Once I'd gotten myself under control I got out of the shower, dressed in an oversized T-shirt and jean shorts, and opened the door and took the tray over to my bed. There was a covered plate (which I knew hid eggs and bacon), a slice of rustic homemade bread, a cup of coffee, and a glass of orange juice. There was also something new on the tray. Wedged between the glass and the cup was a letter.

A letter with a logo I recognized: Caltech.

I reached for it and turned it over. My address in the Hamptons and been crossed out and Sandleholm Manor's written in Rose's handwriting instead. Pushing the tray to the side, I opened the envelope, my hands suddenly a little shaky.

It was a form to defer schooling for a term or year.

Staring at the letter, I wondered if this was some weird cosmic fate thing giving me a sign. Like, don't give up, there is a way to be okay. There is still some hope; your future might not end up like you hoped but not everything is ruined.

On impulse, I reached for the pen on my beside table and filled in the box for "spring semester." My heart rate sped up as I watched the little ticked-in box and I felt dizzy. It was a crazy reaction to something so small. But the idea of leaving James and everything that had happened between us behind made me feel like I could breathe again.

But how could I leave? James and I were bound together by the mate bond. It might not have been fully completed, but it was still there. I wasn't sure what would happen to it, to us, if I went to California. If I did go . . . that would be truly giving up on us.

Except hadn't I already done that? I thought I had . . . but the fact was, as long as I had the bond with James, I would have hope. And that felt like the cruelest part. Hoping with my heart when my head knew James was out of reach.

I ate my breakfast and thought about things some more, staring down at the form. Could I leave? Did I want to? Should I stay and hope for a miracle? Needing to talk to someone, I called Sorelle, but there was no answer. Maybe she was in class. Since I couldn't talk about it I decided I needed a distraction or else I'd go crazy with all the unknowns and worries plaguing my mind. I checked my Facebook and then email on my phone to see if there was anything interesting.

To my surprise, there was. An email about a red specialty series. I'd half forgotten I'd set up an alert for red specialty series Porches located within a hundred and fifty miles of here. I'd wanted to see if I could replace Markus's stolen car, although I'd been doubtful of ever getting a hit; it was too specific. I'd expected to hear from a car dealer (I'd emailed a few of those too) but instead there it was. A Ms. Roderick in Quebec City was selling a number of cars, one of them a red specialty series.

Maybe this was what I needed. Buying a gift for someone, making a mistake right.

I called Ms. Roderick, who was glad to hear I was interested and, since she was at home for the rest of the week, she said I could stop by anytime.

"Is today too soon?" I asked, suddenly wanting to do something. Anything to distract myself from my sad thoughts about James, the future, and the arrival of the Caltech letter.

Ms. Roderick said that would be fine and rattled off an address.

HALF AN HOUR later I'd put on some real clothes and a little makeup and was ready to go. I wasn't exactly feeling great but having a mission made me feel better. I'd go and look at the car. If it was nice, I'd buy it, and at least Markus might stop hating me for losing his car. And it would give me some time away from everything to think. Or not think. I wasn't sure what I wanted most, a distraction or to come to a final decision about what to do.

"Megan?" Trist said. He was at the bottom of the stairs looking up at me as I was coming down. "Are you going somewhere?"

"Yes," I said, continuing to walk down to him. "I'm going . . . eh, shopping." Buying a car was kind of shopping.

"On your own?" Trist sounded like this was the most shocking thing he'd heard all year.

"Yes?"

"That won't do," he said seriously. "I insist you must take me as a chaperone."

"It won't be any fun for you," I said. I was also a bit worried about him spacing out or thinking I was Nora again. I mean, I could probably handle it, but still. "I'm just going to look at a car—"

"I shall have to suffer through it," he said stoically. "You simply cannot go running around on your own."

Part of me wanted to keep on arguing. What kind of day away would it be with James's dad tagging along? But then I figured it was fine. Maybe I could ask him about warrior mate bonds. And what might happen if I actually decided to leave and go to California.

"All right." I smiled at him. "Come on, then."

CHAPTER 42

James

He hadn't meant to invade her privacy, to see anything . . . All he'd planned was to leave the wolf statue. The form had been right there, though, on her bed, drawing his attention. He had only thrown a quick glance at it, then realized what it was and been unable to resist taking a closer look.

Admission forms for a university: Caltech, which he vaguely remembered Megan mentioning the first night they'd met her parents. The school in California.

On the form she'd marked down that she'd be there for the spring semester.

He'd thought giving her a little space would be good; let her come to him when she was ready. But California was not a little bit of space. It was a whole continent of space. He clenched his fists, which made him realize he was still holding on to the wolf statue. It felt stupid now. She wanted to leave, was planning to. Something so small wouldn't be enough—not that he'd thought the wolf itself would change much. It was just a way to try to get her to talk to him.

If she truly wanted to leave, what could he do? Other than tell her of the possible consequences for them both and the pack. If she decided to go after that, he couldn't stop her. Not unless he gave in to the mate bond, and by this point, he wasn't even sure that was what she wanted anymore. She was going to leave and he'd be powerless to stop her.

No. He put the wolf statue on the bedside table. No. He'd make her stay.

Yet if she really wanted to leave, he couldn't stop her. Or he could, but he didn't want to. If being here made her miserable enough to want to leave, then he wouldn't keep her. But he would fight hard to make her stay. Maybe, if she asked, he'd even go with her, he realized; go to California.

Still, he wanted to go find her and tell her she had to stay. Tell her that she couldn't come into his life and make him suddenly want things he didn't think he would ever have and then just shut him out. Leave.

He barely resisted the urge to punch a hole into the wall next to her door. He took a breath. Getting upset would only push her further away, would only make her want to leave more. And he needed her to stay. She'd crept up on him, but now he was sure he wanted her close.

Was letting her in, totally and completely, something he was willing to do in order to not lose her? He wanted to say no. He wanted to be able to let her go. He should have tried that back the first night they'd met, before she'd gotten under his skin like she had. But it had been futile even then, he supposed. He'd kept the red ribbon, still had it in his pocket. And that had been back when he was sure he hated her and wanted as little to do with her as possible.

Megan had crept into his life and his heart. She'd made him see himself and the pack in a different light. She cared about everything even though she didn't have to. She wanted to love and feel and live fully, no holding back, and somewhere along the way she'd made him want that too.

Suddenly he knew the answer to Robin's question. Did he want Megan to stay badly enough to let her in? Yes.

Now he just had to find a way to show her he was willing to really let her in and wanted her around, something that would be enough for her to want to stay. Something that was more than a carving of a wolf and more than words. Something she cared about, some concrete thing or action.

With surprising ease an idea came to him, making him suddenly smile.

CHAPTER 43

"Trist," I said as we got on the highway. "I wanted to ask you about mate bonds."

"Why?"

"Well," I said carefully. "You're the only warrior Alpha I know who's had a mate."

"I suppose that's true," he agreed. "Ask, then."

I tried to think of how to put this, what I wanted to know. In a normal pack I knew there was a way to break a mate bond, at least for omega wolves, simply by staying away from each other, but I'd never actually heard of anyone doing it. I knew there were some mated couples that spent time apart. Months working in different cities or continents. A few even belonged to different packs. But if that had been possible for me and James, wouldn't he just have left me back in the Hamptons?

"How are warrior mate bonds different? James said they were. That I didn't have a choice but to come with him."

"There is more magic," Trist said, "Magic binds harder and it takes more when denied."

"Right," I said, even though that didn't really clear things up all that much.

"There is a drain. Even the way things are now with you and my son," he continued. "Over time the pack will weaken."

"Can you sever a warrior wolf's mate bond? Or is it totally impossible?"

"I don't reckon a lot of people have tried it," Trist said, watching me intently while I watched the road.

"But what about an uncompleted one? That must be easier?"

"Do you know what the mate bond is, Megan?" Trist asked. "It's an invitation."

An invitation? That wasn't what the mate bond was. The bond meant you were destined for each other, a perfect match found with magic.

"It's more than that," I protested.

"Once completed, of course," he agreed. "The bond helps to protect you and your mate and even your pack. It makes us stronger. But an incomplete one takes. So I suppose you might be able to destroy an unconsummated bond . . ."

I shook my head and looked away from the road. "What about love? I mean, that's what the mate bond is about. You know, true . . ." *Love.* I thought *love* but I didn't say it.

"Him being bound to you doesn't guarantee he will love you, nor does it force you to love him," Trist said seriously. I noticed for the first time ever that Trist had eyes almost like James's. That made his words somehow penetrate deeper. Like James was speaking to me himself. "That's up to him, up to you. Do you understand?"

I thought about that as we drove on. Trist was wrong. The mate bond wasn't about protection or strength. It was about finding the perfect person. Wasn't it?

Except James clearly didn't think I was perfect. And maybe I didn't think he was all that perfect either. We'd had our ups and downs (mostly downs, to be honest) but he had started to trust me. Hadn't he? He had told me about Marisol and his past. Back before it all went so wrong. Did that mean he'd started to feel something more for me than what the mate bond required? I didn't know.

MRS. RODERICK LIVED A little bit outside of Quebec City, close to the water, in a house that was big enough to almost be a mansion. It was set far back from the road and made of stone and logs and was three stories high. There was a tall iron gate that stood open when we drove up.

A minute after I knocked, a small, middle-aged woman in a fancy white suit opened the door.

"Hello," I said. "I'm Megan. We spoke on the phone."

"Of course. Hello." She gave me a weak smile. "Let me get Pete for you. The cars belonged to my late husband and I'm afraid I don't know a lot about them."

First I thought Pete was going to be her son, but he turned out to be her dead husband's mechanic. He came to meet us and he took us over to the garage where the car was. It had a little damage to the side but it ran beautifully and everything looked good under the hood. I had Pete take a picture of me in the car and sent it to Tommy, who sent me back a thumbs-up.

Trist had been silent during the last hour of our drive and so far he'd mostly kept it up while we were here, which I thought was good, rather than having him start calling me Nora or spouting off something else that might make Mrs. Roderick A) not sell me the car and B) figure out he was an ancient werewolf. He had quietly taken up Ms. Roderick's offer of a cup of coffee and was currently studying the art in the office.

Even though he seemed fine, I wanted to get away from the humans and back on the road. But the paperwork was taking forever. Still, I knew enough to make sure to read all the documents before signing. When I explained to Ms. Roderick that it was a gift, she said it was fine with her if I needed to keep it in her garage for a little while, which was so totally nice of her.

"Thank you," I said once we were done. I had the key and the title. This would make things right. Markus would understand I hadn't meant to lose his car and that I was sorry enough to go out and find him a replacement.

"I must admit you don't seem especially excited about acquiring this automobile," Trist said once we were back on the road, apparently finally having picked up on my less than stellar mood.

"I'm fine," I said. But this whole thing had kind of made me wish James would buy me a car. Not an actual car car (although I wouldn't say no to one) but for him to do something like this. Something that showed he was sorry and that he wanted me in his life. But I doubted he would. He was fine with me ignoring him, with me keeping the bond closed. I'd thought maybe if I distanced myself, keeping the bond closed would get easier, but it had only gotten harder. I realized I wanted to forgive him. I wanted him to tell me he was sorry. I didn't want to go to California. I wanted a metaphorical car I was never going to get.

"WE SHOULD JUST pull over and ask for directions," Trist suggested.

"We're not pulling over. Besides, even if we wanted to, there is no one to ask," I said. "We're in the middle of nowhere."

That might be a bit of a stretch. We'd gotten off the highway to find a late lunch but so far only found an empty town and confusing winding dirt roads that weren't on the map. The GPS in both the car and my phone had stopped working somewhere back by the highway, so asking Siri for directions was out of the question.

"We passed a farm not two minutes ago," Trist said.

I gritted my teeth as we passed a boulder that looked familiar. Had we driven past this place before? No. I did not get lost. I'd never ever gotten lost before. . . . That sign was familiar too. We *had* been here before.

"Fine, the next time we see—" There was a *boom* and for a second I thought the SUV was going to tilt over on itself. It didn't, but the whole car began vibrating. "What the—?"

I pulled over since the car did not feel drivable, giving Trist a worried look.

"I believe, my dear," he said as I reached the shoulder, "that we hit something."

"But," I said. "But . . . I've never hit anything before. I mean, we didn't hit anything. I didn't see anything. I'm a really good driver."

Or I'd always thought so. Clearly this part of my life needed reevaluating too. I'd lost one car and now I'd blown a tire on another. Because I was pretty sure that was what had happened. Just a flat. Still, the whole pack was going to think I sucked at cars when I didn't.

I knew that shouldn't be a big deal, but somehow it was. But then, thankfully, I realized I could fix this without anyone back at the manor ever being the wiser.

"I'm going to change the tire," I said as I took the key out of the ignition and reached for the handle.

Trist got out too as I checked the car over. Yup. A flat tire. Just my freaking luck. With a sigh I headed to the trunk. There was a medical kit, a box of tools, and a duffel full of random clothes in there. I lugged them out and then got the cover off to reveal . . . nothing.

There was no freaking spare tire.

I swore and kicked at the stupid flat, which hurt my foot more than it did the car.

"Such language," Trist said, but I ignored him.

How could there be no spare tire? Markus slaved over these cars! There should be a spare. But no matter how long I stared the metal bowl where the tire should have been, it remained empty.

All right. It would be fine. I'd call a tow truck. Get the car fixed.

"Perhaps we should find a way to contact my son," Trist said, sidling up to me.

"Maybe," I said, even though calling James . . . well, that was not happening. Nope. Nuh-uh. I was still feeling way too confused about the bond, Caltech, and everything. The idea of spending an hour in a car with James was about as appealing as eating my own shoes. Unfortunately thinking of eating, even my own shoes, made my stomach rumble. I glanced to Trist. I bet he was getting really hungry too.

"Let's just start with finding someone to tell us where the heck we are," I said, grabbing my bag from the car. "And some food."

"YOU SURE YOU can have it done by the end of the day?" I asked the mechanic. The tow truck had dropped us off here a little while ago and the mechanic guy had just agreed to fix the flat.

"Sure thing, sweetie pie," he said, chewing on a toothpick. "No problem."

"All right," I said, and joined back up with Trist over by the garage doors.

If we'd been hungry back at the car, by this time we were both starving. I did some quick googling and discovered a decently rated sushi place within walking distance of the garage. I'd been dreaming about sushi for weeks now and no way was I passing up getting some while we waited for the car to get fixed.

Once we got to the place, despite the fact there were no customers in the restaurant as we entered, I remained optimistic. The emptiness was probably just because it was kind of late for lunch and a bit too early for dinner. I mean, the place looked nice enough; smallish, clean, and bright, with a large aquarium taking up one wall.

We got a window table and a pretty Asian girl handed out menus to us.

"Fish?" Trist said after having scanned the laminated page.

"Yes," I said, putting my own menu away to study him. He didn't look happy.

"Raw fish?" He said it like most people might say dog poop and rotting garbage.

"Well, yes. I guess. I'm not actually sure if it's raw or not," I said. I had a human school friend who was obsessed with sushi and apparently there were all these different kinds, and the most common ones are kind of cooked.

Hearing this didn't seem to make Trist feel any better.

"Raw fish and rice?" Trist said after another minute. As if to clarify this really was what we were going to be eating.

"It's good." I smiled at him. "Trust me."

"I'm not sure I do," he said.

I frowned. "Why not?"

"You're planning on leaving; that's why you asked me those questions about the bond earlier." It was a statement, not a question, but I felt the need to answer anyway.

"I'm not," I said. "I was just . . . thinking about it. And I don't want to leave. I just don't know if I can stay without . . ." I trailed off and we sat in silence for a minute.

"You know, she taught me to play chess," he said suddenly, moving the soy sauce and toothpick holder into the table, like two makeshift chess pieces. "Quite ironic. One step ahead, ten steps ahead. Think, think, time, time."

"Trist?" I frowned.

He looked up at me with his James-like eyes. "Sail at your own peril. For once lost, we stay forever . . . empty. Then time lies and forever ends."

"Trist, are you okay?" I asked. He was talking like he had that first night we'd met, but he seemed focused enough on me. Not like he was spacing out.

"Quite all right," he said, and nodded. "Just remember about time."

"Okay," I told him just as the waitress came over to take our orders, not sure what it all meant.

UNFORTUNATELY TRIST WASN'T impressed with the sushi, so afterward—since the garage still hadn't been in touch—we stopped at a steak house a block down from the sushi place. I had a steak too, since we sort of had both lunch and dinner to make up for. (Sushi might be tasty but it's not very filling, at least not when you're a werewolf.) By the time we were done with our second meal, the mechanic still hadn't called and I was feeling kind of nervous about the fact that it was getting dark.

The guy had said he'd get back to me soon. But for all I knew he might have gotten sidetracked and forgotten all about me and

Trist. And I knew I absolutely did not want to get caught out after dark. One wraith encounter was enough to last me a lifetime. So I decided to call Tommy, only to get voice mail. Urg. What was the point of having a cell if you didn't pick it up?! I pondered who to call, then decided Robin was my best bet.

"Yeah?" Robin answered on the second ring.

"Hi," I said, trying to think of how to best explain the situation.

"You back yet?" he asked before I figured out how to tell him about our unfortunate situation. I guessed Tommy must have told Robin I was off buying a car.

"Um, about that," I said, "I have a tiny favor to ask." I explained about the flat tire, walking to find someone to get directions for the tow, and the mechanic not calling me back. "So if you could come pick us up . . ."

"I'll take care of it," he said.

CHAPTER 44
James

"What do you think, kid?" James asked Lucy as he set the last armchair down in front of the fireplace. She bumped the chair a few inches to the left and then smiled. "Right. Don't know what I was thinking," he said dryly, but was secretly amused and pleased.

He'd decided that the perfect plan to show Megan he wanted her in his life was to finish her project, the "hangout" room, and he'd spent the day doing just that. He'd remembered most of what she had so excitedly told him about this room the day everything went wrong, all of her plans on how she wanted it, and done his best to place the furniture the way she'd described.

Lucy, who had shown up to assist, was surprisingly helpful. Something about the way she'd puff a pillow or insisted he move that chair a few inches . . . well, those things were somehow important to making the room feel *right*. That was the best way he could explain it.

"You know, you have a knack for this," he told her, thinking of her as something more than an odd mute creature he didn't understand for the first time. "Maybe you should become one of those decorators?"

Lucy tilted her head as if thinking this over, but before she could decide what she thought about that idea a voice interrupted them.

"James," Robin said, suddenly having appeared over by the doorway to the room. He sounded serious, which was never a good sign with Robin. He was almost always cheerful.

"What is it?" James asked as he turned. Robin had his phone out and looked uncertain. He grimaced but said nothing. Lucy watched them both. "What?" James asked again.

"Megan just called," Robin said. "Her car broke down. She's with your dad . . . in town."

"Megan's in town?" James asked. He quickly searched the pack bonds for Megan and realized Robin was right. She wasn't anywhere near the manor house. He threw a glance toward the window. It was starting to get dark. "Where?"

Robin gave directions in a tense voice as James walked over to him.

"She called you," James said, trying to not think how that hurt both his heart and his male pride.

"Yes," Robin agreed. "She did."

"Thank you," James said, "for telling me."

"Yeah." Robin stuck his hands in his pockets and shrugged.

James nodded and walked past Robin, hurrying toward the stairs. His beta followed but Lucy scampered off somewhere else.

He needed to find Megan and get her back here before night fell and the wraiths came out. What was she thinking, running off again? Hadn't she realized, didn't she understand, how dangerous it was?

Fishing out his phone, he found Megan's number. It rang. Once. Twice. Three times. No answer. After a while he got a cheerful Megan telling him to *leave a message and I'll get back to you. Probably.*

"What's the bloody point of these things when the person you need to reach doesn't answer?" James growled as he marched down the corridor, Robin on his heels. "Get whoever is patrolling tonight and tell them I need them in the field early."

"Will do, boss," Robin said, and once they got to the entrance hall, he ducked off toward his rooms while James continued outside and to the garage.

CHAPTER 45

I felt little tendrils of fear wrap around me as I watched the sun descend while we waited for Robin on the edge of a large half-empty parking lot. Maybe it was because the last time I'd been away from the safety of the manor after sunset James had almost died or just the nightmarish wraiths all on their own, but even though I knew Robin was on his way, I couldn't stop myself from feeling terrified.

Trist, too, was looking at the setting sun, but not at all with the expression of worry I was sure was on my face. He looked almost . . . excited. I wrapped my arms around myself and felt my phone buzz. Again.

I checked it real quick. It was James. Again. I wondered if Robin had told him I was in town. A tiny little part of me hoped he had. Hoped James would care enough to come along with Robin. Was sure that if James showed up, all this fear I was feeling would go away.

The more I pondered our situation, the more I wanted to talk to him. I wasn't sure how the conversation would go. My dream was still for him to apologize for being an ass and then declare his undying love as we rode off into the sunset . . . except not the sunset because wraiths, but still . . .

I was certain that wouldn't happen. But after talking with Trist, I felt like it was time for us to talk about things. The future and what and how things were going to be between him and me. I wasn't sure what Trist meant about time and all that, but I knew I didn't want to lose any more being confused and sad.

A car door slammed hard and Trist turned over to look and muttered, "About bloody time."

I turned and realized it was James. James was here. Everything would be okay.

"James?" I cried, hurrying toward him, wanting to get closer, to know he was really here.

James was walking our way, looking less than pleased, but still totally droolworthy, in the dusk. How could he look annoyed and stern yet hot at the same time? It was so not fair. That, along with the fact that he had come at all, made my heart speed up.

"Hi," I said once we were within speaking distance. I wanted to hug him, but was pretty sure he wouldn't hug me back, and that was too depressing to think about.

"It's late," he said by way of greeting. His eyes were flashing with anger but he didn't feel angry. He felt upset. Wait! I realized I was opening myself to the mate bond and shut that down. I was *not* letting him back in. I wasn't ready for that.

"We got a flat tire, and the guy was supposed to fix it but he didn't call and—"

"I know, Robin told me," James said, stopping me from babbling on. "Let's get you two home." He moved closer and indicated for both me and Trist to start walking across the parking lot.

"There was no spare," I said slightly defensively, even though James wasn't accusing me of anything. "If there had been I could have fixed it."

"She was quite angry about that," Trist said.

"I'm sure you could have," James said absentmindedly, scanning the lot as we headed toward one of the pack's SUV. "May I ask what you're doing with her?"

"Chaperoning," Trist said. "It's given me nothing but trouble. She made me eat fish, I'll have you know."

James's lip twitched and he glanced at me, which was a surprise and made me feel better. James was here, James was smiling (well, almost). That meant he was sure we were safe. But the longer he looked at me the more serious his eyes got, and even the hint of a smile dropped away.

"Hey," I said, grabbing his wrist, stopping him and letting Trist get a few steps ahead. "I . . . uh, thanks for coming to get me, us."

"Sure," he said, but the seriousness was still there. Somehow he seemed almost more guarded than usual, which was saying a lot.

"What's wrong?" I said. "I can see something is."

"Yes," he said, "but this isn't the time or place."

"But—"

"Trust me, Megan, we're going to have a chat when we get home," he said. James wanted to have a talk? That could be good, right? I mean, maybe we'd actually be able to get something worked out between us. James might even have changed his mind. I mean, a girl could hope. Maybe he did care, a little at least. "And I'm going to explain just what's wrong and we're going to finish this once and for all."

Once and for all? What did that mean? That didn't sound good. That sounded final. Like the end of something, not a beginning. What if . . . what if James had realized the same thing I had begun to worry about? That this wasn't working? What if he wanted to break the mate bond? I mean, maybe that was why he had pulled back that night. Maybe he wanted an out for later?

Someone screamed and then a wolf howled and both me and James froze for a second. Then we rushed toward over to the car and Trist.

Except . . . Trist wasn't there. I'd known he wouldn't be—the howl had been a big clue—but the pile of torn clothes still somehow seemed shocking.

I'd barely had time to draw in a breath before another woman screamed somewhere to our left. Then more voices joined in. Even though the din wasn't very coherent, between the *oh my God* and *n-nooo* I did hear the words *monster, wolf,* and *huge.* James and I stared at each other. We both knew what had happened.

Trist had turned wolf. Right in the middle of town.

"Go home," he said, pressing the SUVs keys into my hand, and took off toward the sounds of freaked-out people.

I debated with myself for only a second—then I ran after James.

CHAPTER 46

raced past several people with their phones out and one woman who looked like she might pass out as she fanned her pale face. I really hoped no one had gotten a picture of Trist in his wolf form.

For a minute I considered stopping and telling these people the wolf they'd seen was just my runaway dog, Muffin. Like Trist had done with the farmer. But this was a group of people, not just one guy. And even though it was getting dark, with the shops and street-lights there would have been enough light to see Trist clearly. Trying to convince them they hadn't seen a wolf might just make everything worse.

So I just ran past the people, following James, who I assumed was following Trist even though I couldn't see any trace of him.

James stopped so suddenly I ran into his back. It didn't even make him stumble although I nearly fell on my ass. James was scanning the street. We'd come to an intersection and he had appar-ently lost his dad. I stepped to one side to look for Trist too.

"Bloody hell," James said, gritting his teeth. "I'm going to have to change to track him." He turned to me. "Didn't I tell you to go home?"

"I assumed you were confused," I said tartly. "You need some backup."

"I wasn't." He scanned the street again before coming back to focus on me. "It's dark, Megan. I need you to go back to the manor."

"But—"

"Look, I can't focus if I'm worried about you being out here, distracting me," he said, not looking at me. The words gave me a warm, fluttery feeling in my stomach while annoying me at the same time. "So I need you to go home, okay?"

"But what if I could help?" I protested.

"Megan." James put his hands on my shoulders. "Please go."

"Fine," I said, even though I wasn't happy about it.

I began running back toward the SUV, heading down a side street, so I wouldn't have to pass the people Trist had scared. When I got to James's car, I walked around to the driver's side and climbed in. It was full dark now. Not safe at all anymore, even if the lit parking lot and the car protected me.

"Time to go," I said as I put the key in the ignition, but I found myself stopping before I turned it.

I bit my lip, remembering James getting so hurt and Doc telling him not to go hunting. Even though his two weeks were almost up and he hadn't seemed bothered by his injury since about a day after it had happened, it still made me a little worried. More than a little. If Trist had gone hunting for wraiths . . .

They could be in trouble. I mean, Trist was probably not on top of his game . . . he hadn't fought in God knew how long and James was still recovering. I knew James had said I would be a distraction, but leaving felt like the wrong thing to do. But what *could* I do, really? I hadn't been able to master any real fighting during my training with either James or Tommy. Just the one jump and bite and duck thing Tommy had been trying to teach me.

But my one kick-wraith-butt move was *something*, and something was better than nothing, wasn't it?

I hesitated for only a second more before jumping out of the car again and, checking that no one was watching, I began pulling my clothes off. If I was going to be any help to James and Trist, I needed to be in my wolf shape. Besides, without my wolf's sharper sense of smell I wouldn't be able to find them in the first place.

Once I was nearly naked I checked the area again. There was a huge truck parked next to mine, which might make for a good spot to change without being noticed, and the lot was pretty deserted. Still, I decided maybe it was better to be safe than sorry and got in the back of the SUV to start my change.

Maybe it was my imagination, or my new determination, but it felt like the change went by faster than ever before. Once I was fully wolf, I nudged the car's door open, jumped out into the night, and went hunting for my mate.

CHAPTER 47

Tracking in the city wasn't something I'd ever done, and it was both easier and harder than tracking in the woods. City scents were all tangled up and stinky. And I had to make sure to stay out of view. One wolf sighting was quite enough for the night. But it was easier because once I did find James's scent, it was strong and clear and *different*, which made it a piece of cake to follow.

I ran through a residential area located behind the strip mall and then followed the trail toward a more populated neighborhood, where I had to duck down next to Dumpsters and into doorways more than once.

The darkness made me tense and fearful, and I was scared a wraith would jump out at me every time I rounded a corner. I'd never been this scared before and it was odd and really, *really* unpleasant.

When I started to sense James through the pack bonds I knew I was getting close. I sensed Trist too, but much more weakly. Then I heard them and I knew I had been right in thinking Trist had gone hunting.

The hissing sound the wraiths made, along with the growl of a pair of wolves, made my already pounding heart speed up as I came to a stop at the alley's entrance. There wasn't just one wraith, but a whole group of them.

Trist had just taken a big bite out of one of them and James did the same, using his dad as a distraction to launch his own attack. I watched for a few seconds in amazement as they worked together to take the wraiths down. They were quick and fierce and I was clearly not needed.

Then it all went wrong. One of the wraiths' claws caught Trist, throwing him hard against a brick wall. He landed in the middle of the alley, his huge wolf body limp.

James jumped in between his father and the wraiths, but he couldn't protect Trist and attack the wraiths at the same time. Thankfully there were only two of them left. James growled and faked a forward attack that made the wraiths float back a little, but then James had to retreat to stay close to Trist.

I wasn't sure if the pack bonds were telling James I was there or if they were too weak for him to notice with everything that was going on. But I needed some way to communicate to him that I was here. That I could help. I could guard Trist while James took care of the wraiths or at least drove them off.

I'd been trying so hard to keep myself from touching the mate bond, not wanting to risk the horrible cold, empty falling feeling I'd gotten when he pulled back before. But the mate bond was closer to me, stronger than the pack bonds. I prayed it was closer for James too, harder to block without notice, and tentatively opened myself up to it.

I could tell he felt it from the way his shoulders tensed, even before I sensed the bond open up between us. A wave of fear and worry and shock that wasn't mine threatened to drop me to the ground.

Trying to think *I know what to do*, and to show him my plan, I stepped forward. If he understood my idea, he'd attack the wraiths for real and I'd step in to protect Trist. The wraiths wouldn't know I was barely passing How to Kill Wraiths 101 and they'd be scared of me like they were of him.

Thankfully he did seem to get the plan. The next time he lunged forward, his attack wasn't faked, and I could feel his satisfaction with getting his teeth into the monster, but there was also a flicker of fear for me and Trist. That fear was a distraction that allowed the wraith to shake him off and slightly to the side. The second wraith descended toward him while the one he'd bitten floated toward me and Trist.

I could practically hear James telling me to stay back and leave it all to him. But the wounded one, which already seemed somehow less solid, was moving my way, our way. I stepped over Trist and gave the wraith my best "big bad wolf" growl.

It hovered in the air and I felt a sort of all-consuming fear take me over, like there was nothing but the fear of death and loneliness and emptiness. Yet through all that I felt a clear sense of knowing just what to do.

It wasn't the move I'd practiced with Tommy. It wasn't even a move I'd seen done. It wasn't mine. It was James's. Somehow I knew it, though, knew everything perfectly, as if I'd done it a thousand times. I dove forward, spun around, and attacked the wraith from behind. It all happened with a lightning-fast speed; I had no idea how I managed it.

When I bit into the wraith, the taste made me want to throw up. It was nasty, like something that had already been gross in life had died, been left to rot for a while, and then covered in salt. *Urg.* My all-consuming fear—which I realized had been partly James's fear for me—faded and as I stood there, not too far to the left of him, the wraith I'd attacked began to . . . dissolve? Fade? In the end, it became one with the shadows it had come from.

For a second I thought about that, and the fact that my bite had been effective against the wraith even though I technically wasn't a warrior wolf. Then I decided it was not important right this second, and scanned the alley for threats but found it empty except for James. He must have gotten the second wraith while I was taking down the injured one. No more of them had shown up. It was just us . . . the mate bond still open and giving me James's feelings, which were a mix of relief, annoyance, anger, fear, and even something I couldn't quite label but that felt almost like affection or caring.

Eyes locked, the mate bond still open, we both began to change back to human at the same time. Just as before, when I was changing in the car, it went faster than normal.

I stood on shaky legs. James did too. His eyes kept flickering between gold and green. Maybe mine were too. I felt my wolf struggle inside me, wanting to go to our mate. I wanted to take a step closer to him too, but I hesitated. He had told me to leave him. That I would be nothing but a distraction. He'd been wrong. I'd been helpful. But I wasn't sure if he'd see it that way.

"You saved my life," he whispered after a few long seconds. He didn't sound the least bit upset. He actually sounded kind of happy, which was hard to believe until I felt it coming through the mate bond too. Then he smiled. As always, James's smile made me feel like I'd just gotten some sort of amazing gift. "Again."

"I kind of did, didn't I?" I said, smiling too, enjoying the warmth of the mate bond, his feelings, reaching out to me. I couldn't believe the mate bond was actually there, open, with feelings from James that were nothing like before. There was still some tension, a struggle for control, but it was so different. Because he was reaching out, not trying to pull away.

Still smiling, he stepped over and put his arms around me, pulling me in close, hugging me. I leaned into it, leaned into him. Let his scent, his warm skin, and the tingles of the mate bond envelop me. I waited, expecting him to pull back. I tried to prepare myself for the cold and the hurt and got ready to pull back as well, to let him go . . . but it didn't happen. Instead the mate bond wove around us, different than before, equal in a way it hadn't ever been before except for maybe that night when James was hurt . . .

"Oh God," I said, suddenly remembering Trist. "Your dad . . ."

We separated and quickly ran back down the alley to where Trist was lying on the ground. There was blood all over his snout and neck and he wasn't moving.

"Is he okay?" I cried. What if I'd gotten James's dad killed? I was the worst person in the world, the worst mate, the worst Alpha . . .

"He's alive," James said, leaning down and putting a hand on Trist's scruffy wolf chest. "The others will be here soon."

"Others?" For a second I thought he was talking about the humans; then I realized I could sense at least two people from the pack, one of them Robin, coming our way.

Hearing footsteps, I crossed my arms over my chest and tried not to care that I was stark naked in the middle of the city. It helped that James was too. In fact, his nude hotness helped a lot. Even with the seriousness of the situation, it and the mate bond still fluttering at the edge of my consciousness were distracting me from thinking of my own lack of clothes.

Robin and Tobias rounded the corner of the alley. They scanned it for threats and after determining there were none Tobias almost immediately turned and headed back the way he'd come. Robin went to kneel across from James next to Trist's massive hairy body. Robin also checked for a pulse and exchanged a few quick words with James about what had happened.

James was worried. I could both sense it through our bond and see it on his face. I wanted to go over and put a comforting hand on his shoulder. Tell him it would be okay. But I wasn't sure where we stood. The mate bond was opened, but I was still as confused as ever.

A SHORT WHILE LATER, Tobias pulled up to the mouth of the alley and helped load Trist into the car. He also got me a blanket, which

278

I gratefully wrapped around myself as a tube dress. Robin and James hopped into the car with James's dad, while Tobias and I found our way back to James's SUV, which still had the keys in the ignition. And an open door. Ooops. At least this time it didn't get stolen and I was able to put my clothes back on.

Tobias drove like a grandmother and it took us *forever* to get back. Once we did, he let me out close to the house before driving off toward the garage. Tommy and Lucy met me in the entrance.

"You okay?" Tommy asked me, and I nodded.

"You hear anything about Trist?"

"Not yet," he said. "They only just got here ten minutes before you."

I KNEW—BECAUSE the mate bond was still open—that James was worried but not terribly. So that meant Trist was probably doing okay-ish. It was still nerve-racking to be sitting outside the medical room just waiting.

It also felt odd to have this sense of James when he wasn't even in the same room. It wasn't clear . . . not like it had been during the fight, but he was still *there*, distorted, like an echo or a barely remembered dream.

I marveled at the fact that he hadn't shut the bond down and part of me kept tensing up, waiting for it to happen. But another part of me thought about how he'd looked at me when we were in in the alley, the way he'd hugged me, and somehow I felt less afraid.

A while later the door to the medical room finally opened and

Markus came out, looking sullen and glaring at us all. So pretty much his normal sunny self.

"How is he?" I asked as I jumped up. "Do you know?"

"Trist is going to be fine; he's resting," Markus said to us. "Doc and James are with him right now."

"Good," I said, glad to hear Trist was doing okay. "That's good."

Markus turned to leave and I remembered something. I'd reflexively grabbed my bag from James's car and still had it with me. I dug into it for the keys to the Porsche and hurried after Markus.

"Wait up!" He didn't, so I picked up my speed and ran past him and blocked his way. "Stop," I said, trying to sound as firm as my dad. This was important.

To my surprise and I think to Markus's too, he stopped. I felt a weird little flutter from the mate bond. I realized I'd just used a tiny little bit of alpha power to give that order. That was new.

I smiled and took the keys out and held them out for Markus. He looked at them in disgust. "I'm not going to park your car."

"They're not for my car! They're for a car just like the one I got stolen," I said, trying not to feel offended at his expression. "Well, it's not exactly the same and it's got a little scrape on it and it's in Quebec City so you'll have to go and get it but . . . but it's my way of apologizing. I wasn't thinking when I took your car that night and, well, I'm sorry."

Markus's expression didn't exactly soften but he did wipe the grimace off his face as he took the keys. He looked at them and I thought for a little bit his eyes looked like Tommy's kind ones.

"Okay," I said, hiking my bag up on my shoulder. I noticed

Tommy was watching from a little way down the corridor. "Well, you enjoy it."

Markus gave a nod, then walked past me. I grinned at Tommy. Then I heard Markus pause at the end of the hallway and I glanced over at him.

"Thank you," he said—and this time he did actually smile!—"little sister."

Sometimes I felt like I'd spent my whole life running from being someone's sister, but right now, I realized I'd missed it, and him calling me sister felt good. Nice. Like being part of a family again.

CHAPTER 48

sank down on my bed some time later, still enjoying the warm
flutter of the mate bond. James was still with his dad, sitting with
him, but I knew we were going to talk soon. I wasn't as worried as
I'd been before the mate bond opened, though.

Which isn't to say I wasn't still worried. There were definitely
things to talk about, and even though it seemed like James was letting me in . . . I wasn't totally sure I could forgive or forget our rocky
start and him pulling back when we were in the middle of making
love. But we needed to talk.

He wanted to talk.

Which was new. I mean, most of the time James couldn't wait
to run away from me. And I'd been doing my fair share of running too over the past weeks. But now I wanted to talk to him, wanted
to understand. I'd been so hurt that night by his rejection of me
I hadn't been able to see anything else. But maybe I should have
tried.

Stretching and looking to the side, my attention was caught by something on my bedside table.

There was a carved wolf statue there.

The wolf had its nose turned upward, howling silently. It was no taller than my hand but the detail was unbelievable. I reached for it, holding it. I traced my fingers along the wolf body, amazed and confused.

There was no message, which didn't surprise me at all, but it was clear who the statue was from. James. Why he'd carved it and left it for me was more of a mystery.

But why the wolf?

Maybe it was a "sorry" gift. Except I wasn't sure what James was saying sorry for. The fact that our first time together had ended badly? Or him shutting the mate bond down? Not explaining? Ignoring me afterward?

If it was a sorry, for any or all of those, I guessed that was a step in the right direction. Kind of how I was saying sorry to Markus with the Porsche. Was this my "Porsche"?

As I leaned back again, I heard the crinkling of paper and noticed the Caltech form still on my bed, partly crushed by my leg. I picked the form up, putting it next to the statue on the bed.

Caltech letter on the left, wolf on the right. Neither was a sure bet for happiness, I knew. Just like I knew I could only have one of them.

"Hey," James said from the doorway. I'd sensed him coming but was still thinking of my options.

"Hi," I said, lifting my eyes from the two objects on the bed. I smiled because of the mate bond's openness and the warm feelings I was getting from him.

"Can I show you something?" he asked, and I could sense that whatever it was, it was important to him. Part of me wanted to agree to anything and everything, just because he was letting me in. But I was still not sure if I could trust this new openness between us. Things hadn't been exactly like this before that night, but they had been getting better. What if I let myself believe and he pulled back again? How could I trust him when there was the memory of that horrible night, of darkness and falling, when the mate bond was jerked away?

"I'm not sure," I said before, putting my hands on my hips. "You said you wanted to talk. So talk."

"It's better if I show you—"

"James," I said, giving him a daggered look.

"It's part of the talking, okay?" he said, and held out his hand. He desperately wanted, needed, me to take it.

I wanted to. The part of me that hoped—hoped James loved me and that the open mate bond and the warmth coming through it would remain—was desperate to. But part of me was scared. Scared that taking that hand would be the first step to saying yes to all those things I dreamed about, to letting my guard down, only to have him shut me out again and leave me in the cold.

James kept holding out his hand. He could sense my struggle or maybe see it on my face, because I was sure emotions were flashing across it.

How could I let him in again without fully trusting him?

How could I learn to trust him again if I didn't let him in?

I took his hand.

WE LEFT MY room and headed downstairs.

It felt nice holding James's hand. He squeezed it, the mate bond possibly having given him an insight into my thoughts. It had been nice hugging him today too. Different kind of nice from making out with him. He stroked the top of my hand and suddenly I felt the two kinds of nice swirl together. Something gentle and sweet could make me want him, and I suspected something sexual might now let me feel this wonderful closeness that came with hand-holding and hugs too.

"Thank you for the wolf," I said, feeling tingly and happy from the mate bond and the small touch, despite my trust dilemma. "It's very pretty."

"I think maybe I should have carved you a car," he said, but smiled, glad that he'd made something I liked. "But you'd probably lose it or break it."

"Probably," I said, an odd lightness settling over me. James was joking. Joking about me liking cars, something I'd told him about the second day we'd met, back when he was still being an ass.

I opened my mouth to say something funny back, but then we entered the Wi-Fi room and I just stopped. Everything was there. All the furniture, right there in front of me. It was just as I'd pictured it. Fully assembled. The car poster on the wall and everything. I let go of James's hand and walked into the room and just took it in.

James had done this, I could sense it from the faint wave of uncertainty and eagerness coming through the mate bond.

Touching the dining table, I wondered if I'd had it wrong all along. . . . He had obviously been listening to what I said that day when I showed him this place. He had to care to pay this much attention. But then why did he push me away that night? Why cut off our mate bond? What had changed between then and now?

"Did it turn out how you wanted?"

"It's nice," I said, turning to him, wincing at how inadequate that word seemed. "Just like I imagined it."

"Lucy helped me," he said.

"She did?" Frowning, I couldn't help but ask, "James? What *is* this?" I knew what I wanted it to be but I couldn't be sure.

"It's a room," he said, walking over to me. "A room for you. To show you with something other than words that I want you here."

Wow. That was exactly what I was hoping for. Except now the reason for it worried me. He had left the wolf for me. He must have seen the form. He knew I had, was, considering leaving.

"Because you saw my letter, right?" I asked, and felt the tension and the need to make me understand. A need for . . . me. It made me want to explain. "Because I checked the box. James—"

"No," he said, looking somewhere over my left shoulder. I felt the mate bond wobble and him pull back a little. "Yes. I had planned to find some way to show you I missed you. The letter, it made me realize I had to do something fast. If this isn't what you want, if you want to leave . . . go live in California . . . we can figure something out."

"But I'm not—" I started. "I don't want to go to California." I winced because that wasn't 100 percent true and he would be able to sense that. Truth was, I did want to go, but I'd just figured out something from Trist's talk of time and leaving in the restaurant. Leaving would mean leaving not only James, but the pack. Even leaving and coming back would change things forever, because I would always have left, and that was time and trust I would never get back. "All right, let's put it like this. I want to stay here more than I want to go there."

"I'm glad," he said, and I felt his relief as he stepped up close to me. "Because I want you, need you, here. With me."

I should have been thrilled to hear those words. Instead fear welled up inside of me. Since day one he had made it clear he didn't want me. Then I'd thought he'd changed, but when I'd opened myself up completely, he'd totally shut me out. That had been the worst thing ever. Even though things seemed different this time, I wasn't sure. I needed to understand what had happened last time.

"I want to believe you," I said, stepping away from him and crossing my arms. "But I'm not sure . . . I mean, what changed?"

He gently put his hand under my chin, tilting my head up. Searched my eyes for a long moment. "I realized everything is better with you," he said finally.

I took that in for a moment as we looked into each other's eyes. I felt the mate bond swirl around us and I knew with certainty he did mean that and he wasn't scared anymore. Not *as* scared, anyway. But I was.

"That night." We both knew what night I was talking about. "When you pulled back from me . . . why? If you—"

"That night, I was afraid. After what had happened before . . . I needed to know that I wouldn't be consumed by the bond," he said slowly. "I thought you understood, but it wasn't until after that I realized . . . that wasn't what you thought would happen at all."

"You thought . . . ," I began. I wasn't sure how to handle this. James hadn't thought we were going to complete the bond that night? That had been the only thing on my mind. "I was so focused on my own desires and fears that I convinced myself we were on the same page . . . I think we both did," I said. "That night and ever since, I've tried not to think about it, or you. I didn't want to understand."

"I didn't either. Not until I realized I missed you," he said. "I hadn't even . . . I didn't know how much I wanted you around. Not until you were gone. Or the bond was."

"The old you-don't-know-what-you-have-till-it's-gone thing," I said quietly.

He didn't smile.

"I know I messed it up. I didn't mean to but I did," he said, honesty and pain mixing in his green eyes. "It's all my fault."

I thought about that.

Part of me wanted to agree, lay all the blame on James. He was supposed to be my knight in shining armor. The perfect mate I'd dreamed about since I was a pup. But he hadn't been. Every step of the way I'd felt like I was fighting him; each bit of information and emotion from him had been a struggle. A two-steps-forward-one-step-back type of deal.

Blaming him would be easy. And he carried enough guilt that I knew he would shoulder this too. But I wasn't blameless in how things had gone between us. I'd been so clear in what I wanted from my mate, from him, that I'd failed to hear what he was saying, not only with his actions, which were clear enough, but even when he used his words.

I'd poked and prodded him to share and then once he did, I'd made the decision to make love with him on my own and told him it would be all right. But it hadn't been. My seduction plan had been for me, not for him or us. I'd wanted the bond, wanted James, and I'd thought that meant he was ready for me, to let me in too. He hadn't been, and I hadn't understood that. Not before and not after, not until today.

"We both made mistakes," I said. He frowned and seemed genuinely confused, as if he couldn't think of a mistake I'd made. I put a hand on his chest and explained, "I had already decided what I wanted before I met you. Then I spent so much time trying to force you to become that. Even when I knew about what happened to you, I thought about me and rushed. That wasn't right of me."

"Maybe," he said after a long pause, then put his hand over mine. The contact of our bare skin touching—or maybe it was our new understanding of each other—made the mate bond coil around us.

This time the strands weren't thin like fine silk, but something sturdier.

"James?" I whispered.

"Do you want this?" he asked solemnly. "I want you, all of you. To be bound to you, bound together. Is that still what yo—"

"Yes!" I cried, not even letting him finish. "I mean, yes. That's what I want too."

"Good," he growled as he cupped my cheek and leaned down to kiss me.

As his lips touched mine, I felt the flare of the mate bond, reaching out, soothing and thrilling at the same time. Lips still locked, we stumbled together over to the couch.

"Too many layers," James said hoarsely after he got my sweater off . . . only to find I was wearing a long-sleeved T-shirt under it.

"That's how you stay warm," I told him playfully. "I learned it in the Girl Scouts."

"Staying warm, huh?" He smiled and tugged at the top. "I can think of better ways to do that."

"Mmm," I said, tilting my head a little. "Really? Were you a Boy Scout?" I teased.

"No," he said, grabbing me and flipping us over so I was under him. I gasped, but didn't pull back. Neither one of us did. Instead, when James slid his hands under my top, his warm hands on my skin, I felt the bond flow over and around us, connecting us even closer.

I wasn't quite sure how James got my clothes off; it didn't matter, nothing mattered other than touching, tasting, scratching, licking, and getting as close as possible. At one point we rolled off the couch and for about a second I was glad to have ordered a thick, fluffy carpet. Then I forgot all about the carpet as James moved in me. Our eyes locked and I thrust my hips up to meet him and felt the mate bond finally bind us together, the warmth and love and security I felt, he felt, we felt, wrapping us up safely. And this time there was no pulling back, no fight for control. We both surrendered to the magic.

"James," I panted as he kissed and nibbled my neck, one hand between us and the other holding one of my wrists. I dug my nails into his shoulder, gripping him with my legs. It was like a storm of emotions and touches, like after all the waiting we couldn't get enough of each other.

"Mine," he said, pulling back to look into my eyes. His were green with flecks of gold. Both wolf and man claiming me.

"Mine," I said back, and smiled.

Check out more books chosen for publication by readers like you.

DID YOU KNOW...

this book was picked
by readers like you?

Join our book-obsessed community
and help us discover awesome new
writing talent.

1

Write it.

Share your original YA manuscript.

2

Read it.

Discover bright new bookish talent.

3

Share it.

Discuss, rate, and share your faves.

4

Love it.

Help us publish the books you love.

Share your own manuscript or dive between the
pages at **swoonreads.com**